In His Footsteps

Ben Steinlage

In His Footsteps

Ben Steinlage

ARPress
45 Dan Road Suite 5
Canton MA 02021
Hotline: 1(888) 821-0229
Fax: 1(508) 545-7580

Ordering Information:

Quantity sales. Special discounts are available on quantity purchases by corporations, associations, and others. For details, contact the publisher at the address above.

Printed in the United States of America.

ISBN-13:   Softcover   979-8-89330-607-1
                eBook   979-8-89330-608-8

Library of Congress Control Number: 2024900576

DEDICATION

I would like to dedicate this to all the veterans I have known and to a good friend BB. It was because of him that I wrote this story. He is also a writer and during a discussion on our hobby we got to talk about Veterans. I wrote two paragraphs of an idea on the subject and challenged him to finish. Once he read what I had written he decided, I should finish it. He said it sounded as if I had a strong message in mind so I should go with it rather than him. You the reader are the true judges to me making a statement or not.

CONTENTS

OTHER BOOKS, BY THE AUTHOR BEN STEINLAGE

You can find them on Amazon, CreateSpace, Barnes and Noble as well as through your local bookstore.

amazon.com/author/bensteinlage

Books that stand alone:
A Fundraiser's Dilemma
A Tusk for Two
For you Mom
In His Footsteps
In the Evening Hours
Nrevac (Cavern)
On a cold night
Sally's Wishes
The Canning Jar
The Legacy
The Tapestry
White Water
Why the Chief

Collections of short stories:
Ant-Hology
A Honeycomb of Smiles
A Sunset Full of Mysteries
    Books one – three
Christmas Ramblings
Shared: Short Stories
    Books one - ten

Western Shorts
A Night Time Read
On A Cold Day
The Petals of A Rose

Bird Boy Series:
Bird Boy
Stand Up to Them

Want to Go West Lady series:
A Deputy and a Cornfield
Edgar
Suspenders
Want to Go West Lady

Writing my shorts series:
Writing my Shorts
More Shorts within a
    Mystery

INTRODUCTION

While I was in the ROTC, I always wanted to be in the service. Unfortunately, I wasn't able to join since I had asthma, and I blew my leg up in my early teens. I've always felt I missed out in doing my duty for my country. I did my best to get to know everyone I could that had been to Viet Nam. I've gotten to know some of the men and women that served in the war, and I have found they all shared some of the same feelings. Every man and woman coming back from a battlefield also returns with some horrific memories.

Though the veterans should be remembered, the same can be said for the noncombatant survivors. These survivors are the war wives and children never to see that lonely soldier again. In writing this story, I would like to bring something to these individuals. All we have given them is our sympathies and a few dollars. Let us not forget the dependents of these great soldiers. Their losses are just as important as those having fought in other battles are.

You have to remember this story is fictional. In writing it, I have tried to portray both the veterans and the survivors, as I have found some of them to be. I have to add veterans have passed on to me the incidents you will read. As this is a piece of fiction, I haven't gone to the trouble of researching the truth to all of them.

CHAPTER ONE

I've been told throughout my life, "Don't worry about your past... Take a breath and live your future as you want. If nothing else, you know what not to do for your kids."

I've asked, "Can it be that easy when you start out with nothing?"

All through school, my fellow students called me "Orphan Boy," rather than Jeff O'Connor. They called me that because I didn't have a father around. The label of being an Orphan Boy never bothered me because my mother had been honest with me. She told me she had met my father who was a soldier. The first night they went out and got drunk. She woke up the next morning in his bed. It didn't take much thinking to know what had taken place during the night. After that one night, they never saw each other again. One afternoon she was to learn that, that was to change.

To mother's surprise, she learned she was pregnant. Not knowing what else to do she went out and found my father. As they shared a cup of coffee, she broke the news to him. He was as shocked as she was to learn he was about to become a father. His greatest fear was that he would never get to know his child. The Army sent him to Vietnam the next day; he knew he wasn't coming back.

Neither mother nor I ever saw him again. She told me he had written to her a few times, as she had written back to him about me. Unfortunately, his fear of not making it home came true, and I was never to know him. As it turned out, mother didn't know him well enough to give me any idea, who or what he was like. Later when I grew up I wondered why we were so poor. I would have thought she should have received a pension of some kind, but she didn't get anything. She fought with the Army because they said he had made it home. As it was, we moved from town to town until she died. On her deathbed, she apologized for not having given me a loving father. In a blink of an eye, she slipped away. I was five when she died, and I thought my world had ended.

My father's mother took me in, and I settled down in one school until I graduated. After graduating, I married Martha, and we had three wonderful children. Like so many, my marriage broke up after six years. I thought we had a good marriage, although I knew down deep something was missing. The last year of our marriage, I found my wife and kids going off without me. At times, I felt left out of their lives, but mine was so busy. One night she gave me the bad news. If I didn't change, she was taking the kids and leaving. In my own way, I tried to be more of a husband and father, but it wasn't enough. Finally, after our trial separation, we decided to end the marriage.

My wife in the divorce court said it was a shame I hadn't had a father to teach me how to be a husband and father. A tear in her eye, she gave me a kiss and walked away. Fortunately, she does let me see my kids whenever I want to. The trouble is that I'm a businessman and on the road a lot. The hours I put in, I didn't get to see them as often as I would have liked to.

The night of the divorce I found myself sitting in a bar having a drink. I felt alone knowing I would be going home, and my children wouldn't be there. All of this wasn't new to me, for we had separated many times. Then after the seventh time we finally realized we were only fooling ourselves and got a divorce. As I drank my drink, a guy bumped into me, and I wanted to hit him. Rather than hit him, I bought him a drink. Like me, he had gone through a divorce only a few months before. After telling each other our stories, we found ourselves crying over our drinks. I finally reached the point I knew I had more to drink than I should have, and I left him at the bar. I went home feeling sorry for myself. My thoughts turned to what my wife had told me.

My dog Skippy gave me a friendly greeting when I came into the house. With every lick he gave me, I knew he was my only true friend, and I never figured out why. I scratched him behind the ears, remembering when Martha and I had gotten him as a pup. He didn't care what my mood was, he was always there for me. He and I used to have long conversations over Martha, the kids or my business. He never answered, which made it easier to talk to him. It was easy to see he enjoyed my fingernails digging into the area behind his ear. As I scratched him, his tail would begin wagging, and all was well. It was clear from the first-day Skippy was my dog, and he didn't want anything to do with rest of the family. It didn't take much for her to let me take him, but not much of anything else.

That night on, I realized I didn't have any friends but Skippy. I didn't socialize with anyone, and that included my partner who used to invite us over for supper. Occasionally, I would take my family to the park for a picnic or to a movie. One of Martha's complaints was not having anyone in our home. I never understood her need for people around her. After a long day at the office, coming home to solitude was all I needed. I didn't need a bunch of people around.

There were many times that she said I was boring. As I ran those comments repeatedly, it got me thinking about myself. For some reason, I realized like other men I knew I didn't have a hobby other than my job. It didn't take much for me to realize what I must have been, a poor excuse for a father and husband. My biggest problem was in not knowing how to change myself. No matter how bad I was, I needed my family back in my life.

Martha might have been right about not having had a father to teach me. A voice deep inside me said, "Your work has always come before your family." As she used to comment, "I think you're afraid to face life so you bury yourself in your work. I wish the kids, and I could be part of that life." I knew there was some truth to her assessment of me. It wasn't uncommon for a customer's call to interrupt me from my family until after the kids had gone to bed. Most of the calls were not emergency calls so I could have taken care of them the next day. If I had done what was right, they wouldn't have kept me from my family. It seemed my customers always came first, and my family got whatever time I had left.

A few nights later, my grandma called me. She told me she had something I should have. I had to tell her I wouldn't be over for a day or two. To be safe I called her before I went over. When I finally made it to her house, I knocked on the door. As she opened the door, I saw she had manila envelope in her hand. To my surprise, she didn't ask me in. As she handed me the envelope, I saw some hesitation in her eyes. It didn't take much to see the envelope was old, and she had never opened it. It's interesting she had kept it so long without seeing what was inside of it. If I had gotten it, I would have opened it right away. I turned the envelope over, and I saw the postmark on it was September 11, 1978.

"Junior, I've had this for many years. I have tried to open it, but I couldn't bring myself to do it… I always thought I was a strong woman, but I guess I'm not. I've decided to open it because in doing so, was long overdue. I guess I'll let you have the honor," grandmother told me as I opened it.

In the envelope, to my surprise I found what looked like a book. As I took it out, I felt a chill go up my spine because it was a diary. It looked to be almost new though it was dirty and had a few tearstains. My fingers began to tremble, afraid what I might find. I looked up at grandma and saw her turn away.

"Once you have read it, I'll tell you the rest of the story," she said. She didn't add anything else, but turned around and went inside. I wasn't sure, but as she went inside, I thought I saw a tear run down her cheek.

I was so dumbfounded I didn't even think about going inside. I found my interest was more in the diary than with her. Opening it, I found written on the first page:

Jeff O'Connor
In search of myself

The name was the same as mine, which made it a dead giveaway. This was something of my father's. It didn't take much to realize it was his diary. From the date on it, I knew he had sent it to her two years after my birth. I found myself staring at the page not believing what it said. I knew either he or someone had sent the diary to my grandmother about the time mother died. I looked up at grandma, and I wanted to scream. Why had she held this from me for so many years?

I didn't say anything as I sat on the steps of the front porch and began to read. I realized I had a lump in my throat, and my eyes were misty as I tried to focus on the page. I wiped my eyes and read father's first couple of sentences:

> *Once I was innocent and then along came the war. Now I'm not who I was for somewhere I must have died. I hope that I'll find myself soon so I can be a good father for my son. Please Lord; help me find the man I once was.*

When I went inside, I found my grandmother crying. I didn't know what to say so I told her, "This was my fathers."

"I know," she answered not looking at me. As she wiped her eyes she added, "You don't have to read it. If you do, I'll tell you more… when you have finished it. Only then what I have to tell you will make sense to you."

I was about to respond to her when the phone rang. I let her answer the phone as I nervously turned the diary over, and over in my hands. I opened the diary again and went to the next page. His writing was so small I could hardly read it. I got the feeling that he wanted to make good use of every page. I read the next few lines, and it said:

> *I just showered, but I still feel dirty. I'm finding myself scared for the first time since I left for Nam. I will reach Oakland tomorrow, and they will muster me out. Gregg and Bill want to go over to Frisco before they go home. I know I shouldn't, but I'll probably go over with them. I can always leave from there if God is willing.*
>
> *Every waking moment over the past three years, I have been either in fear for my life or waiting for this day to come. Unfortunately, I don't know Janis or the son I have never seen. I don't know what to do with them. I know I have screwed up their lives just as the war did me.*

"That was Martha," grandma told me.

When I heard her hang the phone up, I asked her "What now?"

"She called to remind you of the movie tonight. She said you promised to take the kids to it," she answered.

"Shit…That's right," I muttered under my breath. Her reminder took my mind off the diary and to my kids. I gave her a kiss on the cheek, and I told her, "I had better get on my way."

"Give my love to the kids," she returned with a smile. As I tried to give her the diary back, she added, "No… that's for you. If at some time you think I need to know more, you can tell me."

As I got into my car, I began to worry about the drive to Martha's place in Glendale. However, it was only a fifteen-mile drive from grandma's place down the San Diego Freeway, which could be treacherous. It was irritating but from where I was, I didn't have a choice. More times than I could count I seemed to catch the traffic when it was backed up for miles. I got on the freeway, and I found it wasn't as bad as I feared. It was moving slowly enough that I had time to think. My first and only thoughts were on the diary next to me. Twice, I pulled out my cell phone to cancel my plans for the night. I didn't make the call because I knew it wasn't right. My kids had to come first, and my father's diary could wait. From the little I had read I had gained more ideas of him than I had ever known. The places and location I had seen in it did give me some ideas.

As I followed the car ahead of me, an idea came to mind. I found the idea exciting, and I shouted out, "In his Footsteps." I decided there was no better way I could learn about my father than to walk in his footsteps. The idea ran through me as if I were a kid again. Then my heart sank with the reality of my business coming to mind. As I thought about the idea, I could see myself getting hold of some military type clothing. I could dress as my father might have and start in Frisco. From there, I could follow his footsteps as noted in the diary. My thinking was it would give what he wrote in the diary more meaning. In ways, it would be like visiting Dodge City because Wyatt Earp had been there. As I wove through traffic, I laughed at the idea.

As I pulled into Martha's driveway, I laughed again at my dumb idea. I announced my arrival by honking the horn. As was the custom, I waited for the kids in the car. Martha opened the door and gave me a wave and holding one finger up. It didn't take a genius to know she meant the kids would be out shortly. As I waited for them, I went over my crazy plan in my head. The more I thought about it, the more absurd it sounded. My train of thought ended as one of the kids began opening the door of the car.

"Hi Dad," Gloria said, greeting me as she got into the passenger seat. At the age of ten, she was the oldest and always sat in front with me.

"Hi Beautiful," I told her, as I kept my eye on the front door of the house. I prayed the other two would be out soon. I knew the movie was going to be starting soon. I wanted to get them there and home, as soon as I could.

The next one in was Jerry, my seven-year-old. He got in behind his sister and announced, "Cory's in the bathroom."

"We can wait for him…," I assured him. It had become a routine to wait in the car for either him or his mother before going anywhere. No matter how I planned a trip one of them had to use the restroom before we could get very far.

"He smells," Jerry added. With a grin, he pinched his nose together.

"I'm looking forward to it," I said under my breath. Once I asked the doctor why my son had such bad gas. We never learned why he had gas problems. The doctor's solution was to continue to give him different medicine. My wife claimed it was from nerves and blamed me for it. The doctor never agreed with her, but he didn't argue either. I came away from the doctor's office with the feeling it was my fault. Trying to get a conversation going, I asked them, "How have you two been?"

"All right I guess… but what's this?" Gloria asked, as she held up the diary.

"Sorry… That's a diary grandma gave me," I explained to her a little louder than I should have. I found an excessively possessive feeling towards the diary running through me. I knew when she got in, it was on her seat, and I should have moved it.

"Oh," she replied with a questioning look on her face.

I knew I should have told her more, but I didn't know what to say. Thankfully, Cory came running out of the house and got in the car behind me. As the kids waved good-bye to their mother, we were on our way. We went to the movie and to this day, I have no idea what the name of the movie was. I found my mind going over the diary to the point I couldn't concentrate on the movie. After the movie, I took the kids out for ice cream, and I believe we talked. As with the movie I have no idea what we covered in the conversation. At least, the kids got out of the car laughing as if they had a good time. With a wave, I drove off toward my place.

On the way home, I regretted my lack of attention to my children. I knew I wasn't the father they needed and that made me mad. I found myself uttering my father's words, "I hope that I'll find myself soon so I can be a good father for my son." As if it was a security blanket, I reached into the center console, and took out the diary. Holding it in one hand, I had a feeling my father was with me. I knew it was ridiculous to feel that way, but I did. I knew that at some point he had held it so some part of him was on it. Holding it in one hand, my idea of walking in his footsteps came back to me. Having that thought to hold onto, I began smiling as I pulled into my driveway.

As I climbed into bed, I sold myself on following in my father's footsteps. My only regret was that mother, wouldn't know what I would find. As I laid my head on the pillow, I told myself that they might be together. For the first time since my divorce, I got a good night's sleep.

I woke up the next morning more determined to make the journey. As I prepared myself for another day at work, I began to make plans. I knew there were a few projects I had to finish before I could leave. The first one was getting my partner to agree to me leaving for a month or two. My problem was telling him why I needed the time off. I didn't know how to explain why I needed the time. Part of the problem was the firm of "Crawford and O'Connor," had a lot going on. As consultants, we had a number of construction projects in one stage or another toward completion. If business kept coming as it had been, this would be our best year.

"Morning Jeff," Ray said, greeting me as I walked into the office. When I didn't respond, he set the papers he held down and followed me into my office. He propped himself against the door jam and asked, "What are we going to do with the Jeffery account?"

"I don't know... I won't be here to worry about it," I blurted out. I saw a confused look on his face. His expression changed as he took a chair. I knew he was waiting to hear the rest of the story. He finally asked, "Is there something wrong?"

In answer to his question, I pushed the diary across the desk to him. I hadn't come up with a way of telling him what I wanted to do. I prayed that if I let him read a portion of the diary it would give him more of an answer than I could.

As he held the diary up, he asked, "What's this?"

"If you would, read the cover..., and the first few pages," I suggested. The confused expression didn't change as he read. He froze as he looked at the cover. He then turned the first page and stopped for a second to look at me. Turning back to the diary, he read a couple more pages. Closing the diary, he looked up at me with a tear in his eye.

"I don't know what to say... If I read this right, it's something I would have a hard time accepting. Knowing you for as long as I have, I know this must be something you have dreamed about...," he started to say but took time to wipe his eyes. As he glanced back to the diary he asked, "When did you get this?"

"My Grandmother gave it to me last night," I answered.

He began to ask, "And...?"

"A good question...," I began to tell him, but my phone rang. I shouted out to Cathy, "Take a message."

"You were saying," Ray, reminded me of what I was about to tell him.

"I know it's dumb..., so is the rest of my life. I think for the first time in my life, I might get to know my father. My grandmother did talk about him occasionally. From what she told me I never learned any more than what my mother told me. As you know, it's not too surprising since she barely knew him. I think I need to...," I began to answer. I found it hard to tell him what was on my mind.

With a curious expression he asked, "You need to do what?"

After a few seconds, I finally got out "Take two months off."

"It isn't that you haven't earned a vacation. After ten years, you've taken what… Three days off," he replied as he sat straighter in the chair. Once he was comfortable in the chair, he held the diary up. As his eyes went from the dairy then to me he added, "With most people I would say, oh this is interesting. Knowing you as I do, I know there's more to it than that. Now that you have the diary, what are you planning to do…? I know it isn't going to take you but a few hours to read it."

"I know… I think it would mean more if I were to walk in his footsteps," I answered.

As he sat up straighter he asked, "Walk in his footsteps… Am I missing something?"

I went into my partially laid-out plans as he shook his head. He agreed it was an interesting idea, but doubted I would learn much. At the end of our conversation, he gave me his blessings as he returned to his office. I also went back to work closing out everything I had been working on. It was bad enough I was leaving him in a lurch. I knew the least I could do was to finish what I had started. It took me the entire day to take care of my projects. With several of my projects not completed yet he would be able to pick up where I left off easily. I did find time to go online and find a source for a suitable uniform of sorts, so I could start my journey making me look like a veteran.

Later, that afternoon Ray came by my office and asked, "When are you going to begin this trip of yours?"

"Probably a week or two… I'll take care of the Jeffries account before I leave. I've gotten most of the other accounts updated for you… It shouldn't take too much longer, and I'll have them caught up," I answered, as I closed another file on my computer.

"I'm not worried about taking care of whatever you have been working on. Don't let the work keep you here if you feel the need to go… My concern is what I can do for you," he told me.

"Thanks Ray… and I mean it," I told him. For the first time, I found I meant every word of it.

Later, that night I went over to my grandmother's place to tell her of my plans. If there was anyone I could talk to, it was she. I felt she would understand my need to do what I was planning. I was also in hopes of getting the information she had hinted at having.

"Good evening, Junior," she said, greeting me. She then gave me a hug and a kiss on my cheek. Releasing me, she asked, "Have you had supper yet?"

"I grabbed a quick burger… I just came over to talk," I told her. I was hesitant to tell her how I felt and what I had planned to do. I prayed she wouldn't give me an argument when I was through telling her. I hoped once she understood what I was going to do and its importance, she would tell me all she knew.

With a concerned look she asked, "What's the problem… is it Martha, my grandchildren?"

"No… it's the diary you gave me," I answered her. As she sat down, I took a seat on the couch across from her. As my eyes wandered around the room, I had to smile. I couldn't find one change to the place in the last thirty years. It looked the same as when she had taken me in. I found myself smiling when I learned it was a Sears's home. I thought of Sears being a store that sold clothes, furniture and tools but not homes. I then learned in the early 1900's Sears made homes in factories. They moved the pre-assembled home to a site and set them onto a foundation and did the finished work. Even as a young man I felt, my grandmother should have a better place to live. When I began making some good money, I offered to buy her another place. She surprised me when she declined the offer. She explained it didn't matter to her if the neighborhood was on the decline. She didn't care what I thought, but she wasn't moving. She told me it was her place, and she would die there as my grandfather had.

"There's nothing I can tell you about it… Your father and I weren't close," she answered.

"You said the other day when I finish reading the diary you wanted to tell me something. I know…" I began telling her then I paused in fear, that I was upsetting her. I picked up where I left off, I asked her, "…or is there something I don't understand. I know mother didn't get one of those telegrams telling her of his death. I also know she contacted the Army to find out what happened to him. They told her he made it back to the states, and they mustered him out of the service.

After a long battle with them, they finally agreed to list him as "MIA." Emotionally, it might have helped her but that's all… Now you have given me the diary I see he did make it back… What's going on?"

"All I can tell you is that he went off to Vietnam against my wishes. When he left, I refused to have anything to do with him…," she stopped, to wipe a tear from her eye. As she gained control of herself, she added, "I have never forgiven myself knowing my fears chased him away."

"But…?" I began to ask why she hadn't tried to find him when he came back. I didn't know if she didn't know he was home, or if she didn't care. I found myself at another point in my life with even more questions.

"There are no buts about it… I can only wish you luck in your search for your father. I don't see anything but disappointment ahead of you, but that's up to you. I don't know what you expect to find, but I know you. I know there's nothing I can say or do to change it. You have this idea in your head, and you have to do it… All I can say is that I'm the luckiest woman alive. I may have lost a son, but I got a second chance in a grandson, and if you need me, I'm here," she told me with a forced smile.

I knew it would be a waste of time, to push her anymore so I got up to leave. As I gave her a kiss, I told her, "I guess I had better get going. I have to finish a few projects that I have been working on back at the office."

"Just remember I love you…All right, I have told you part of what I wanted to, I do have something to add when you get back," she replied as she stroked my arm.

"Goodnight grandma," I said, leaving. As I shut the front door, I thought about what she had said. I found it irritating, but I knew she wasn't giving me any more information until I finished reading the diary. I also knew I should go on ahead and finish. I then would learn what she was holding back. The problem with that idea was that it didn't fit into my plan. Throughout my life, I had done everything my way, or I didn't do it at all. I decided not to deviate from my plan. I wanted to feel my father's experiences one-step at a time. This meant I would take only one sentence or page until I finished it. I headed for home not knowing what else she had to tell me.

Originally, I thought I would be on the road in a week or two at the most. I found I had more to do than I thought I did. It took almost three weeks for me to close everything out. Then, there was the personal side to my life. I sent out checks to cover my bills for the following three months. I wasn't planning to be gone that long, but I wanted to be safe. All of it went better than I had planned except for reading more of the diary. I was afraid if I read it before I needed to I would back out of my plan. The day came when I was ready to leave. I knew before I left, I had to tell my kids I was going to be gone. To resolve that idea, I had to go through Martha.

With hesitation, I pulled my phone out and dialed Martha's number. When she answered the phone, I asked her, "Can you get a baby-sitter…? I need to talk to you tonight about something… I can't think of better time than over supper… Yes. It's important."

She gave me every excuse known to mankind why we shouldn't meet. After a few tries, I told her where to meet me. I didn't want her to interpret my invitation to supper as a date. I needed to tell her what my plans were. I thought I would leave it up to her to explain it to the kids. Not knowing if I would make it back, I didn't want my kids to grow up not having answers.

On my way to the restaurant, I made one last call to my grandmother. I needed to tell her I was leaving in the morning. I was in hopes she would tell me whatever she was holding back from me. As with my last visit to her, she wouldn't tell me anything. Her only comment on my plans was she would tell me when I got back. Closing my cell phone, I felt I was on my own without any help.

I got to the restaurant and found Martha's car in the parking lot. I found it interesting she would be waiting for me. In all the years that I had known her, she was always late. As I got out of my car, memories of the restaurant came flooding back to me. The first time I took her to the restaurant was to propose to her. That one trip led to others to celebrate our anniversaries. Now, at the onset of an adventure of my life, we were back there again.

As I went to the front door, I could hear the surf pounding the beach in the background. Once inside I found nothing had changed, and I almost felt at home. As I walked through the door, the window to the wine cellar greeted me with its red velvet curtains. I was glad they hadn't covered the old wainscoting with plasterboard. To my left was the lounge with a few customers at the bar. To my right was the dining room. I could see the English décor I had always loved with brass chandeliers. At the door, framed in red velvet, the maitre de was standing at a podium ready to greet me.

"May I help you sir," the maitre de asked as I walked up to the entrance to the dining room.

"I'm meeting a woman… She may already be here," I told him. In checking out the dining room, I saw she was waiting for me at a table. I pointed her out to him as I went over to join her. Seeing her, I knew she'd had her hair done for the evening. Unlike her normal hairdo, her hair was full of highlights as well as soft flowing curls. To my satisfaction, the highlights in her hair glistened from the lights of the dining room. Her full red lips began to bring back memories. Setting her hair off, she was wearing a simple blue dress. I saw what I had seen when I first saw her many years ago. Once again, I was wondering why she hadn't gone into modeling. Remembering why I was there, I set the diary down on the table in front of her. I greeted her with, "Thanks for coming."

"Just explain to me why I'm here," she said in greeting me.

"I can tell you… It isn't for what you might think," I answered her as I pushed the diary towards her. I saw her look down at the diary, and hesitate at picking it up. When she touched it, she looked as if she thought it would bite her. She sat it back down and looked up at me. When I saw her reaction, I nodded for her to pick it up. I then told her, "Grandma gave it to me the night that I took the kids to the movies… Grandma's had it since 1978 and never opened it."

"I can't believe she didn't open it… I wonder why. If it was from my son, I sure would have, no matter what I thought of him," she replied as she picked the diary up.

"Afraid of what she might learn… I don't know. I haven't read all of it yet, and that's what I asked you here for," I confessed to her. I had a lot to tell her, I let her read a few pages. When she looked up at me, I told her, "I have to go and find him."

The waiter asked, "May, I take your order sir?"

"Yes… A Tom Collins… and nothing for my ex-wife," I told him. Having looked over at Martha's drink, it was still full. I would have bet she hadn't even touched it.

"I'll be right back," he said as he turned to walk away.

As she read the diary, I looked out the windows at the traffic. Turning the other way, I could see the surf coming in. As I watched the waves, come in I wondered why I hadn't taken her for more walks on the beach. I prayed when I got back that I would see moonlight glistening in her eyes again. Her smile and pearly teeth had always aroused me, for some reason. I had those types of thoughts many times during our marriage. In the end, something always came up; being a job, or weather, and I never told her how I thought of her. Here was another time I wish I could have told her how I felt about her. For some reason, I just couldn't tell her.

"This is something else… I've read stories like this… A bottle found on the beach and all, but this is strange," she said. She raised the book up as if to stress a point she asked, "What if he isn't alive? In fact, what makes you think he is?"

"I have to find out… I figure he sent it to her since there's no return address. If he had died and the police sent it to her, there would be a return address… Now that it's thirty years later, he may be dead. I find it a shame she didn't tell someone about it before now… It might have been a cry for help or understanding," I replied to her.

"I can't believe grandma didn't tell you anything else, if she knew something," she stated as she set the diary down.

"I tried to get it out of her, but she won't say anything else. She promised to tell me the rest of the story after I read the diary. Who knows what she might be holding back?" I answered as the waiter brought my drink to the table.

"The rest of…" she started to say. The waiter coming to the table interrupted her.

As he sat my drink down, he asked, "Here you are sir… Would you like to order?"

"Thanks… Give us a couple of minutes," I answered him as I kept my eyes on Martha. I found myself forgetting my real reason for asking her to have supper. Many ideas were going through my head and none of them had anything to do with the diary. I got control of myself and began thinking about what I wanted to eat. I told her, "We should probably order."

"I guess… I'll have the Beef Wellington it's always been my favorite," she answered, not opening the menu. Taking a sip of her drink, she asked, "You never answered me… What if he isn't alive?"

"Then the dream is over, I guess," I replied as I looked out the window at the surf. I wanted to change the subject, but it was important she understood. One day I prayed we would be back together, and our conversation would be on a different subject.

"Tell me what I can do to help you… I know how much this must mean to you," she said.

"The kids…" I started to tell her. Sipping my drink, I told her what I had in mind. I explained to her that I didn't think I would find him, but it might give me a better understanding of him. As I told her, my main concern was what might happen to me. Later, after our meal came, I told her I didn't want to leave the kids without some answers.

As our waiter removed our dishes, I asked Martha, "Would Madame or you like some dessert?"

"You know what I like," Martha answered. Not looking up at me, she was fingering the diary again.

I asked the waiter "Would you do something for me?"

"Yes sir," he replied.

"I would like you to witness this for me," I answered as I pulled a piece of paper out of my pocket. As I handed him my driver's license, I told him, "To verify I'm the one referred to in the document."

"What's that all about?" Martha asked.

"Just a minute," I told her.

"This is a little irregular," the waiter said taking my license. Looking at the license he went back to read the paper.

"It would be a great help to me since there aren't any banks open this late," I told him. He gave me a questioning look as he signed the papers as a witness. He handed everything back to me. Taking it, I told him, "Thanks… Both of us would like a Cognac."

"Yes sir," the waiter said as he left the table.

With him being on his way I handed the papers to Martha. I then told her, "This will make it easier for you. If I don't come back by December first, you get everything I own… the house, my investment properties, investment holdings, the bank accounts… and the business… or my share of it."

"I get the feeling you're afraid you might not come back… Isn't that a little melodramatic," she said as she read the piece of paper.

"I'll be back… I'm just making sure everything is in order while I'm gone," I assured her.

Later she told me how great supper was. To finish the night we had a cognac as we used to do. As we walked to the parking lot, she gave me her promise to tell the kids why they wouldn't be seeing me. When we got to our cars, she gave me a gentle kiss on the cheek.

"Good luck," she said as she started her car. While backing out she added, "Call me if you need anything."

I didn't know what to say so I waved and shouted out, "Thanks."

As I watched her drive out of the lot, I realized my trip was to begin the following day. With nothing else to do. I decided to take a walk on the beach, and I headed that way. I stopped, to look back in the direction Martha had driven, and I wanted to kick myself. As I turned towards the beach, I knew I should have invited her for a walk. I was about to step up onto the sidewalk, and I heard a horn honk. Turning around I saw Martha staring back at me with a sly grin on her face.

She cried out, "Want to go for a walk, stranger?"

"I was just thinking it might be a good night for one," I called back to her. With her suggestion, memories came to me. We used to go for walks on the beach prior to the birth of our son Jerry. In thinking about us strolling down the beach, I remembered that it was on one of them, we got the idea that it was time to have children. It then hit me, that it had been seven years since we had taken a romantic stroll. As I watched her come closer, I wondered why it had taken so long.

She asked, "What are you waiting for?"

"I guess I'm getting cautious and slow," I returned as I let her slip her arm into mine. As I let her balance herself on me, she took off her high heels.

We walked and walked the beach until our legs almost fell off. It was two-thirty in the morning, when we finally said good-bye to each other. As she pulled out of my driveway, I found myself wondering if I wanted to look for my father or not. I tried to go back to sleep, but I couldn't get the smile off my face. I finally got out of bed and began pulling out what I would need for my trip to Frisco. I had everything packed and ready before I went in and took a shower. As I walked into the bathroom, I saw my reflection in the mirror. What I saw made me glad I always wore my hair short. It saved me from having to get a GI haircut. I was also glad because if it were any longer the few gray hairs, I had, would show even more. For some reason, I had a feeling as if my whole life that I had been waiting for this day to come.

CHAPTER TWO

By daybreak, I was outside my house in fatigues, combat boots, and a carryall bag with a few changes of underwear in my hand. An ex-soldier supposedly wore the fatigues I had bought on the internet. When I got them, I pulled off the insignia and Master sergeant's stripes. I wanted to give everyone the impression, I had been a soldier, but I didn't want a cop to arrest me for impersonating a soldier. I thought leaving the threads showing where everything had been, gave the jacket more of an authentic look.

In making my plans, I decided my father wouldn't have had much money. If he were to have traveled anywhere, it would've been by bus. I decided to make my way to Frisco by bus. Once I had packed everything, I called a cab to take me to the bus station. As I waited for the cab, I was wishing I could be on my way to the airport. Then, going back to the diary, I knew he had sent home a good portion of his check. Like him, I would be getting to Frisco without much money in my pocket. I did take a couple of hundred dollars to start with. I decided to leave my credit cards, phone card, and everything else at home. I knew if I took them, I would use them. For my own safety, I did plan to carry my driver's license. I knew if worse came to worst I could always phone someone to come to my rescue. As I ran a mental check, I waited for the cab at the curb in front of my house.

Once the cabdriver pulled in front of me, he asked, "You called a cab soldier?"

"Yes, I'm the one that called you," I answered as I threw my bag in through the window onto the backseat. For some reason, I took my field cap off and put it under my arm. Then opening the door to get in I told him, "The bus depot."

"Yes sir," he returned as he flipped the fare meter arm down. He looked at me in the rearview mirror and added, "A good day for a trip."

"It looks like it's going to be one," I replied as he drove off. As he made our way down the street, I looked back at my neighbors' places. The area in Montebello was older than my place was. It wasn't elaborate, but it was all I needed. Ray kept saying I needed to move to a better neighborhood, but I couldn't see it. My neighbors were nosey enough. I wondered how many had seen me get into the cab dressed as I was. I wondered what they might be saying about me. I turned back around and laughed to myself as I watched the road while the cabby drove me to the bus depot.

As the cabby drove, I turned my attention to everyone else on the road. I had found it entertaining to watch people in their cars as they drove. There were the drivers who were singing with their radios, or laughing at who knows what. I enjoyed watching the expressions on drivers' faces. As we made our way to the bus depot, I saw some of them smiling, but most of the drivers had frowns on their faces. Then, the ones I feared the most, with cell phones plastered to their heads. As I watched them, it was hard to believe there weren't more accidents. For years, I had never accepted or made calls on my phone while I was driving. Since the Blue-Tooth's came in, I now feel okay to use my cell phone occasionally. Still, as I watched the different faces, I wondered how many were facing anything such as, I was about to do.

The cabdriver turned on to US 10 west and headed toward downtown Los Angeles. He took it to the Alameda exit and headed south. As we went through the city, I tried to remember where the bus depot was. About the time, I remembered it was seventh the driver turned onto it. As he made his turn, I saw the depot sign ahead of us.

"Twenty-seven dollars," the driver said as he pulled up to the curb.

I reached into my pocket, and pulled out my stash of money. I gritted my teeth as I counted out thirty dollars and handed it to him.

In my normal life, I would spend more than that for lunch. For what I had on me, it represented a good chunk of my money. As he took the money, I told him, "Keep the change."

As he pulled away, I was glad I had grabbed some extra money off my dresser. When I originally laid out my plans, I had forgotten about cab fare when I went to the bank. I looked at the money in my hand thinking how much I depended on plastic. The balance might have looked like a lot of money, but I knew it wouldn't last long. Over a tenth of what I started with was gone already. At the rate, I was going; the two hundred that I had planned to use on the trip wasn't going to last long.

When I got inside the depot, I found it interesting. The last time I was there, it was full of people, traveling all across the country. As I looked around it looked deserted compared to last time I had been there. It was hard to believe they were still in business. I recognized the rows of lockers, the seats, and the doors going out to the buses. Then, the middle of one wall was full of vending machines. As I looked around, I also saw the off-white tile floor and the dirty yellow walls. As I remember it, there were rows of seats in the center of the waiting room. I would have bet they were the same discolored, nicked, and scratched plastic seats I had sat on as a kid. I didn't want to think about the tons of gum stuck to the underside of them. The dirt, cigarette butts, and wrappers covering the floor matched the thought of the gum. Then seeing the prospective riders I began to worry about myself. It wasn't for what I had on because there were many outlandishly dressed men in the depot.

As strange as it sounded the worst I could have done was to have taken a shower. Most of the weirdo's I could smell ten feet away. Then as I took a seat waiting for my bus, I got the feeling I did smell. I didn't know if it was me or not, but people would walk past the empty seat next to me and take one four or five away. My wife more than once said people could smell my attitude, and that's why they stayed from me. I found myself beginning to think she might be right. That morning in the bus depot, for some reason, was worse than usual. Little old ladies also walked a wide berth around me. I went as far as bending my head trying to detect an odor from my fatigues, but they smelled clean.

Rather than taking the first bus, I hung around and sweated for a few hours, so I could take a later one. It was good because I could bluff my way through a couple of conversations with a few service men I had met. I also picked up some of their frustrations as I talked to them. I gained a feeling for the attitude I should be portraying.

The ticket to Frisco cost me a little over fifty dollars. After I paid for the ticket, I had a little over a hundred dollars to hold me for two months. I found a knot form in my stomach, a little scared at what I was about to do. My life was a mess compared to a year earlier, it wasn't as bad as it might become. In the back of my mind, I knew I would be missing everything I held valuable. I knew it wouldn't be that bad if I came up with some answers. My life had revolved around who and what my father might have been. I knew I had to get over that hurdle in my life. I found myself saying, "Doing what I'm about to do will make room for others."Something told me this was more of a dream than a reality. I prayed that I was man enough to go through with it. The time came to either do, or die. I decided to go ahead no matter what it cost.

"Bus 6544 to San Francisco is now boarding," came over the PA.

"Here we go," I announced aloud.

The man standing in line with me asked me, "What?"

"Sorry… I have a bad habit of talking to myself," I explained to him.

As I stepped forward, the man behind me stayed where he was, rather than keeping up with me. As I moved forward, again I noticed he kept a good distance from me. Once again, I raised my arm up to make sure I didn't stink. I didn't find an offensive odor about myself, so I figured it was his problem. I forgot about him and kept my eye on the passengers ahead of me. I could hear a mother yell at her child from somewhere behind me. It brought back memories of Martha yelling at our children to behave. I found myself wondering if she was still yelling at them.

"Scotty, get back here," the mother yelled out to her son.

"I want to play soldier," the little guy cried out to her.

I turned around and found the little boy a few feet from me. I didn't say anything to him, but I waved my fingers at him. He gave me a scared look and ran back to his mother. Once he found her, he grabbed her leg and stood beside it and looked at me. Again, I waved at him trying to dispel his fear. Not getting a reaction from him, I focused my attention on the head of the line. It wasn't easy keeping my mind on what was happening. My problem was seeing his mother, and she brought me back to Martha's visit a few hours earlier. Having her in the same bed with me again brought a tear to my eyes. I found myself wishing I knew what she had been thinking of.

"Your ticket please," the ticket agent said as I got up to him.

He startled me with my thoughts being on Martha. As I gave him my ticket, I told him, "Sorry…I was thinking about something else."

"I've been known to do that… I've been thinking about going home," he replied as he punched my ticket. Then handing me back the ticket he reached behind me and told the man, "Ticket please."

As I walked out to the bus I heard, the man behind tell the agent, "Yes sir."

I found myself hesitating at the first step. I had flown or driven to Frisco many times, but I had never taken the bus. The idea of all of those bodies in one bus didn't sound like fun. For as long as the line had been, I knew the bus was going to be full. It wasn't difficult to find a seat. To my surprise, there were four or five double seats open. I walked halfway down the aisle and took a window seat. Rather than putting my bag in the overhead area, I threw it under the seat ahead of me. Sitting in my seat, I found myself already bored. I watched the rest of the passenger's board the bus. There were little old ladies, men of all ages dressed neatly and sloppy. One guy looked like he was in his twenties was sporting an earring and a boom box. I had to smile thinking how typical the passengers compared to what you see in movies.

It wasn't long before the woman, and the little boy got onto the bus. The kid walked past me and gave me a little wave as he picked his nose. He took his finger out of his nose and said, "Hi mister."

"Hi," I returned smiling at him. He reminded me of Jerry when he was at that age.

"Get on down there Scotty," his mother told him.

As the other passengers got on, I noticed they seemed concerned to where they would be sitting. There were few empty double seats available so it was hard for them to find a seat to themselves. Then, as the bus began to fill up, the selection got more difficult. As the bus filled up, leaving fewer places for people to sit alone, they had to sit with strangers. Most of the passengers would look at the seat next to me and walk right past me.

A man having just passed me asked the man behind me, 'Mind if I take this seat?"

The frustrated mother leaned over and told me, "Sorry if he bothered you."

"No problem," I assured her. I took a good look at her, and found her attractive but not as beautiful as Martha. She was a good ten years younger, but she had some of the same striking beauty traits that Martha had. I didn't want to be obvious, so I turned my attention to what was going on outside my window. Not having anything better to look at, I watched the clean up men sweep the floor of the garage. Then, tired of watching nothing, I pulled the diary out of the bag. It wasn't hard to find the last passage I had read. I looked back out of the window, and nothing had changed. I turned my attention back to the front of the bus when I heard the door, to the bus close. I muttered, "I guess I'm on my way."

As the bus pulled out, I turned my attention back to the diary. As I was about to start reading, the diary slipped out of my hands. As it hit the floor of the bus, something fell out of it. I reached down, picked up the diary, and laid it on the seat next to me. Then with difficulty, I picked up the piece of paper. As I picked it up on the backside, I saw the words "Kodak." I also saw scribbled in pencil were the words:

Remember I love you

Your son

Jeffery

I didn't have to turn it over to know whose picture it was. As I turned it over, I saw a man in uniform, and I knew it was my father.

My grandmother had shown me pictures of him and commented how much I looked like him. As I looked into his eyes in the picture, I muttered, "Thanks for putting your picture in the diary for me... I meant to get one from grandma." Tucking it into my pocket, I began to read:

> *...a son I have never seen. Will I screw up their lives as well as my own?*

> *I know I should go home, but I don't feel as if I have one. I know I have a wife and a small son, but I don't know what to do with them. I'm scared because I have never had the chance to get to know Helen. What will I do if she doesn't like me? Then, even if we did know each other, I'm not the same man, that I once was. The worst part of it all is that I can't go back to mom's place. I ruined that by joining the service. Not having gotten a letter from her in three years, I know what she thinks of me. My only choice is to head out on my own. After a while, in Frisco, maybe I will be able to shed some of my guilt and start a new life with Helen. At least, she wrote to me and told me about Jeff Jr. If there is anything I would hold against her is sending me copies of the paper with all the lies in it.*

I wanted to read more, but I couldn't. In the diary, my father confirmed what grandma had told me. The rest of it was beginning to bring back memories I hadn't thought about for years. I remembered her reading a letter from him. He told her the news stories she had sent him were a pack of lies, and she wasn't to send him anymore of them. Shaking my head, I put the diary back into my bag.

From the aisle a little boy asked, "Can I sit with you mister?"

I looked back at his mother to see if it was all right with her. I found she was staring out her window, not seeming to know he had left her side. Then turning to the little boy, I told him, "Sure."

He crawled into the seat and just sat there. He didn't say anything but occasionally he would look up at me and grin. I could see myself at his age acting as he was. I found myself wondering if his father was in the services, and he just missed his father. I finally got the nerve to ask him, "Where's your daddy?"

After a short pause, he got down from the seat without answering. Halfway to his seat with his mother he gave me a grin. Then, as he crawled back into his seat, his mother took notice of him. I couldn't hear what she whispered to him, but it wasn't any of my business.

Turning to the buildings we were passing, my thoughts went back to my search. I wanted to cry because I knew what I was about to do was dumb. I could have just as easily flown to Frisco, read the diary, and walked the streets that he did. The fear that it wouldn't be the same kept coming back to me. If I just had gone there, walked the streets, and prayed, I would have returned home not gaining anything. I had already walked the streets of Frisco, and I knew I didn't get what he had from it. Walking the streets as he did would give it more meaning.As these thoughts went through my head, I fell asleep somewhere along the way.

A voice woke me asking, "Did I wake you?"

"What?" I asked startled by the question. Opening my eyes and sitting up straighter, I saw it was Scotty's mother.

"I guess I fell asleep," I managed to get out of my mouth.

"I'm sorry… Being alone with a little boy is a little frightening… I thought you might be willing to keep me company with him liking you so much," she told me.

"No problem… You have a cute little boy there," I replied not knowing what else to say. As the words came out of my mouth, Scotty was crawling into her lap. Then looking at the little boy I added, "Hi again."

"He's good most of the time," she told me with a smile.

As Scotty was moving around I couldn't be sure, but I knew her smile went all the way around her head. To my surprise, I noticed she had dimples that Martha didn't have. I reminded myself not to get any ideas that I had messed up one family already. I had no wish to involve myself with someone on a bus. Our little chat covered many different subjects about her and her son. I learned she was a single mother about to make a new start. She didn't know what she was going to do, but she was going to try. Then when there wasn't anything else to say we both went back to our own thoughts. The only distraction was Scotty jumping on and off her lap, running up and down the aisle.

Thirty or forty miles out of Bakersfield as I was looking out the window, I felt a hand go up and down my leg. The hairs on the back of my neck began to rise with everything else. I turned to her and wanted to ask what she thought she was doing. Then seeing the smile on her face I came up with one of my own.

"I sure wish we were a couple," she blurted out.

"Well… I… don't know what to say," I admitted. Having never been a lady's man I didn't know what to do. I married the only woman I had ever dated. Therefore, what she was doing might have been normal it wasn't to me. Not knowing what else to do, I pushed her hand off my leg.

"I'm sorry… It's just that I'm so confused… I spent my last buck on these tickets. I don't know what Scotty, and I are going to do tonight. If I'm lucky, I'll find a waitress job tomorrow. If I do, then I'll have tips to live on," she told me with a tear in her eye. She then leaned over into the aisle and cried out to her son, "Leave the driver alone and get back here."

Not knowing what to say I just sat there like a bump on a log as grandma used to say. Shaking my head thinking of her son, I wondered what they were going to do. What was facing me was bad enough, but it was my choice. I couldn't imagine what I would do if I were in her shoes. Then, with a tear, Scotty climbed back into her lap.

Feeling sorry for him, I told his mother, "I can give you fifty dollars if you think that would help."

"I didn't mean for you to give me any money… Don't get me wrong, for I can use it. I would hate to have him go to sleep on a park bench hungry," she told me with another tear running down her cheek.

Reaching into my pocket, I pulled out my stash of money. I swallowed hard as I pulled out fifty dollars and handed it to her. Hesitating, I told her, "The least I can do."

"Oh, I appreciate it… I can get a cheap room and something for him to eat," she said, taking the money from me with a smile. She lowered her head as she added, "It isn't an imposition I hope."

"Don't think anything of it," I told her as I tried to smile. All I had left was a little over fifty dollars and change. I found myself thinking, "I haven't even got to Frisco yet, and I'm almost broke."

We both fell into silence the rest of the way into Bakersfield. It didn't take long before the bus pulled into the garage of the depot. The woman beside me began grabbing for her bags. I figured I had been wrong about her going to Frisco. From her actions, I knew she was getting off in Bakersfield.

"We'll be here for fifteen minutes," the driver announced.

"We get off here," Scotty's mother told me. She moved her son into the aisle and pushed him towards the front of the bus. With a smile, she added, "Thank you again."

"Good luck," I told her as I tipped my hat to her.

Once the bus stopped, she walked on down the aisle. Halfway down the aisle Scotty came back and gave me a wave good-bye. I waved to him as I said, "Be good for your mother."

He was still grinning, as he ran back to his mother and the two of them got off the bus. I followed them as they walked away without waving goodbye. I said a short prayer it would work out for them. Then, to my surprise, the woman walked up to a newer model car and put her son into the backseat. As she opened the passenger door, I could see a man in his twenties behind the steering wheel. The woman got in, grabbed his neck, and gave him a passionate kiss. Releasing him, she laid her head back and laughed as she looked out at the bus.

"Well soldier, it looks as if you got the shaft," the man replied from behind me.

"And I didn't even get her name," I added. Martha was always saying I should put more faith in people. I wondered what she would have said if she had been in my shoes.

CHAPTER THREE

It was seven o'clock when we pulled into San Francisco. I got off the bus hungrier than hell. I hadn't had any breakfast or lunch, and it was almost suppertime. My first impulse was *to* go to a restaurant and get something to eat. Then as I walked up to one, I saw my reflection in the window. The image looking back at me wasn't what I was used to. I could almost hear the image tell me I didn't have enough money to buy anything. Even if I did, I doubted they would let me in. I knew I had to find a way to earn my next meal.

The reality of what I had gotten myself in, hit me hard enough to knock me off my feet. I began to play with the idea of giving up and going home. I knew if I had a credit card on me, I would catch the first flight home. I knew I could call Martha, and she would wire me some money. I would still be in the mess I was in for a while. Giving that idea some thought I knew I couldn't call her. I didn't want to admit to her that my idea was dumb.

Sucking in my stomach, I decided to make it work no matter how much it hurt. I had to find a job first, but the question is where? Right then my first concern, or want, was food. I decided to find a restaurant and get a job. The trouble with that idea was that I never had done anything but get water or coffee in the kitchen of my own home. I had never worked in a restaurant and had no idea what I could do. Then from the back of my mind, something shouted out, "Wash dishes dummy."

Standing where I was, people walking by kept giving me funny looks. I wanted to ask them what their problem was, but I didn't. I wondered if it was the fatigues, I was wearing or what. I found their reaction to me funny since I wasn't in the best part of town. I had learned around the bus depot to expect the unexpected. Then a hunger pang hit, and I forgot about the stares I was getting.

Not that it made any difference, but I walked to the closest corner to see where I was. Reaching the corner, I saw a sub shop and different little restaurants. I prayed one of them had a job for me. From the street sign, I saw I was at the corner of Mission and Fremont. I knew it didn't make any difference where I was; I gave a shrug as I walked to the nearest alley. With what I had on, I couldn't see anyone but a soup kitchen allowing me inside the place. I was in hopes by going to the rear of a restaurant where I might find someone willing to put me to work.

For some reason, I felt like I was playing a game of "Monopoly." On my first roll of the dice, it got me to a property called "Frisco." Now it was time to roll them again. I prayed I wouldn't land on "Chance," and get the card that says, "Go to Jail, and Do not pass go."

"Humph," a woman said, passing me just before I got to the alley. Then a few feet from me, she told her friend, "They should lock those drunks up."

As I turned around, I asked her, "Who's drunk…, I know I'm not, are you?"

"I don't think he's drunk," the friend commented. She looked over at me, giving me a disgusted look.

The first woman asked her friend "Why is he dressed like that?"

"Does it make a difference…? You're not wearing the same outfit your friend is," I reminded her as I walked on.

"He has a point… He's probably just back from Afghanistan or Iraq." I heard her friend tell the other woman.

Looking back as I turned into the alley, I noticed the two women looking at each other and then at me. Not caring what they thought, I continued walking down the alley to find a job. I found myself giving it a second thought seeing the alley. I knew there was paper and whatever in the gutters of the street, but it was nothing like the alley. Even with the lighting being dim, I could see pieces of signs and boxes against the backs of the buildings. The worst was the stench from a dumpster with flies buzzing around it. The thought of the women took my mind off the stench, and I found myself muttering, "Stupid bitch."

From the sidewalk, the alley wasn't at all inviting with all the shadow's hiding everything. I knew that in daylight, I wouldn't hesitate walking through it. I was a little worried about what I might find in it. Taking a second look, I couldn't see anything that worried me. I didn't see any, but I knew there were rats in it, and I can't stand them. I told myself that if I didn't bother them, they wouldn't bother me.

As I walked up the alley, I was thinking about the woman's outburst. I wasn't sure what her problem was, and I didn't care. My main concern was getting something in my stomach. Still, the woman's comment did bother me. It wasn't long, and I would have a better understanding of what bothered her about me. I would learn there is a side of this country I didn't know existed. What I was to learn I would find hard to believe, and I wouldn't have any idea how to fight it.

I found the door to the first restaurant. I sucked in a breath and smelled rotten food from the trash cans. The trash can next to it was a dead giveaway, it was easy to tell it was the right door. As I was about to go to the door, a man came out with a bucket in his hand. He began to pitch the contents of the bucket into the alley. With a questioning look, he lowered the bucket when he saw me.

From five feet away he screamed at me, "What do you want?"

"My wallet and everything I…," I began to say, but I stopped, seeing him aim the bucket at me.

"We don't want any bums like you around here," he screamed as he let the contents of the bucket fly.

"Excuse me," I returned as I sidestepped the water that he had thrown at me. As I looked back at him, I wondered where he got off calling me a bum. I knew it had been a few hours since I had taken a shower but I had taken one. I have also shaved and my fatigues were clean so I didn't see what the problem was. Frustrated, I headed towards the entrance to the alley. He didn't bother me since I knew the area had several other restaurants. I prayed one of them had something I can do for a meal.

"Don't bother to come back… We don't like your kind," he added, as I continued down the alley.

"You don't have to worry… I won't," I yelled back to him.

Because of his attitude, I had a little hesitation as I made my way to another restaurant. Then with another hunger pang, there was no question. I had to either get a job or spend some of my stash. As hungry as I was, I hadn't thought about sleeping. I saw an open screen door, and I went up to it and knocked. I didn't get an answer, and I wasn't sure what to do. I decided to open the door and go in when a Chinese man greeted me.

He gave me the impression that he was too busy to talk to me. He still asked, "What you want?"

"I just got back to the states, and someone stole everything but this one bag…, my money and identification. I would like to know if you have something I can do for a meal?" I asked him.

"I…" he began to say as he stared at me. I didn't know if I should run or wait for him to decide. From his expression, I thought he might want to help me. First, he looked back through the door, but before he went inside, he turned to me with a grin.

"I'll don't care what it is… I'm not asking for a full-time job," I assured him. I realized how that might have sounded so I added, "If you have one, I would love it."

"You clean floor… I feed you," he offered.

"A deal," I told him. Then, as he opened the screen door, I went inside. As I looked around, I found the floor to be a mess. Fish heads caught my attention once I got into the kitchen. I could see them all over the place. The floor was a mess with vegetable trimmings and a fine film of oil over it. I wondered where the health department was as I looked at the mess. The stench was so bad I wasn't sure if I wanted to eat. For a couple of minutes, I watched the cooks working their woks and my hunger came back. The man who gave me the job pointed to a broom, mop, and bucket next to some shelving.

"And the garbage in cans," he ordered, as he walked away.

As I looked around the kitchen, I got the feeling the cooks were in their own little world. They didn't even look up when he told me what to do with the garbage. As time went on, I noticed they did speak to each other a little in Chinese. Not once did they say anything to me. I didn't care what they were doing, but I had a job to do. I put my bag on a shelf and grabbed a broom. I had to admit I wasn't the most skilled sweeper in the world, but I was doing my best. The man who gave me the job grabbed the broom from me and showed me a squeegee. He then motioned for me to use it to get everything up. After he watched me for a few minutes, he finally left me to my work.

"Didn't your mother tell you to stay out of fishnets?" I asked the first fish head I saw.

As I swept the floor, the beady little eyes kept looking up at me. I could almost hear his cry for help. I began sweeping cabbage leaves over the heads as if I were dressing them. This game helped me get through the mess. After a while, I found I wasn't looking at them as a dead being, but garbage. Once I'd reached that point, it went faster. The thoughts of all the fish that I had eaten came to mind. From all the garbage on the floor, I found myself wondering if I could ever eat in another restaurant.

After a half hour, the floor was clean, or at least I thought it was. Then I saw the cooks were still throwing their garbage on the floor. I could see where it saved them time, but it didn't make it easier for me. As I made my last swipe with the mop, the cooks began putting food away. Then looking at my watch, I saw it was nine-forty-five. I found myself thinking it was a little early for them to close, but I didn't mind. I was as bad as a dog waiting for a bone from his owner. As I waited, the cooks continued putting the food away, which worried me. Then when I saw the cooks wrapping up their tools, I began to worry they weren't going to feed me.

As my thoughts of eating took me to the meals, Martha used to fix. I could almost taste the stew she used to make. Visions of her pies began to make my mouth water. Then the owner came into the kitchen carrying a large sack. No one had to tell me it was full of food. It was far more than I had expected, but I knew it was the leftovers from the buffet table. I doubted I could eat all of it, but I was going to try.

"You leave now," he said, handing me the sack. He motioned with his finger for me to move. I got the idea he wanted me to leave. As I began to move, he repeated, "You leave now."

"Yes sir…Thank you," I offered as I held the sack up as a salute. I knew my welcome had ended. I didn't want to argue so I made my way towards the back door. As I held the screen door halfway open, I remembered my bag. I stepped back inside and pointed to my bag. I then explained, "I almost forgot my bag."

"You take," he replied as he grabbed it and handed it to me. He didn't say anything as he motioned for me to leave.

"Thanks, again," I said as I went down the alley. I opened the sack, and I saw several to-go containers. The aroma of the food reached my nose, and I felt a smile on my face. As I began looking for a place to sit, I felt my stomach saying, "Thanks."

The first place that made sense was the bus depot. There were lights, air-conditioning, and chairs where I could sit and enjoy my meal. I went into the depot, and no one gave me any grief. I took a seat, opened the sack and the aroma of the food rose, and tickled my nose. I knew my hands were dirty, but I was too tired to use the restroom. I wiped them off on my leg, and they felt a little cleaner. I reached inside the sack and began taking out the different containers. I placed all of it on the seat next to me. I found the man at the restaurant hadn't given me a fork or spoon.

A man behind me asked, "Can you spare some of that?"

I turned around, and I saw a kid in a set of fatigues as I was wearing. He was about my size with red hair and stubbles. I had the feeling he was four or five years younger than I was. From his stance, I got the feeling that he'd had a bad day. Other than that, I could tell he was a corporal in the army. On his upper arm, I could make out a patch that said Afghanistan. I knew I couldn't eat it all, and I told him, "Help yourself, I have plenty."

"Thanks… I lost all of my money in a crap game this afternoon," he said, sitting on the other side of the food.

"Sorry but they forgot to give me a fork," I apologized to him. Then with a shrug, I told him, "I guess fingers will work."

"I'll get us a fork," he said. He got up and headed to the fast-food area.

When he came back, he handed me a fork and a napkin. In his other hand, he had a bag, which he put on the floor. Then as he took a seat, he told me, "I'm Fred Crawford."

"A pleasure to meet you Fred… I'm Jeff O'Connor… and thanks for the utensil," I returned. I wanted to eat more than talking to someone. I didn't bother to say anything, but I motioned for him to dig in. For as fast as he was eating, I knew he was as hungry as I was.

"I appreciate this," Fred said as he took another bite.

"As you can see I have enough for four or five," I replied as I took a fork full myself. As I wiped my mouth, I asked him, "What's your story again?"

"Like I said, I lost my money in a crap game," he answered. He wiped his mouth and told me, "They mustered us out this morning. I didn't have enough money for a flight home, so I decided to take the bus… I was sitting over there and three guys asked me if I liked to play dice. Like an idiot, I said yes, and I went out back with them… It didn't take long, and they had what money I had. I can't prove it, but I think they set me up."

"So, you're stranded here like I am," I replied. In ways, I was in the same straight, but at least it was my decision. I knew I couldn't help him, but I had to ask him, "I don't really have the money to help you… but how much is it going cost, to get you home?"

"Oh, I have the ticket to get home… Then my parents will be there to help me," he answered.

"Where's home" I asked him.

"Oklahoma City," he answered with a smile. He then waved his hand as if he was pushing the food away. He added, "That's enough for me."

"I agree with you, enough is enough… It was good though," I commented. As full as I felt I knew I couldn't eat another bite. Then as I began putting the leftovers into the bag, I thought of Fred. I asked him, "Want to take this with you...? You're going to get hungry between here and there."

"If you don't mind... I doubt I'll find anyone but a fellow soldier that'll help me," he answered with a smile and a shrug.

"What do you mean...? There are many good people out there," I told him, not understanding what he meant.

"You mean wearing that, you haven't had problems?" He asked. As he sat back in his seat, he didn't wait for me to answer. He told me, "I flew home last year on leave to attend my brother's funeral... he was, killed in a car accident. Anyway, at the Kennedy Airport, everyone looked at me as if I had a disease... In fact, one woman walking by called me a baby killer."

"Why would she call you a baby killer?" I asked, not understanding.

"I kept my temper, but I caught up with her. I asked her what she was talking about...," he began to tell me. With a pause, he added, "She told me she had heard about the villages we had leveled... and the women and children killed when we leveled them."

"And..., what did you tell her?" I asked him when he stopped.

"I didn't bother... You know how it is. Only someone that's been there understands," he answered. As he looked up at the ceiling he added, "Why don't they understand... When someone is throwing mortar shells, fifty caliber rounds..., what are you to do? You either take them out or walk away. If it had been up to us, we may have done it differently, but we followed our orders.... What were we supposed to do if we didn't agree, just walk away? Those times many of our guys lost their lives..., for nothing. I saw it happen day after day, and you find it builds up inside until it almost drives you nuts. Then the order came to take the village anyway we had to. I don't know if there was a different way, but we had our orders. We threw everything at them, we had. As each shell went off, I said this one is for Dave, then Robby and so on. As with the others, there wasn't any thought to who was or wasn't in the village. It was a target that was trying to kill us, and we got the job done," he answered. As the last word left his mouth, he lowered his head and a tear fell. As he turned to me, he added, "I guess it's the same in any war… A soldier doesn't ask questions. His duty is to take orders and act on them. Then the damn politicians, who sent us there, are saying they didn't approve of the war. If they didn't approve of it, why did they send us?"

"I know what you are saying," I replied. I lied in that I had never been in the service, and I didn't know firsthand. My understanding came from what he said as well as the expression on his face.

"I know it's none of my business, but I don't understand why you are wearing your fatigues," he told me.

A security officer asked us, "Waiting for a bus?"

"Yes… Oklahoma City," Fred answered him, holding his ticket up to him.

I found myself swallowing hard waiting for him to ask to see my ticket. Then as he walked off, I relaxed and went back to our discussion. I told him, "The same group of guys must be the ones that got me into a crap game earlier. After I lost all the money I had on me, I went to get my bags and found someone had stolen them. I don't have anything else to wear, so I removed my stripes and badges… I did that because I don't want everyone to know I just got out of the service."

"Well, within twenty minutes of boarding, I'm putting on civilian clothes. You will never see me in anything green, tan or brown ever again," he said as he looked around. Then he told me, "I'm keeping my dress uniform, and I'm throwing the rest of it out. I even wrote my mother and told her to throw out my western boots. I'll wear wing-tips before I wear another pair of boots."

"As I said, I wouldn't be wearing this if I had something else to wear," I told him.

"My father owes me…. If he had told me why he never talked about Vietnam, I wouldn't have joined," he replied.

"What do you mean?" I asked him. I got the feeling he had joined the service for the wrong reason and wasn't happy about it.

"I've known all my life he fought in Nam. Then, once I was old enough, I asked him different questions about his tour…. He never told me anything. Now that I'm back, I don't think I'll be talking about my life as a soldier. If I could, I would tell my friends I was out here working for an Uncle or something…. Unfortunately, too many know the truth, so I can't lie," he answered.

"My father never told me anything either… I would love to know more about his tour other than where he went," I confessed.

"I can't wait until we walk into the house…" a woman was telling her husband as they passed us.

"And to tell them we're expecting. Something tells me…," the husband returned as they walked on.

"I remember that feeling of excitement at the birth of my first one," I commented, as I watched the couple walk away.

"If I have anything to say about it, I will never have kids… I wouldn't want any kid of mine in some war. Don't get me wrong, I believe in fighting for my country. I don't like the ridicule you get when you come back from a war," Fred replied.

Fred looked at his watch, and a worried look came across his face. As I looked at the clock on the wall, he gave a shrug. He then looked over at the rest room, back at me, and shrugged his shoulders again. With a grin he got up, and added, "If you want these once I've changed, you're more than welcome to them."

"Yes, if you don't mind… Since I don't have anything else to my name," I assured him. I didn't want them, but they would work as a change. After cleaning the restaurant, what I had on was filthy. I figured if nothing else I could take them into the rest room and use the soap in there to wash them.

"I'll be right back," Fred assured me as he turned towards the rest room. Stopping, he handed me the bag of food and told me, "I don't think I need this right now."

With a big smile a little boy asked, "Are you soldiers?"

"We were," I answered him.

"My father was a soldier…, and a bad man killed him," the little boy said with a sad look.

"I'm sorry about that…. He might have been one of my friends. When did he die?" Fred asked him.

He was so young he didn't know when his father died, and it didn't matter. All he knew was that his father had died as a soldier. I figured Fred needed to feel close to the kid with his regrets in seeing so many men dying for nothing. I found it nice the two of them had each other for a minute or two. Fred and the boy had lost something, and they were both reaching out.

"Long time ago," the little boy answered. Once he said his piece, he turned with a smile and walked away.

"I'm sorry," Fred called out to the little boy.

On the other side of the lobby area, a mother was weaving in and out of the aisles of chairs. She stopped when she saw the little boy coming up the other side. I could see her breathing deeply as if she was out of breath trying to keep up with him. I wanted to laugh as I watched her shake her fist at her son as she tried to head him off. As a parent, I understood the frustration.

"I'll be right back," Fred told me.

"I'm not going anywhere," I replied as I looked around the lobby. Most of the people in the lobby were so involved in themselves, they had missed the fun. Then turning back to the mother and child, I saw they were sitting across the lobby.

"1438 to Bakersfield is now boarding," the PA announced.

A couple of minutes later Fred came out of the restroom. I saw he had a red pullover and a pair of jeans on. When he got back to me, he was panting as he picked up the sack of food. After he set the food into his bag, he grinned and threw his fatigues at me. He then told me, "Thanks, and I wish you luck."

"You too," I returned as he went to the boarding area. I felt funny having some man throw his clothes at me. I caught them and stuffed them into my bag.

As the bus drove off Fred waved goodbye to me through a window on the bus. As I waved back to him, I found myself yawning so I got up to go outside. I didn't know what else to do, so I was in hopes going outside would wake me up.

As I walked up and down the street, I found myself wishing I smoked. If I smoked, I would have fitted in better with everyone else on the street. Then with a little chuckle, I realized smoke would cost money, and I didn't have any. As I got control of myself, I began working out a plan for the night. I didn't know what else to do, so I went back into the depot.

I went to the ticket agent, and asked her, "Are you open all-night?"

"Yes sir," she answered with a questioning look.

"Earlier someone stole my money and everything I had… I've called my wife and …," I began to tell her as I looked around the lobby. I had forgotten some depots had a Western Union office in them. I wanted to get my story right, but I didn't see one. Since there wasn't one my story would hold some water. I added, "I'm waiting for Western Union to bring a check to me."

"I see," she replied, as she went back to her work.

"You'll be here the rest of the night?" I asked her. I had almost walked off when I remembered that I had forgotten to tell her where I would be.

"Yes," she answered, looking up at me.

"When they get here, I'll be by the television," I told her. Then as I turned to walk off, I added, "Thanks."

"My pleasure… I wish you luck," she returned as she went back to work.

With what I thought was a good story I headed to where the television was. I would've preferred a quieter place, but it was the most logical place. I took a seat in front of a television hanging from the ceiling and looked around. It was obvious it was the most popular place in the lobby. As luck would have it, there was only one seat left. I had to sit next to an older man and a little girl. As I was about to take a seat, the man shifted to one side, for some reason. The little girl didn't realize I had taken a seat. If I had a choice, I would have watched something other than what I was, but it was better than nothing.

"This is where it gets good," the little girl said from my elbow.

"Oh," I replied, looking at the little girl. I had just reached down to get my father's diary. With the little girl speaking to me, I let it fall back inside the bag. For some reason, I felt obliged to watch the show with her. I figured dad's diary could wait.

"The prince is going to save her from the dragon…. You'll see," she told me.

"I'll have to watch it then… I wouldn't want to miss it," I told her. I looked over at her and had to admit she was a quiet little blonde, with a big smile. I in turn had to smile back at her.

"Don't bother the man," the little girl's mother told her daughter.

"She's fine… In fact, she reminds me of my little girl when she was that age," I told her. As I was talking, thoughts of my daughter Gloria came to mind. I wished she was beside me keeping me company. Her smile was something that always brought about one to me. I knew when this was over, I was going to take her out and buy her a new outfit.

The woman reminded me of the woman on the bus coming up from LA. I did my best to forget about her as I looked at the little girl's mother. I saw that unlike her daughter, she was a brunette. I could see she looked tired with their bags down next to her feet. I was glad to see there wasn't anything that said she wanted to talk. I relaxed a little and sat back to watch the television with her daughter.

Somewhere between the prince saving the young lady, and a late-night talk show, show, I fell asleep. I found myself with the feeling that a hand was on my shoulder. Then, with a little tighter pressure, it was shaking me. The shaking wasn't painful, but my joints were aching. Then in response to the shaking I asked, "All right I'm awake… What do you want?"

"You have to get out of here…We don't let bums hang around here," a voice said above me.

I looked up, and it was a security guard. Baldheaded, and a little overweight, he looked to be the same age as I was. As I sat up straighter, I told him, "I'm waiting for a Western Union messenger… Ask the woman at the counter… She knows about it."

"You had better, be right about it… If you're lying, I'll have you thrown in as a vagrant," he warned me as he walked off.

As I yawned, I noticed someone had turned the television off. It was just as well with the lobby as empty as it was. There was a man a couple of aisles over asleep with his feet on top of his suitcase. Then, there was a couple asleep with their heads against each other. The mother and daughter were gone so I figured they had gotten on their bus. Then, off by the luggage department there was a janitor sweeping. Otherwise, there wasn't anything going on other than the security guard going to the ticket counter. I could see the clock on the wall, and it said it was three-thirty. I still felt tired, so I settled back to try to get some sleep. I was just drifting off again when I felt someone kicking my boots, and I gave up on the idea of sleeping.

"Yes," I answered as I opened my eyes.

"She confirms your story…. If the messenger isn't here in the next hour or so, I want you out of here," he told me with a scowl.

"But…," I began to protest.

"All of us have problems…. There are two missions not that far from here. If you need help that's what they're there for," he told me as if he cared.

"Where are they?" I asked as I rubbed my eyes. Then as he took out his pen and notepad, I asked him, "And how is the messenger going to find me?"

"That's your problem…. They can call Western Union and give them your location," he answered as he kept drawing a map.

"I guess that's true," I replied, too tired to care.

"Here… with these two places there are also different churches around," he replied as he folded a piece of paper. He then tossed it at me as if he didn't want to touch me. With a look of disgust, he turned to walk away. Before he went very far, he turned and reminded me, "An hour from now I don't want to see you here."

"Yes sir," I responded as I tried to figure out what I was going to do. Still in need of some sleep, I didn't know what to do. I also knew

I was going to be getting hungry soon and needed to take care of that problem.

Since I was awake, I thought I would read a little of my father's diary. I reached into my bag and took it out. I flipped to the page I had turned the corner over, and I began to read:

> *I guess the lies are nothing short of being what they are, just lies. I don't know what else anyone can expect from politicians. The politicians irritate me to no end, but they are not my main concern right now. My concern now is what I am going to tell my wife and son. Worse than that, what will I tell Saint Peter when I get to the pearly gates?*

As I read, my eyes were burning, and I knew there was no point in reading any more. I finally folded the page back and put the diary into the bag.

I didn't know what else to do, so I continued to move on. The only possibility I had was on the piece of paper the security guard had thrown at me. As he said, there were two addresses on it. I looked at the addresses and saw he had drawn a rough map to where they were from the depot. One place was on Market, and the other was on Polk St. I looked back in the direction he had gone and wondered how he knew of the two places. I had a feeling he had been homeless once himself. If he had been, it would explain why he had memorized their locations. I didn't want to cause any trouble, so I got up and grabbed my bag. I didn't feel like walking but there wasn't much more I could do.

As I left the bus depot, I saw the security guard outside having a cigarette. He brought a finger to the brim of his hat as a salute to me. I returned the salute in a good military fashion. The expression on his face said he was proud of getting rid of another tramp.

"Say hi to the rest of your friends," he shouted out to me.

"If I had any," I shouted back to him. I had a feeling I knew what he meant about my friends. I found myself smiling with the thought I could probably buy him and his family out. My thoughts went to that, but it wasn't what you were worth but who you are. I might not have liked him for his thoughts, it was his right to think any way he wanted. I wished I knew for sure what his feelings were.

I found myself wishing I had a jacket as I pulled my shirt collar together. The air was damp, and I felt a chill run down my back. I didn't need to worry about walking against the lights with so little traffic. Then, in the distance, I heard a siren and thought better of it. I found myself moving my feet around trying to take the chill off. I looked back at the bus depot wishing I was inside it. If I were there, I would have another hour before the guard was going to throw me out. That extra hour of heat sounded like heaven. Then I realized if I had stayed, the temperature would have dropped, and I would be colder. I found myself asking, "What do I do now, dad?"

The way it looked on the map, the mission on Market was closer. I didn't count the blocks, but it seemed as if I had walked forever. As I walked the streets, I noticed the lack of people around. A good nine hours earlier, the street was bustling with people. There weren't enough to keep you from getting anywhere, but there was enough. For as few cars as there were on the street, I figured most people were home in bed. I would have given anything to have a bed to crawl into for a few hours. "If I'm lucky, I'll find a bed yet tonight," I said to myself as I got to the mission.

I opened the door and found the place had a musty smell. The odor I smelled reminded me I wasn't home. There were two sets of doors with one being open. I hesitated for a second when I saw three men were talking at a table. It didn't take much to figure that was a dining area leaving the other door as the way to the dorms. I almost decided to go elsewhere when I noticed one man getting up.

"Good evening," he said, greeting me.

"Good evening," I returned. I couldn't be sure, but the guy didn't look much older than I was. He had a pencil line beard that followed the curvature of his jaw. As with his beard and goatee, his black hair had a touch of gray in it. I felt a little uneasy, for some reason, with his voice and the way he stood. It wasn't the first time I had felt uneasy with a man in my presence while in Frisco.

"In need of a bed…, we just happen to have a couple of empties," he offered as he motioned towards the second door. Then with a smile he added, "You're welcome to take anyone you want… We change the bedding daily."

I held my bag up to him, questioning if I should trust my roommates. There wasn't that much in it, but it was all I had. I saw he didn't understand, so I asked him, "What about my bag?"

"Most of our guests are honest. You might want to use it as a pillow," he suggested.

Some man in the dining room shouted out, "Hey Charlie… Are you coming back, I haven't finished the story?"

"I'll be there in a second," Charlie called back to him. Then with a smile, he asked, "As you heard, I'm Charlie… I work here three nights a week. Your name is?"

"My name is Jeff," I answered him as I walked through the door.

"Glad to meet you Jeff," he said, as he let the door close behind me.

There was a dim light on, so I couldn't see much of the barracks. On each side of the room, there were beds. I didn't count how many beds there were, but I guessed there were two dozen. To my left, there was another door. I had a hunch that if I were to go through it, I would find more beds. From what I could see, most of the beds in the room I was in were empty. I took the first bed I came to and laid on it. It wasn't the most comfortable bed in the world. It was better than the chair at the depot.

As suggested, I laid my bag where the pillow should have been. I laid my head on the bag, and I found myself wishing it was more comfortable. As at the depot, I hadn't been in the bed only a few minutes, and I fell asleep. Some time later, the sound of people walking around woke me. I kept my eyes closed in hopes of going back to sleep, but it didn't work.

"We've… got a new member… in our club," some man told someone with a little difficulty.

"Looks like it… I wonder where…," another replied. I couldn't hear anything more since they had left the room.

A third man asked, "Hey you two, where do you think you're going… I thought we were going together?"

"Time for some coffee," the second one answered him.

In the other room, I could hear someone singing. I wanted to shout out, "Don't give up your day job," but I knew it didn't apply, since none of them worked. I tried to relax and get some sleep. For as few men as I had seen a few hours earlier I figured I had a chance. I had an idea what the day might bring so I decided I would get as much sleep as I could. The nap I took at the depot wasn't worth much. I knew if I ever saw the security guard again that I owed him my thanks.

From somewhere I had a feeling people were talking and walking past me. As I shook myself awake, I saw men getting up. Then, two were going past my cot, and I let them go on their way. I wanted to shout at them to be quiet, but I knew it wasn't worth it. I knew if I continued to lie where I was any longer, every muscle in my body would be aching. I stretched out with my eyes closed, and I rolled over. Then, before I could get up, I heard another voice coming towards me.

Someone asked, "…are you going today?"

"I don't…. You know if I didn't know better, I would say I know that new guy," a second voice said as they passed by me.

I don't recognize him," the first voice told his friend.

"You weren't around then…. This was a good twenty-five or thirty years ago," the second man told him.

"He surely wouldn't look that…," the first man was saying as they left the room.

I sat up and saw them through the barrack's door. I could see the two going to the front door. One was a good twenty years older than I was. I figured the other man to be about sixty years old. He had white hair, a red stocking cap, and a beard. For a brief second, the thought of his beard came to mind. He was wearing everyday clothes of clean jeans and a sport shirt. His hair or beard somehow didn't say he was a homeless person. He would just be a man with a beard. As I dropped my feet to the floor, I realized what the older man had said, "I know that I knew that guy." I got to wondering if he might have meant my father. As I straightened up, I grabbed my bag and took off after the two.

I ran outside through the front door not saying anything to Charlie. My intent wasn't to be friendly but to gain some knowledge of my father. I had the feeling the man I was after had known him. Once I was outside, I looked up and down the street and didn't see the two. I ran to the corner, and I didn't see them anywhere around. I had the feeling I may have imagined hearing and seeing them. The only thing I could figure was that they had gone up an alley. If I were right, I knew I would never find them. My only hope was to talk to the guy later at supper. Not knowing what else to do I went back inside the mission to decide what I was going to do.

"So you have returned… Did you forget something?" Charlie asked as I closed the front door.

"The two men who left a few minutes ago…. Do you know their names?" I asked him.

"I don't know who you are talking about," he answered with a confused look.

"One was older… In his sixties, white hair, beard, and a red stocking cap," I told him in hopes, he would recognize the men.

From the dining room, next to the door a man told us, "He's talking about Jake and Phil."

"Of course, those two… I didn't see them leave but that's them," Charlie said with a smile.

"I guess I can talk to them later… I wish I could have caught up to them… I hate waiting," I replied. I felt bad not having caught up with the two. I had nothing better to do, so I looked around the dining room. There was only one man sitting alone. All I knew was I wouldn't want to get into a fight with him. He had to be six-four if not taller and about three hundred pounds. In guessing his age, I would say he was in his fifties and had seen better days. He wasn't fat, but he looked to be out of shape. Whoever he was at least I knew I hadn't imagined seeing the two men.

"I doubt they'll be back for a month or so…. By the way I'm Carl," Carl said walking up to us. Then with his hand out, he asked, "And your name?"

"Jeff," I told him as I took his hand and shook it.

"If you have nothing else to do, you might as well as grab some coffee and oatmeal," he offered as he motioned for me to go into the dining room.

"Sounds good to me... I haven't had much to eat," I told him. It didn't take much for me to follow him into the dining room.

"Watch out, Carl's apt to talk you to death," Charlie warned me.

"I'll remember that," I returned. I didn't know what else to do, so I followed him into the dining room.

"Don't pay any attention to him... Go on ahead and help yourself," Carl told me as he went to a table. He reached over to the table and grabbed his coffee cup. He took the cup to the coffee urn and filled it. As he turned to head to the table, he gave me a nod.

I went straight to the chow line and dished up some oatmeal. It wasn't my favorite breakfast food, but it was better than nothing. Then turning toward the coffee urns, I saw some toast. Picking up a piece, I saw it was a little soggy, but I knew I could eat it. It wasn't much but I had the main part of my breakfast, so I went over and got myself some coffee. I thought about setting my bag on the table and come back for the coffee. I didn't want to chance on someone stealing my bag. I finally put my left arm through the straps and picked up my bowl of mush. With my right hand, I managed to get some coffee and tried to decide where to sit. Seeing Carl's insistence in me joining him, I went over to his table.

"Have a seat," he offered as I walked up to the table.

"Morning Carl... I guess we'll see you later," an old man said, with a wave as he left the dining room.

"Morning Gabby," Carl returned with a smile.

"All right... I don't know anyone else here anyway," I replied as I sat my coffee cup down. Then setting my plate and silverware on the table, I took a seat. I got the feeling I should say something. I finally got out, "It looks like it's going to be a beautiful day."

"I guess so... I won't see much of it for as late as I work," he told me.

Where I was sitting, I could see everyone else in the room. There was about every bum imaginable sitting around at the tables. The youngest one had to be in his twenties and the oldest in his sixties. Most of them looked as if they hadn't showered for months. Some were wearing shirts, with sweatshirts and coats. I doubted if they had washed their clothing in months. As I looked at the other men, I knew shaving wasn't something anyone in the place did. As I took my first bite of food, I couldn't see anyone of them in mainstream society. I couldn't imagine letting myself go as those men had. Then thinking about it, I knew, after a time I probably would look like them.

"Where are you from?" Carl asked as if he was trying to be friendly.

"Originally Los Angeles," I answered as I took another bite. As I swallowed, I told him, "They mustered me out of the service yesterday. As luck will have it, someone stole almost everything I owned while I was waiting for my bus… money and all… That's how I wound up here. If I can make enough to get me home, I'll be gone."

"I see…," he started to say, but I interrupted him.

I said, "To make it worse I met a woman, with her little girl. The woman conned me out of the few dollars I had left last night… I tell you it was really stupid of me."

"That's for the shit's," he remarked. Then as he lifted his cup he asked, "What did you want with Jake?"

"He made a comment he thought he recognized me… Then he realized I was too young to be the man he thought I was," I answered, as I bit into the soggy toast. If it wasn't for the hunger pangs, I wouldn't have been able to get it down. I found myself wishing I had kept the food I had given Fred the night before. Even if the food were cold, it would have tasted better than what I was eating.

He asked, "So he thought he recognized you. What's the big deal?"

His question was understandable but still curious. I wasn't sure how much I should tell him, but I decided to be partially honest. I told him, "My parents separated and my father came to Frisco. From what the family has learned he was a homeless person."

"So you think Jake might know him," he replied with interest.

"I don't know…. It might be worth waiting around for Jake to come back and ask him," I told him.

"Trust me, I've run this place for the past two years... I know Jake, and he isn't all there. I'm not saying he didn't know your father, but I wouldn't put money on it," he warned me.

"If there is some truth to it...," I stopped, knowing he knew the man better than I did. Since my grandmother had gotten the diary thirty years ago, it was too much to ask. Still, if there was a chance, I had to stay around until he came back to the mission. As it was, I had planned to walk in my father's footsteps for two months anyway. With an empty bowl in front of me, I told him, "If I hear you right, he might come back sooner... I would like to find out what happened to my father."

"No skin off, my nose as they say," he replied as he took another sip of his coffee.

"I sure wish you had an idea where I might find him," I told him as I looked out of the window beside me. I found it hard to imagine him working on the mission. It had to be difficult to look the guys in the face. Not one of them had a smile on their faces. Every one of them looked as if everything had drained from them years ago. It was good someone was giving them a place to stay and a bite of food.

"For as rough of a deal as most of these men have had they don't talk much. Then in Jake's case, it's hard to believe anything he says.... One day he's a minister, the next the owner of a car lot," he told me as he sat back in his chair. Then waving at another man leaving he turned his attention to me. He added, "From what I understand he's been coming in here for over thirty years. That's after they mustered him out of the service after Nam, and he became a resident of this place... Like so many of us, he lost his self-respect, confidence or whatever. Society didn't want or appreciate them.Because of society, they had to fend for themselves... As it is, I might be able to give you some information that might help."

"What's that?" I asked him. I found the prospect that this Jake could tell me something about my father excited me. I then realized it might be a waste of time talking to him. I was a little worried about talking to him. I was afraid I might get nothing but wild stories from him. No matter how it turned out, I knew I had to talk to him. If I were lucky, he might be able to tell me what happened to him.

"A place you might find employment… A day labor office is better than nothing is… Unless you have something else in mind," he answered as he wrote down an address.

"Dressed as I am, I don't think I can go and apply for an executive job," I replied.

"No, people will either take you as a druggy, radical or something worse," he added.

"I guess you're right about that… I have already heard reactions from a few people," I said, agreeing with him. However, I had only been in the city for a little over twelve hours, and I had gotten enough ridicule already.

As he looked up at me, he asked, "If you were to get any job you wanted, what would it be?"

"I have an engineering degree… When I get home, I'll be looking for a position in the construction field… I was a construction worker before joining the service," I answered. I had come close to telling him I was a partner in a consulting firm. Thankfully, I had a mouth full of coffee, and I had to swallow it. While I swallowed, I had the chance to get my thoughts straightened out.

I let his comments about my clothes drift off, and my thoughts went back to working. I knew working day labor wasn't my cup of tea, but it would be better than working at the mission. If worse came to worst, I would, but I was praying he had another idea. I was more than willing to go back and sweep up fish heads than work at the mission.

CHAPTER

I left Carl at the mission to search out a job somewhere. He was good enough to give me the address of the day labor outfit. It was a fair distance to walk, but I was full and up to it. As I began walking, different thoughts came to mind. From what I had learned from one of the residents at the mission, it was better than the one on Polk Street. After hearing what he had to say, I was glad I hadn't gone there. As it turned out, the one I was at, I learned about Jake. From the way it looked, he was the only one that might know something about my father. If he did know anything, it meant my father probably also stayed where I was. Looking up into the sky, I said a prayer to my father:

> *Father if you can hear me, this is day two with twenty-eight to go. I have a life as you did, and I have to go back to it. In the next three weeks, I want to learn about you and your life.*

It surprised me hearing the prayer coming out of my mouth. I wasn't what most would call a religious man. I figured a prayer wouldn't hurt for what I was doing and wanted to learn. As I rubbed my chin in thought, I felt stubbles on my chin, and I wanted to kick myself. I also wanted to laugh at the thought of becoming as bad as the other residents at the mission had become. In all the excitement, I hadn't even showered, brushed my teeth, or shaved. I took a vow, that I would wash Fred's fatigues and take a shower if one was available, as soon as I got back to the mission.

Though I felt dirty, I still found myself in a good mood. A driving force was the hope of learning something about my father. Then, there was the day itself. The sun was out with a couple of small clouds overhead. A slight breeze was bringing in the smell of sea salt, which I had always loved. I had a full stomach, and everything was good.

As I scanned, the skyline I could make out the Transamerica, I knew not far-off there was the Embarcadero Hotel, Marriot, and the Wells Fargo buildings. In thinking about the Wells Fargo building, a smile came to my face. A customer of mine told me one day I needed to see the black kidney shape sculpture the bank had commissioned. The local people had named that sculpture the "Bankers Heart." I could imagine what the bankers thought about that. The landmark that said San Francisco to me was the Coit Tower on Nob Hill, which I couldn't see from where I stood. Another favorite place of mine was the Wharf.

I found many memories coming back to me as I stood waiting for a light to turn green. One of the funniest memories happened in China Town. Martha and I had gone to supper at a restaurant a customer had recommended. I didn't have any problem finding the place. I parked the car and we went straight in, sat down, and ordered our food. The place was nice enough, but we were looking forward to a quiet supper. When our meal came, we were talking about our kids being at their grandmothers. My wife had commented on something when the waitress brought our food to us. Once she left, I went straight to eating my meal, rather than going back to what we had been talking about. I picked up the chopsticks, planning to take a bite of rice. Then as I thought about her last comment, I stuck the chopsticks into the rice and left them there, standing straight up as I played back what she had said. It wasn't long, and the waiter was at our table. He asked if there was something wrong with our meal or if someone had died. A little confused, I told him we hadn't eaten anything but a bite of rice. He explained that chopsticks stuck in a meal, as I did with mine symbolized death. I apologized and laid them down. From that experience, every time we had Chinese food that memory always came back to me.

I had many memories of different places in Frisco. With regret, I knew I wouldn't be seeing any of them on this trip. I prayed this would be my most memorable trip anywhere. If I succeeded in my search for my father, I would have answers to all the questions I had as a child.

From somewhere I heard someone shout out, "What in the hell do think you're doing?"

When I came out of my trance, I saw I was in the way of a man making a turn. I looked up at the light, and it was red. As I went back to the curb, I told the driver, "Sorry."

"Get off the drugs and you might live longer," he told me with a disgusted look, as he drove on around me.

Somewhere during the exchange, the light had changed and people were walking around me. As they walked around me, a few were giving me a funny look. Since I had stepped out against the light, which made me look dumb, I took his look as agreeing with me. I had a hard time associating what I did with being on drugs. Lost in my thoughts as I wasn't paying attention to what was going on. I had been in his position one or two dozen times, and I understood his frustrations with me. The rest of the way to the Day Labor office I tried to keep my attention on what I was doing.

I didn't have that much farther to go before I was at the Day Labor office. It was easy to recognize the place. In front of the building, there was a line of four to five dozen men and women standing along the outside wall. I found it interesting that most of them had a suitcase or a paper bag sitting beside them on the ground. As I lifted my bag, I felt at home. Even from a block away, I could see something going on in front of the building. With the place being a one-way street, cars could pull up in front of the office. I saw a couple of cars stop in front of the office. When one of the cars stopped, a man would go up to the car and get in. My guess was the drivers of the cars were picking up workers.

As I got to the corner of the block, I saw a man step out from the office. He looked around and then shouted out, "Anderson."

"Here," a man shouted back not far from me. A man leaning against the wall broke free of the line. He went over to the man from the office and took a piece of paper from him. Looking at the piece of paper, he looked up at the man and said something. Then with a wave to his friends, he came towards me with a smile on his face.

"I take it, you got a job," I commented as he passed me.

"It might even become a full-time position," he boosted with a grin. With a wave, he continued to head the way I had come from.

"I wish you luck," I called back to him. As I continued to the door of the office, a couple of others went to cars. Not understanding what was going on for sure I decided to ask someone. I picked out one man out and asked him, "What's going on?"

"What do you think… We are waiting for jobs," he answered with a confused look.

"I know that… Does that piece of paper he's carrying mean he has a job? The others are just getting into cars as they drive by. Do I have to go in and sign up or… do I just stand out here and wait for someone to come by?" I asked. From the irritated look on his face, I knew I should have gone inside to ask my questions.

"I don't care what you do," he replied.

"Don't pay any attention to Jim… He had a rough night," the first man's friend told me. He nodded his head at his friend as he added, "He hasn't had a job for a while. He's out here keeping me company… Most, of us here, have jobs already, and we are waiting for rides… I assume you're looking for a job."

"Yes," I told him. Unlike his friend, he had a friendly and helpful attitude.

"You have to go inside and fill out an application. Unless you have special skills, the jobs are first come, first serve. If you are a smoker, you'll probably find you will want to wait out here with us… There's no smoking inside," he explained.

"Thanks," I told him. Then to his friend I offered, "I hope you find something."

"Yeah," the man returned in a curt voice.

I got the feeling from the tone of his voice I might be in trouble if I got a job before he did. I felt funny being around men like these men. I couldn't see myself sitting around the mission all day doing nothing. If I did find a job, I wasn't buying booze with my paycheck. As I grabbed the door handle to the office, I looked back at the line-up of people. They looked like a group of vultures sitting on a fence waiting for a piece of meat to come by.

"Sorry," a man said pushing his way between the door and my body.

"Sorry," I returned, apologizing for blocking the door. I caught the door and held it for a minute. As I went inside, I swallowed hard knowing I had to go through with it.

Then, as I let the door close, I saw the sign on the door. It told me they opened at seven in the morning. I looked at my watch and saw the time was eight-fifteen. When I thought of all the people, standing around it was understandable why they opened at seven. I had a feeling anyone showing up after seven was out of luck. I also knew I had to get more than a couple of hours sleep that night. I prayed that if I got a decent night of sleep, I would be able to get to the office before seven.

I found as many inside as there were outside waiting for jobs. The ones waiting inside I figured were mainly non-smokers. The ones outside against the wall were smokers or tired of the stench in the office. Some were using their time waiting for a job by sleeping on the sidewalk. When I saw those asleep, it reminded me where I began my night's rest the night before. From the way it looked, the men had their own dress code, and I found it interesting. The ones dressed as the average person, looked out of place. A few even looked as if they had taken a bath, which surprised me. I knew those that had bathed and dressed as the average man did, were serious about getting a job. If they wanted a job, they had to be presentable. It looked as if the place needed a fresh coat of paint on the walls, floor, and the ceiling. I also was thinking that a little soap and water wouldn't have hurt either.

As I looked around, I saw to my left a couple of women at a counter who were helping people. Then, I saw on the ledge of the counter, a stand with a number holder on it. I had a feeling I would be waiting awhile when I saw ninety-nine on the card. When I saw what number I had, I could see myself waiting for a couple of hours. I then realized that as few people as there were in the room, I didn't have a long wait ahead of me.

From behind me, I heard someone say, "And there's a late sleeper."

"He might as well as go home… coming in this late," another man replied.

I turned around and saw two older men sitting behind me. When I turned around and they could see me, they had a guilty look on their faces. I stood where I was, not saying anything to them.

As I was about to take a seat, I heard a woman shout out, "Ninety-nine."

I turned towards the counter, and I saw a woman motioning for me to come over to her. She had a pleasant smile but was on the heavy side. I nodded towards her, and her smile got even bigger. She was one of those women you wouldn't mind knowing no matter what her size was. Unlike most women, she knew who she was, and she wasn't making any pretense of it.

"Hi, I'm Bertha… I take it, you're looking for work," The woman said, greeting me.

"I'm Jeff, and you have it right. I could use a few days of work," I answered as I sat my bag on the counter. I saw her interest in the bag, and I told her, "A change of underwear in case if I get too excited… I'm sorry, but it was a rough night sleeping in a chair at the bus depot."

"No problem… I need to register you," she told me. Then with a smile she commented, "You're new around here."

"They mustered me out…," I went ahead and told her my story. As I was telling her my story, she handed me a form.

As I took the form, she told me with a frown, "I doubt there will be any calls for workers at this hour… You need to get here earlier if you want to work."

"I realize that now… I didn't find out about this place until late… Tomorrow I'll be here earlier," I assured her as I started to fill out the form. There wasn't too much for me to fill out on the form. I had to give her my name, the mission's address, my social security number, and experience.

As I finished filling out the form she asked me, "Other than playing soldier. What have you done?"

"Worked in construction," I told her, being halfway honest.

"No Union Card I guess," she replied with a faint smile.

"Sorry but I don't belong to a union… Then, like I said, I only want to make enough to get home," I told her.

She asked, "Your family won't send you any money?"

"I have two problems with that…. My mother doesn't know I'm out of the service, and I want to surprise her. The second is she can't get out, and I don't want to worry her," I lied to her.

"In the morning, just remind me who you are. I'll keep this on file," she told me as she took the form from me. Then with a smile she added, "You might get lucky and someone will drive by offering you work."

"I have nothing better to do, so I'll hang around," I replied. Then turning to walk away, I told her, "Thanks… I appreciate your help."

"Good luck," she returned as she set my number to one side.

The second woman called out, "Number one."

When I turned to face the counter, one of the women had put the old cards back starting the rotation again. Instinctively, I looked around for the person that held number one. It wasn't long, and a young Hispanic man walked up to the counter. Holding his baseball cap in his hand, he gave me a grin. I told him, "I wish you luck."

"Gracias, senor," he returned with a smile.

As I went back outside, I wondered why he wasn't in the valley working the fields. Then, realizing that was stereotyping, I let the thought go. I could feel the sun on my face, and I felt better than being inside. Most of the men were still standing against the wall smoking their cigarettes. I felt chills going up my back from the looks they gave me as I walked past them. Not wanting to start any trouble, I walked to the other side of the building. A couple of men were talking, and they didn't pay any attention to me.

"Good morning," I offered as an introduction.

"Yeah," one said, as he turned to look at me. After he looked me over, he went back to his conversation with his friend.

The two of them were my age or a few years younger. Both had what I would call military haircuts. From the way they were standing, I knew they hadn't been out of the service for long. They still had a military look about them, so I figured they might give me a better idea what it was like just getting out of the service. I was afraid I might say something wrong, so I didn't say anything to them. I played it safe and kept my mouth shut. After sitting on my haunches for a while one of the men looked over at me. I told him, "I wouldn't mind if we got some work."

"Yeah… that would be good," the second man, answered. His answer sounded as if he had a chip on his shoulder.

"Garrison," Bertha called out.

"Yo," a black man answered. He was at the far end, and it took him a while to get to her. He took a toothpick out of his mouth and asked her, "You got something for me?"

"It's your lucky day Mr. Garrison," Bertha told him, as she handed him a sheet of paper. As he looked at it, she warned him, "They won't come after you… You have to find your own way."

"No problem… Got it covered," he assured her.

"Good luck," she told him. Not saying anything else, she turned to go back into the office.

As he looked at the piece of paper, he asked, "Am I reading this right… 7:00 PM?"

"Yes," she answered. With a short pause, she told him, "If you don't have any more questions I need to go back to my desk."

"I guess, I have everything," he told her.

I stood up and stretched my legs. I have never been as bored as I was sitting there waiting for a job. Boredom was only part of my problem for I was aching in every joint of my body. I was doing my best to stick it out, but I didn't know how long I would last. I checked my watch, and saw it was ten-thirty. When I saw what time it was, my stomach began begging for some lunch.

Other than walking back and forth, I stood in that one place all day. A couple of times Bertha came outside, and we would talk for a few minutes. Each time that she came over to me, a couple of men would come and go from the office, and comment about something as they passed us. I found it interesting for in most cases, they never said anything worthwhile. As it turned out it had to be about as boring of a day as I had ever experienced.

The only way of staying awake was by counting the cars going by. With everyone treating me as if I were a leper, I had to do something. On top of not being able to talk to anyone, I didn't have anything to read or look at. The buildings across the street were vacant, and a cat came out of one of them to add to my excitement.

Then, three o'clock came around, and I was dying of starvation. I looked around and saw everyone was leaving, so I decided I might as well follow their example.

I knew the first step would be as hard as the last one. It seemed with every step I took; my bag got heavier and heavier as I made my way to the mission. As I made my way back, I wondered if they were serving anything for supper. I knew I would have to break down and buy myself a candy bar, if they weren't serving supper. It wasn't something I wanted for the enjoyment but found myself feeling faint. I didn't know if it was from hunger, the heat, or lack of doing anything. I wasn't sure why but something told me, I would feel better if I had something to eat.

"So, you didn't do any good today… You never came over to talk to us," a woman's voice said.

I realized the woman I had just passed must have directed the voice at me. When I turned around, I saw a smile on her face. To my surprise, I recognized her from the Day Labor Office building. She was one of the ones I saw standing against the wall. I would have had to be blind not to have seen such an attractive young woman as she was. I found her maturity refreshing, but she looked like she was in her late teens. I found myself wondering if she would also be asking me for money. If she was looking for financial help, she was barking up the wrong tree. I threw caution to the wind, giving her a smile as I told her, "I thought I had a disease from the way all of you acted."

"Sorry… I just need someone to talk to and there aren't many back there that care," she replied with a smile. She then pointed to a bus stop bench and asked me, "Mind talking for a few minutes?"

"Don't mind at all," I told her, as I motioned for her to take a seat. As I took a seat next to her, I asked her, "Other than needing a job, what's the problem?"

"Not much… I ran away from home with my boyfriend to have his daughter… He left me a couple of hours before I delivered her. Now I'm stuck with his older sister, not knowing what to do…" she rattled off as she looked down at her feet. She looked back at me and added, "Other than being broke, I don't have any problems."

"Sounds like you have a good attitude… At least you have his sister," I replied wondering how people could get themselves into such situations. I wanted to laugh, thinking of Martha. As with her, many people I knew accused me of having a bad attitude towards my fellow man. I never knew what to say or do for people in trouble. As a solution, I have given money regularly to several causes. On a personal level, I was the first one to walk away from my problems. It was a little different in that I had no one to talk to, and I needed help. I didn't see how I could help her, but figured I could stop and listen.

"She's leaving in a few days, and that's the biggest problem… I don't know what I'll do when she goes," she said with a tear in her eye. Then, with a cute little smile, she asked, "What's your problem?"

As what was becoming my standard introduction to people, I told her my story. I got the impression she didn't care what my problems were. I knew she was worse off than I was, but I continued with my story. I ended my story with, "… I'm Jeff."

"Sorry, I was thinking about my daughter… My name is Karen," she answered as she looked off into the distance.

The delivery trucks going by didn't make it easy to hear what she had to say, but we managed. I noticed I could hear the conversations of people walking by. I couldn't take her anywhere so the bus bench was the best I could do. To make it worse, a car with a bunch of kids in it came by. One of the kids flipped me off and shouted out, "Up… yours."

I didn't pay any attention to the kids and asked Karen, "How old are you, Karen?"

I asked her the question in fear of getting into trouble. While I waited for her answer, I watched what was going on around us. A couple of people were now at the bus stop waiting for the bus. I didn't see any interest in our conversation from any of them.

"Eighteen," she answered after a little pause. A woman pushed us to one side by setting her bags on the bench. She looked up at the woman and told her, "Sorry, let me move down a bit."

"Let's go down a ways," I suggested. I knew the young woman wanted to talk, but I also wanted to get back to the mission. I couldn't do much for her so walking wouldn't hurt. I didn't feel our conversation was something everyone needed to hear.

Not saying anything, she got up and joined me as I walked down the block. We continued to walk in silence until we found a block wall we could sit on. I asked her, "What can I do?"

"I don't know… I got myself into this mess, and I guess it's up to me to get myself out of it… At first, I thought you might give me some answers," she said. Then with a look of defeat, she lowered herself to the sidewalk. Once she was on her feet she gave me a fake smile, she added, "Don't worry about it… I'll work it out."

"Right offhand I would say you should go back home… I have to admit I have never been in your position. I can also see where it might be hard to do… They may be upset with you, but I can't believe they would shut you out. You need to be with your friends and your family… Your daughter also needs them," I suggested to her.

"It's not that I don't have the money because I don't… I'm scared that they wouldn't let me come back… You can trust me, when I say I haven't been the best daughter in the world. In fact, this time, I may have gone too far," she confessed.

As I shook my head, I told her, "At least you understand the seriousness of your situation… Your parents must have done a good job of raising you. I find it hard to believe they would shut you out… Where are you from?"

"Portland," she answered with a questioning look.

I reached into the end of my bag, pulled out a pen and a notepad. I wrote down my office number and Ray's name. As I handed it to her, I offered, "When you feel you can face your parents, give Ray a call. Remind him that you talked to me, and he will get you a flight home… It's bad enough that your daughter probably won't know her father…

I know what it's like not having known my father. Why make it worse by depriving her of her grandparents?"

"If you can do that for me… why not for…" she began to ask.

"Don't ask… What's your last name?" I asked her. If I were going to listen to her, I wanted to know her full name. While I listened to her, she reminded me of the woman on the bus. That conversation cost me a few dollars I couldn't afford. I knew she wasn't trying to get something, for nothing. I got the feeling that she had approached me because she just wanted to talk to someone.

"Benson," she answered, as she continued to read the piece of paper. As she raised her head, I could see she was crying.

"Well Miss Karen Benson, I had better get going… I hope I get to see you again, and your daughter. If I don't, I wish you luck," I told her, as I stepped away from the wall.

She began to cry, and she wrapped her arms around me. As she released me, she said, "Thanks… I don't know when or even if, I will ever be ready… Unless you leave San Francisco, you'll see my daughter. This weekend I'll bring her to the mission."

"I would love to see her… But right now, I had better get a move on," I reminded her. I gave her a little wave as I left her standing next to the wall. I found myself with a warm satisfying feeling for having taken a few minutes to listen to her problems. It didn't matter, but I had a feeling that I wouldn't be seeing her again. I did find hearing her problems made me think of my grandmother. I took a few minutes on my way back to call her. The conversation was short, but I let her know I was all right. I also told her where I was staying. Once again, she didn't have anything to add to my father's diary.

The rest of the way back to the mission wasn't too exciting. My stomach was still growling, and my legs were sore. My mind was active with the thoughts of Karen and her little girl as well as thinking about Jake. The prospect of having to stay on the mission for a month didn't sound like fun, but I knew I would do it. Whatever it took to meet Jake and learn about my father, I was going to do.

As I entered the mission, a man I didn't recognize asked, "Need a place to sleep?"

"Any luck today?" Carl asked as he came up to me. Then turning to the man, I didn't know, he said, introducing me, "This is Jeff..., he checked in last night."

"Hi," the new man said without introducing himself.

"Joey's not too talkative," Carl told me, as he ushered me into the dining room.

"Ok.... Sometimes that a good way to be," I replied as I followed him. As we entered the dining room, I saw a few men sitting at tables. When I didn't see Jake among the men, it disappointed me. It wasn't that I didn't believe Carl when he said he only came by once a month. I was in hopes that he might change his routine and come back by the next day or two. I remembered Carl's question and I told him, "I had a good time today standing around for nothing."

"Tomorrow's another day so don't worry about it and get something to eat. You might want to turn in early and get a good night's sleep... You'll have a better day tomorrow," he suggested as he pointed to the steam table full of food.

"I don't know if I can handle two meals in one day," I replied jokingly.

"Give it a try.... You might, get to liking it," he said.

I got myself a few hot dogs, vegetables, mashed potatoes and a cup of coffee. Then, sitting down across the table from Carl, we talked while I ate. I found I could talk to him as if I had known him all of my life. I learned a bit about him, his wife, and children. By saying what he had I was reminded of my own children. It was from the pride he had for his children that got me to liking him. A feeling welled up inside of me, that I wished I was a part of my family's life. Martha probably wouldn't have divorced me if I were more like him. I had learned that I wasn't the type to interact with people, but it didn't mean I didn't care.

As Carl started to leave, I asked him, "Say..., have you got a minute,"

When he retook a seat, he asked, "Sure.... What can I do for you?"

I asked him "Well these men... How long do most of the men stay here?"

"Fifty percent of them have been here from three to five years.... Some will eventually rape, rob, or kill someone. Then there are those few who will make something of themselves. Most of them will drift off to an alley or another mission," he answered.

"Why…? They could do so much better," I replied.

"Many reasons…. We don't have time to go into them. Some say they've lost their will to live, no feeling of self-worth…. Others say society put them here. Your guess is as good as any. I don't judge. I just look after them," he answered.

"I'll shoot myself before I lower myself to their level," I commented.

"Some do shoot themselves and others use booze… It's a shame," he added. Then with a smile, he got up and added, "I have some work to do."

"Thanks," I told him as I went back to my supper. The thoughts going through my head didn't help the taste of the food. In the men, I could see I tried not to put my father behind their faces. I prayed my father pulled himself out of his depression.

I finished my meager supper and went into the barracks. I found someone had taken the bed I used the night before. With that being the case, I took another one back further in the room. I sat my bag down and walked into the other room to check it out. I wanted to talk to Jake, so I went to check to see if he might be in the next room. What I found were the two restrooms separating the two rooms and more beds. I found in the one rest room I hadn't used that morning, that it had four more showers. I touched my chin and felt the stubble. I also knew I had to make a trip to the shower soon. I muttered softly, "I'll return."

"Excuse me," a rough looking man said going past me in the little hallway.

"Sorry," I replied. I briefly watched him walk on and gave a shrug. I didn't give him much thought as I headed for the bed I had picked out for the night.

"I'm Bill," a man said introducing himself to me.

I introduced myself to him by saying, "I'm Jeff…. Been here long?"

"Not for a while…. My wife threw me out for my best friend some time back, and I stayed here one night," he answered as he fluffed up his pillow.

"And now you're back," I replied not feeling like another conversation. With everything going through my head, I didn't want to go to sleep either. I still had to call Ray and tell him about Karen.

"Yep…. The first night was because I didn't have a place to go. Then I got an apartment, and I thought everything was going all right," he told me.

"What happened that brought you back here?" I asked. He had tweaked my curiosity, hearing what I had. I gave up and sat down to hear his story. I got the feeling that he was younger than I was, but had a rougher life. For some reason, I had a feeling he had been as blonde as I had been when I was younger. I found the thought strange, and I let it go. For some reason, I felt something was wrong with the guy. He was a little too well groomed for a homeless person. From his hands and body, I would have guessed he worked with his hands. He was slim in build, but he still looked powerful somehow. His clothes looked old, but they were clean and pressed. The pressed clothes and his stature didn't fit the picture of a resident of a homeless mission. I still felt safe talking to him.

"I got to drinking…. Because of it, I lost my job and the co-operation of my ex-wife by not letting me see my kids. She said if I were too sober up, she might, but not drunk," he answered, as he lay down on his bed.

"You loser," someone shouted out from across the room.

With a smile another man asked, "You expected more from him?"

"I don't understand their excitement. That baseball game is three years-old…. I don't know about you, but it's dumb getting excited over a rerun that old," Bill commented.

"I guess when you don't have a life, it doesn't take much," I replied. I had to laugh at the concentration I saw in the faces of the men watching the game. I found myself wishing a game could interest me as much as it did the guys watching it.

"Don't I know it," Bill said.

"What?" I asked. My attention was on the other men in the room and not on what he was saying.

"Nothing," he answered.

My mind went back to him saying he was a drunk. He didn't show any sign of being a heavy drinker. I had to tell him, "You don't act like any drunks I've known."

"Haven't had a drop for most of a month now… I'm trying to get back on my feet for my kids," he answered with a smile as he propped himself against the wall. He went to ask me, "What's your story?"

I told him my stock story, and we talked the rest of the evening as we watched a little television. I finally got up, went in, and took a long needed shower. As I showered, I washed Fred's fatigues, so I could wear them the following day. The idea of wearing what I had been for another day turned my stomach. When I got back to the bed, he told me the best place to put my washed clothes was under the mattress. He explained the mattress would soak up the moisture in them, and they would be dry by morning. Not knowing what else to do, I did as he suggested. We finally went into the dining room and had a cup of coffee. We ended the night with the understanding that we would go to the day labor office together the following morning.

Bill fell sound asleep, but I sat back in the dim light and read part of my father's diary:

> *Not knowing what else to do, I asked a cop for advice. He told me of a homeless mission on Polk. In telling me about the place, he suggested for me to go there. The idea of sleeping with a bunch of drunks didn't seem that inviting but I don't know what else to do. I still had to start somewhere, and it was out of the weather.*
>
> *If I get lucky, I might find a job tomorrow and work my way back to being a respectable human being.*

I found myself wishing I had gone to the mission he had rather than the one I was in right then. I began wondering if I shouldn't move there rather than stay where I was. In thinking it over, I began to worry about not getting to meet Jake if I moved. I decided I might go over there to the other place the following night and ask around. I decided I would wait on moving until I saw what they could tell me. If I didn't learn anything of interest, I would stay where I was.

The next morning, I woke up at four and lay in bed for a while. Finally, at five, I got up, went in, and shaved. All I had to do before leaving was to put my fatigues on. I reached under the mattress and pulled out the clean fatigues. They were dry, but they had the pattern of the bedsprings on them. When I saw the chevrons on the jacket sleeves, I pulled them off first before putting it on. Then as I buttoned up the last button, I saw Bill sit up on the edge of his bed rubbing his eyes. I greeted him with, "It's about time."

"Careful, I don't wake up easily… I feel hung over," he warned me.

"Excuse me… I've never had that problem," I replied, thinking it funny. I decided to take pity on him by offering him, "Want some coffee?"

"Yeah," he answered as he fell back onto the bed.

I needed to get him going so I went to the dining room and got us some coffee. When I got back to the barracks, I found him sound asleep. I sat the cups down on the floor, shook him until he woke up. As he opened his eyes, I told him, "Here's your coffee."

"Thanks," he replied as he took the cup into his hand.

We headed for the day labor office after he showered, and we had breakfast. The walk wasn't as pleasant as it had been the day before. There was a slight drizzle making it a little uncomfortable walking. For the first time in Frisco, I missed my car. We finally got there a little wet, but we weren't too bad.

"Little damp out there," Bertha said, greeting us.

"At least we're not soaked to the skin," I pointed out to her.

"I'll pull out your registration form. If something comes up I'll let you know," she assured me.

"Number twenty-three," she called out as I left her.

"Surprise, surprise… I think there's a woman who wants to talk to me," Bill said holding his card up to me.

"You had better get over there before you disappoint her," I replied as I pushed him along his way.

I took a seat not far away and waited for him. Then, once he had his registration form filled out, I followed him outside. At first, I thought he was going outside for fresh air. I was to learn his reason was that he was a smoker. I don't smoke, but I didn't mind if he did. As he smoked, I noticed the drizzle had let up, but the humidity was climbing. As I stood outside with him, I wasn't getting wet from the rain, but from sweating. We finally began to talk about our plans for our future.

"I told her construction or anything… I need money, and I don't care what she finds for me," Bill told me once we got outside.

"I know what you mean," I replied as I looked around. From what I could see, the men against the wall hadn't changed positions. I would have bet none of them ever got a job. I knew I would have to be desperate to hire any one of them.

I got the feeling they didn't bother Bill. He talked to a few of them as we made our way to the office door. When he came back to me, he smiled and related some of the conversations he'd had. I told him of the reactions to me. I had gotten the day before.

"I don't know what to tell you… It might have been your body odor yesterday. I don't have any problems getting them to talk," he replied.

I looked around to see if Karen was around, and I didn't see her. I told him, "I have to make a call."

"I'll hold the fort down," he promised.

"Be right back," I told him as I went inside. I knew I should have made the call the night before, but I got to talking and forgot to make the call. With a feeling of regret, I found the phone, and I made my call to Ray's house. Once he answered, I told him what I needed him to do for me. I also gave him some of the highlights of my time in Frisco to satisfy his curiosity. He told me he would check on Karen and buy the tickets if she called. I assured him that I would keep in touch and call if I needed anything.

As I looked at my watch, I saw it was eight-fifteen. When I looked up, I saw Karen coming down the sidewalk. I found myself smiling, as she got closer to me. She gave me a wink as she went into the office to check in. I gave her a little wave as she went in.

"When she grows up, she'll be a beautiful woman" Bill commented.

"That's the single mother I was talking about," I told him.

"Shame she's so young… If I were her father, I would think about killing her," he boasted.

"I doubt it," I replied, not believing him. It would be disappointing, but I wouldn't kill my daughter if she got into trouble. I might think about killing her child's father if I ever caught him, but not her.

I found myself waiting for Karen to come outside, but she never did. I thought about going inside and saying hi. As I was talking to Bill, it didn't seem right for me to leave him alone. Not being a talker, I let him carry the conversation as I had the night before. Most of my contribution to the conversation was a yes or no. I found myself glancing at the door occasionally, as we continued to talk. I had a feeling that she wasn't a smoker, and she probably was waiting inside for a job.

My feet and back ached from standing and doing nothing. I was about to squat down again when a royal blue Chevy, crew cab pickup, stopped in front of the building. I could see the driver look us over, and I had no idea what he was thinking. I was hoping he was looking for some workers.

"I'm moving and I need a few hands," the driver shouted out.

I expected Bertha to come out and give us a job, so I didn't do anything. Then when she didn't come out. I wasn't sure as to what I should do. I looked over at Bill, and got the feeling that he was as confused as I was. From the way it looked, the other men didn't want the job either. Though that wasn't a good sign, I still needed a job. So as the driver put the truck into gear, I shouted out, "Hold it… We're willing."

"Get in," he told me as he looked off into the distance.

I was in for a surprise for there was a woman in the passenger seat. I grabbed the handle to the backdoor and threw my bag in ahead of me. As I got in, I looked back at the men standing against the wall. I got the impression they didn't care if we took the job or not. Their lack of reaction didn't settle well with me. I was a little worried when I felt the truck begin to roll. My concern about taking the job left me in the street. As the truck was rolling down the street, I jumped into the truck. As I closed the Door, I saw Bill, was already in, seated and watching my every move.

"I have to warn the two of you, I can only pay you five bucks an hour… You have to remember you won't be paying any taxes so you should break even," the driver said as he pulled away.

"That's more than I'm making now," Bill told him as he gave me a shrug.

Not having worked for wages for so long, it took me a minute to get my thoughts together. Then, thinking about wages, I wondered how much I made as half owner of the firm. I began thinking about wages as if I had been out of touch with reality. I wondered why I hadn't asked Bertha how much they paid. Then, rolling it all over, I figured anything was better than I had gotten the day before.

"I'll also be paying for your meals," the driver offered as he brought the truck to a stop. Then, turning back to me, he asked, "A deal?"

"A deal," I told him, agreeing with his offer.

"Should be good for a few dollars," Bill whispered to me.

I nodded my agreement and watched the road as the driver drove us to our destination. As advertised, the streets the man was taking were up and down. I began to wonder if he was going to take Lombard Street. For as many hills as we were going up and down, he might as well take the most crooked street in the world.

As I chuckled to myself, I went back to what Bill had said. I had to agree with him the job would be worth a few dollars to us. Even if we got in eight hours, it was only forty dollars, which wasn't much. That little money wouldn't get me far unless I could work a week or two. Then I might have enough to rent a studio apartment, but not enough to keep me in food. All I had to look forward to was saving a few bucks and staying at the mission. I was looking forward to the opportunity of meeting Jake.

"We're almost there… and we appreciate what you're about to do for us," the woman sitting in front announced.

"It's our pleasure… We're going to appreciate the money," Bill assured her, with a wink to me.

"I'm Paul and this is Ann," Paul said, introducing them to us.

"I'm Bill and my friend, here is Jeff," Bill said, introducing us to them.

"Nice, to meet the two of you," Paul said as he turned a corner.

"Maybe we should have told you, but our place is on the third floor," Ann warned us.

"As young as I am, and with Jeff needing the exercise anyway… I don't see any problem," Bill said with a little chuckle.

"I hope you're speaking for yourself," I told Bill, with a grin, thinking he was cute. We found ourselves in an older neighborhood full of Victorian duplexes made in the early nineteen hundreds. Where they once were a single family occupying each floor, someone had converted them into four or six one-bedroom apartments. The pickup we were in wasn't new, and I found it hard to believe these two would hire someone to help them. I asked them, "Where are you moving to?"

"El Paso, to work with my brother… The way he talks, I should have been there six months ago," Paul answered.

"Never been there," I replied.

"I was there once," Bill said as he leaned forward to look around. When he turned back to me, he added, "It's too hot there for me… I also prefer a little more change in climate."

"I'll get used to it," Ann said with a smile as she patted her husband on the shoulder.

"Ann's never been there either… We'll see what she thinks of it after the first year," Paul said with a laugh.

"Just as long as we're together my love," she said with a smile to him.

"Have to be newlyweds," Bill whispered.

"Yeah," I replied, remembering being in that position once in my life. When Martha and I got our divorce, I knew I would never be a newlywed again. I figured if I wasn't good enough for Martha, no one would want me. Then as Paul slowed down, I saw a moving van ahead of us. When I saw that moving van, I knew we had arrived.

"That's our place up there," Paul said, pointing to the apartment house on our left.

As the two of them lead the way, I took it slowly. I wanted to work, but I couldn't do anything until they took us up there. When I looked over at Bill, he was grinning ear to ear.

"I must be a lucky charm for you," he told me with a grin. From the expression on his face, he felt a need to explain what he had said. He added, "You didn't get a job yesterday. Then I go with you, and we get a job… It seems that I'm good luck for you."

"I'm not going to argue… but it could be the other way around. Now that we're here I just want to get going at it," I told him. As we chatted, we were going up three flights of stairs. When we got to the top step, I wondered if I was going to make it. The idea of going up and down the stairs all day didn't sound easy. I had a funny feeling sitting at a desk as I had for so many years, hadn't prepared me for what was ahead of me.

"Come on in boys," Paul said as he opened the door to the apartment.

As we walked inside the apartment, I had a feeling it was a one-bedroom apartment. I casually commented, "Not that bad of a place."

"Suited us for the time we were here," Paul replied. With a nod, he added, "There's stuff on the back porch… The washer and dryer also go with us."

"Should keep us busy for a few hours," Bill said as he looked around.

I looked around and there were a few boxes taped and marked. It looked as if they had just started packing and there was a lot more to box up. It was easy to see we would be there for a few hours boxing and loading the truck. I looked over at Bill and the other two waiting for directions.

"Bill, why don't you go with Ann to the kitchen? Jeff and I will start in the bedroom," Paul suggested.

"Sounds good to me," Bill said, agreeing with him. Then as he followed Ann, he added, "Might as well start somewhere."

Are you ready?" Paul asked me.

"Lead on," I told him. I was willing to do anything to get the job finished.

As I walked down the hall, I saw my guess was right in that this was a one-bedroom apartment. Once in the bedroom it looked as if they had already started. Most everything was off the walls and there was a stripped-down bed, so everything was ready to box up. I began boxing up the bedding as Paul boxed up the clothes. After we filled each box, we labeled them and stacked them in the corner. After half an hour, we had everything boxed, labeled and the bed broke down.

"Why don't you begin taking down the pictures in the hallway and living room," Paul suggested. Then with a smile he added, "I'll start in the bathroom."

"Whatever," I told him as I made my way into the hallway. I didn't know why but Paul wasn't as friendly as he had been. For the first half-hour that we worked, we hadn't said more than ten words to each other. I didn't mind, but I did find it interesting.

As I was stacking the different pictures against the living room wall, Bill stuck his head out of the kitchen. He asked me, "How's it going?"

"I only have the pictures on the walls of the bedroom to box up," I answered as I began taking down the pictures around me. When I looked back at him, I asked, "What about you?"

"I'm almost done in here… I can't believe a small room such as the kitchen could have held as much as it did," he answered, shaking his head.

"It shouldn't take but a few more hours," I suggested.

In response, he shook his head to say he agreed with me. He went back into the kitchen where I heard pots and pans banging. While the two of them were having their fun, I was finishing taking down the pictures. In the bathroom, I could hear Paul loading up a box of what sounded like bottles.

"On the porch there's some cardboard you can cut up to put around and between, the pictures," Paul told me. After telling me what to do, he turned towards the kitchen, and he shouted out, "I'm going after Burgers… Do you need anything else my love?"

"No," she called back.

"I'll be back shortly," he said as he gave me a nod before he went out the front door.

Once he got back, I had all the pictures covered with cardboard and bundled. I had taken them into manageable groups about the same size and tied them together. Looking around I saw some vases, and with Ann's help, I began to box them up. Exhaustion began to set in, and I wondered how much longer we would be at it. I looked around, and something told me we had another two or three hours before we would be through packing everything. I wasn't sure about then, but if I were right, it meant we would make twenty-five dollars. I might not have been much, but it was still better than I had made the day before.

"Soup's on," Paul shouted out as he came into the apartment.

"My stomach just said, thank you," I told him after I let loose with a belch. As he sat the burgers down on the dining table, I walked over to him. When I heard footsteps, I saw Bill and Ann coming into the dining room.

"Hope the two of you, don't mind colas…, I meant to ask, but I forgot," Paul said as he began handing the burgers out.

"Just as long as it's wet," Bill told him.

"Doesn't matter to me… Anything has to be better than the coffee, I've been drinking," I told him. The four of us sat on the chairs around the table and ate our burgers. There was a little conversation with most of it being about Paul and Ann. The job was one reason they were in a hurry to move. The other reason for the rush was that Ann was pregnant with their first child.

After eating, we finished packing. Paul and I began the task of hauling boxes down to the truck. We hadn't made many trips when Bill began loading the truck with us. The three of us agreed Ann shouldn't be doing any of it, and we left her upstairs. Between the three of us, we loaded everything into the truck by four o'clock. With the last piece of furniture loaded, I found I could barely walk. The only problem I could think of was the walk back to the mission.

"We'll leave the truck here…, and take these two back first," Paul told Ann.

"That makes sense. There's no reason to fight the traffic with the truck," she said, agreeing with him.

He turned to us and asked, "Ready?"

"If there's nothing else we can do," I answered him.

"Then let's be gone," he said as he motioned for us to get into the truck.

As I got in, I commented to Bill, "I hope you're happy. I got that exercise you talked about this morning."

With a grin, he replied, "Don't forget I was going up and down the stairs like you were. Trust me, I don't care how lumpy the bed is it still sounds good…. Something tells me I've been on the wagon too long."

"Guess so," I replied as I gave him a slug in the arm.

"It didn't take as long as I thought it would," Ann told her husband.

"The two of them did most of the work…. We found two good workers," Paul told his wife.

"That we did," she said agreeing with him.

As we rode back in silence, I found myself thinking about Karen. I knew the only place I could catch her was at the office. I knew it was getting late, and I looked at my watch. I saw it was after four o'clock and I doubted I would be able to catch her there. My only hope was that she might have found some work. If she did, she might be getting back about the same time we were. As I thought about her, I wished I had time to hunt for the father of her daughter. If I were to find him, I would make him pay for leaving her and his daughter.

"Here you are," Paul announced, as he brought the truck to a stop.

Bill and I got out, and I noticed there were hardly any traffic around. Standing to one side as Bill was, I waited for Paul to get out and pay us. Before I realized what was going on the pickup took off.

"Suckers," Paul shouted out as he drove off.

"Asshole," Bill shouted back to Paul and his wife.

"I had a feeling, they would stiff us," I told him, as we walked to the curb.

He asked, "How so?"

"Not one of the other guys jumped at the chance to work for him…. Then there was the apartment. There wasn't anything in it worth anything. I had the feeling they are working on a shoestring," I explained to him.

As he gave me a look that he wanted to kill me, he asked, "Why didn't you say anything?"

"And have to walk back from there…? A meal was better than nothing when there's that distance to walk," I told him. Then, to rub it in, I added, "Yep, you're lucky for me."

"Aw, shut up… I guess we both got the shaft," he said as we began our trip back to the mission. Then with a grin, he asked me, "What do you have planned for excitement tonight?"

"I think I'll grab a bite of supper first… Then I might walk up to the mission on Polk," I answered. I began to think after reading my father's diary it might be a good idea to see the place. I also wanted to see if what I had heard about the place was right. I wasn't going over with any expectation of finding anyone that remembered him.

As if he didn't understand he asked, "Why, are you thinking it might be a better place?"

"I have to see someone…. It shouldn't take long. I don't know when I'll get back to Market Street, I might not even try. I would like to, but I might have a better idea when we get there," I explained to him.

When we got to the day labor office, I didn't see anyone around. I wasn't too surprised, knowing everyone usually left by three o'clock. I expected a few would be coming back some time after five from their jobs. I looked through the front door to see if anyone was inside. I could see a light inside and almost went in, to see if Karen was there. Then, before I knew it, the doors opened and Bertha stepped outside.

"I was wondering where the two of you were," she said, greeting us. She turned to Bill, and asked him, "Have a good day?"

"Yeah… we had a great day if getting the shaft is having a good day," I told her.

"So they stiffed you… I'm not surprised," she replied with a straight face. She added with a grin, "I warned you about taking jobs without checking with me. We guarantee payment…. There are those out there that are willing to take advantage of men like you."

"They did that," I assured her.

"They fed us," Bill added.

"You haven't had supper at the mission yet… The burgers were better," I commented.

"So it wasn't a total loss then," she said with a grin. Then, as she was walking away, she turned and added, "I think I might have something for you tomorrow, Jeff."

I asked, "With pay?"

"With pay… I'm waiting for a call. Once it comes in you'll have a job," she answered with a wave.

"Doing what?" I called out to her.

"Come back in the morning and I'll tell you," She shouted out.

From her expression, I knew I had to wait until morning to find out what the job would be. As I caught up with Bill, I wondered if my father had to go through this bullshit.

CHAPTER FIVE

We left at 6:30 the next morning for the Day Labor office. I was looking forward to seeing what Bertha had for me. Since I had learned any job the agency gave me was a guaranteed paycheck, it made me feel better. There were two questions in the back of my mind. The first was what I was going to be doing. The second was how long I had to wait for that call to come into her.

"Since I was asleep when you got back from Polk Street… How did it go?" Bill asked as we crossed the first intersection.

I almost didn't hear him because of an irritated truck driver. From what I could see, a driver had pulled halfway out of a parking space and stopped. The car blocking traffic was bringing everyone's tempers to the boiling point. The truck driver's solution was honking his horn. The horn made it difficult to hear on the street being narrow and the high-rise buildings. I wanted to shout out that losing one's temper doesn't solve anything, but I knew it would be a waste.

"Idiots," I said as we crossed the rest of the way through the intersection. I turned to Bill and told him, "I can't say the trip over there was a waste of time, but I didn't learn what I was hoping to."

He asked, "How was your trip?"

"I was in hopes of finding a man I had seen at our place… I was in hopes he went from one place to another," I answered Bill.

"And he doesn't," Bill replied, getting the wrong idea.

"Oh, he does… but as with our place it's only once a month," I told him. Then, deciding to tell him the interesting part, I added, "What I found out blew me away… I have never known of a wealthy bum before. He gives each of the shelters a hundred-thousand dollars a year… It seems he stayed at both missions thirty years ago, and now he wants to help both of them… In saying thanks, he comes back once a month."

"He could give me a few of those dollars," Bill said with a shrug.

I have to say I found it hard to believe when I heard the story. In doing simple math, he gave six million dollars to the missions. I found it sad more of the rich weren't doing as he was. I thought it funny thinking most people thought he was a bum. All of it had an unreal atmosphere to it. I couldn't wait to meet the man when he came back to the mission.

"And you would just spend it," I said, ribbing him a little.

As I gave him a stupid grin he asked, "Your point is?"

"Degenerate… baby, killer," a woman shouted out as she passed us.

"What…? I wonder what that was all about." I asked. I didn't understand what was wrong with the woman and her outburst.

"It's your fatigues," Bill answered without explaining.

I found myself rubbing myself down and checking out my fatigues. I couldn't see or feel anything wrong with them. They might have the funny little pattern in them from the bedsprings, but she couldn't see that. Even if she could have seen the patterns, they wouldn't make me a baby killer. Not understanding, I asked him, "What of it?"

"Trust me, I know…. Your outfit says Army, and that's a big negative, to some," he answered as he shook his head.

"I don't know what you mean," I asked, still not understanding. I found it hard to understand how the Army correlated with being a negative.

"My grandmother taught me… Oh, how she taught me… In fact it was her attitude that separated us for a longtime. After thinking about it for a couple of years, I began to understand her feelings," he began to tell me. Then, stopping, he looked at me with a tear in his eye.

He added, "I never knew my father…. After my mother died, I never learned any more about my father, other than he was in Vietnam…"

"Sounds familiar," I replied, as he got his thoughts together.

"No matter the politics, news coverage, or reality, she felt soldiers were nothing but murderers… The baby killer comes from the children killed in Nam. Grandmother didn't understand casualties of war. She didn't understand what it was like to live in a war-torn country. Obviously, she had never been in a battle. The only gunfire she had ever heard was in western movies, so she didn't understand. She didn't understand what a soldier needed to do when a sniper is shooting at him from a hut in a village. When that soldier returns fire the children in or around the hut became casualties. What the public didn't understand is some of those snipers were children. What are soldiers, supposed to do…, not shoot back? You have to protect yourself… which means you, shoot the ten, twelve-year olds and go on.

People like my grandmother only saw what the newscasters portrayed, and they formed her opinion. That opinion was that a man joined the service, because he couldn't handle a job or a normal life. It didn't matter if he was a draftee, or if he joined on his own back then… Since father was in the service, she thought of him as an outcast. She referred to him as that bum, or why would you want to know about worthless… I never learned anything about him," he answered.

"Oh," I replied, wishing we had more time to talk about it. When I heard, what he said made me wonder if my grandmother had the same problem. She had kept the diary for years, and she had more to tell me. Whatever she had to tell me she was holding back on it also. As I grew up, I didn't hear how my father did in school, what his hobbies were, or anything else about him. When I pushed for information, she would send me to my room. I learned not to bring him up to her.

My mother was a different matter in that she never did anything wrong. She was the one that suffered without help from her husband. She had a child to raise, even though she was sick.

"That thought scares you?" Bill asked, with a concerned look.

"No…. You got me to thinking about my grandmother… and like you, I never knew my father. Though he was her son, she didn't approve of him, so she wouldn't tell me anything about him. In hearing what you said, I wonder if that wasn't her problem with him, also," I answered, still running memories through my mind.

"People are strange," he commented. Then after walking a few feet, he smiled and added, "This is dangerous.... Both of us at the same mission broke, screwed, nutty grandmothers, and we don't know our fathers."

"It's scary, isn't it," I commented. I barely knew him for two days, and I was finding we had a lot in common. The funniest part of it was that in those short two days, I had learned more about him than I knew about my partner.

"At least you sound as if you are getting a job today with pay," he commented.

"Talk is cheap… We'll see when the day is over. You might be the one that gets a job," I reminded him.

"If you get the job, I'll get the coffee in the morning," he offered with a smile.

"Thanks… I probably won't get my coffee until ten for as late you like to sleep," I replied.

"You'll get your coffee… It may be a little late, but you'll get it," he added.

Both of us laughed, and then we fell into our own thoughts. I was thinking about the possible job we may be getting, Bill, Karen, Jake, and my father. I found it hard to believe so much could happen in just a few days. My life had been so predictable until then, and then at that point I knew what a bore my life had been. My marriage to Martha and having my three kids were the exciting parts in my life. Now I was adding the memory of the foulest oatmeal and coffee I have ever had on my tongue. All of this was because I had to walk in my father's footsteps.

"Good morning," Bertha's voice came from behind me.

In deep thought, I hadn't realized we had arrived, and I turned to her. Seeing her smile, I returned, "Good morning."

"Good morning, Ma'am," Bill added with a bow.

As she typed, she commented, "A beautiful day isn't it?"

Not having noticed, I looked up into the sky and had to agree. The sun was bright in the sky, and the humidity wasn't as bad as it had been. A flock of seagulls was flying overhead in search of food. It looked like she was right about it being a beautiful day.

"Jeff's in dreamland today…, but we have a bet, if he gets a job or not today," Bill told her.

"Oh," she replied with a sparkle of interest in her eye. She had just begun inserting the key in the lock.

"If he gets the job, he gets coffee tomorrow morning. If not, he has to wait until I wake up…, which might mean waiting until Christmas," he told her.

"I'm glad to see you can still laugh," she replied as she opened the door.

"That's all we have and it doesn't cost anything," I reminded her.

"True… Most people that I deal with have forgotten that," she replied, as she let us inside.

"I think I'll begin charging you for the good times," Bill suggested to me as we walked inside.

"Good luck in collecting," I said as I slapped him on the back.

"I strike out again… Are you telling me I've paired up with another deadbeat?" He replied as he walked up to the counter.

"Give me a minute to turn everything on," Bertha told us.

As we stood at the counter, I could hear the door open behind us. I turned briefly and saw a couple of men walk in. I nodded and greeted them, "Good morning."

"Huh," one of the men answered in a sour voice.

With a shrug, I turned around and waited for Bertha to come back to the counter. As I turned around, I heard the doors open again, and I saw who it was. Once again, I was in hopes of seeing Karen, so I could see how she was doing. Instead of her, it was three more men.

"A friendly sort," Bill commented.

"Yeah," I replied as Bertha took her seat behind the counter. Then reaching over she picked up some number cards and handed them to me. As I took them, she asked me, "Would you hang them up for me?"

"Sure," I told her as I took them. I checked to make sure they were in their proper order and hung them on the peg.

"You will owe me coffee tomorrow morning. You just got a job," Bill announced with a smile.

Not understanding what he was talking about I asked him "What?"

"You just got a job… She gave you the job of hanging up the cards," he answered, as he nodded toward the numbered cards.

"Yeah, and the guy stiffed us… That wasn't part of the deal," I reminded him of our deal. I realized what he had said, and I gave him a shrug.

As I turned back to Bertha, she smiled and reached out with her hand. I had a feeling there was something in it, so I accepted whatever it was. As she continued to smile, she dropped a little piece of candy into my hand.

"I wouldn't want you to feel cheated so here's your pay," she said with a chuckle. She then handed me a piece of candy.

"Thanks… I think," I returned as I popped the piece into my mouth.

"It's coffee in the morning," Bill said.

"I've already logged the two of you in," she told us with a nod.

"Thanks," I told her. Then, as we left the counter to go outside, I told Bill, "For as good as it tastes it is worth getting you, coffee… Especially for as bad as that coffee is"

"I think I'm getting to like that woman," he returned as we went out the door.

"Yeah right," I replied, as I held the door open for a man going inside. He reached around me and held the door for himself. Not caring, one way or the other, I let the pressure of the door off my arm. I was finding it hard accepting the rudeness I had experienced during this trip to Frisco. I knew there were many good people around the city. What surprised me was most of them had a negative streak running through them.

As Bill lit up, I watched the parade of labor hopefuls coming from all directions. I couldn't remember seeing so many solemn disgusted looks on so many faces. Though I found it hard to take, I felt everyone should take a minute out of their day and see these people. I knew I wasn't any different from anyone else. Like them, most of my life was going to and from work. After working, anything left had gone to my wife and children. The only time I knew anything about the rest of the world was when I turned on the television.

"You trying to solve all the problems of the world?" Bill asked as if he had read my mind.

I asked, "What are you talking about?"

"You were so intent on those going into the office… I figured you were trying to think of some way of helping them," he answered.

"I doubt there's anything anyone can do for them," I replied, letting the thought drop.

"You're wrong… I got myself into this mess. I can't hold my wife, grandparents or anyone responsible. I did it and only I can change myself and become a worthwhile person," he told me, as he lit another cigarette. Not adding anything more to his little speech he walked on down the sidewalk.

I could appreciate his thoughts, but I wondered if it was that easy. Then, remembering where I was, I still had my own problems. I was thinking about his comment when I turned towards the office. I was beginning to think Bertha would never get the call about the work she promised. It's even more frustrating with the door to the office opening and closing every two seconds. I finally gave up and sat down against the building to wait for her. As my backside hit the cement, I noticed Bill talking to an old man. I gave them a shrug, and watched the traffic go by.

As Bill came back over to where I was, I looked up at him. Once I saw him, I noticed Karen coming down the street. To my surprise, she had a smile on her face and a bounce in her step. Seeing the change stirred my interest in finding out. It would be good to hear something was going right for someone.

She gave me a smile and a wave. As she opened the door, she told me, "I need to talk to you later."

"All right… Later," I assured her.

"I'm glad she's not my daughter," Bill commented as he watched her go inside. Then turning back to me, he asked, "I wonder how long before you get your job?"

"A good question," I answered as a woman drove up in front of us.

As the car stopped, Karen came running out of the office. She waived a piece of paper as she passed me. With a smile she told me, "I got here just in time for this job… See you later."

"Yeah…, have fun," I told her as I gave her a wave. Then turning back to Bill, I saw Bertha come walking out of the office. I asked her, "Something for me?"

"I think so… I got the call from the Construction Company and what they want you to do. They have a couple of trucks that they need unloaded… And Bill, they told me they needed two men, so if you want to go, you can," she told him.

"I guess so… At the moment I don't have anything planned," he answered with a grin. As he turned back to me, he gave me a thumbs up. He then continued, "I guess we get our own coffee in the morning."

"I'll hold you to that," I told him.

"It's a roofing company… They want you to unload a truck for them," she explained.

"As long as it pays… It's got to be better than sitting here on the sidewalk," I told her.

"Oh… Here is your contract, Jeff. Mr. Simpson should be by in thirty minutes. He should be calling out your contract numbers. I didn't give him your names… Once you have completed what he has contracted you for, have him sign this. When you bring it back, I'll pay you…," she told us with a questioning look. Then as I took the contract from her, she asked us, "Any questions?"

"None that I can think of," I replied as I looked over at Bill.

"Me neither," he assured her.

Before she went inside, she turned around with a grin. She then went back to Bill and handed him his contract. As he took the piece of paper from her, she added, "Sorry about that."

"I understand… You don't love me anymore," he replied as he put it into his bag.

"I don't love you any less," she returned as she went inside.

"That's good to know," Bill told her, as he gave me a wink.

As she was going inside, I reminded him, "She's a little old, for you."

"Not to tease," he told me as he took a long drag on his cigarette.

When I saw his eyes light up, I asked him, "Where are you getting all of those cigarettes?"

"With the last few bucks I had, I bought three cartons… If I don't make some money soon, I'll have to quit," he answered as he took a big draw on it.

"Maybe you should give them up." I suggested.

"Number 07935 and 36," a man called out from a pickup.

Since I had my contract out and Bill didn't, I checked on the contract numbers, and it matched. When I saw the truck, it brought memories of the day before to mind. Though this job was going through the office, there was still a chance we might not see any money. We had to make sure our employer signed our contract. If we didn't, we would be in the same kettle of fish. I knew as with everything else in life, there were no guarantees. Not knowing what else to do I decided we had nothing to lose. I turned to Bill and told him, "It's him."

"Early isn't he," he replied, as he put his cigarette out and followed me.

"Mr. Simpson?" I asked the driver. I wanted to make sure he was the right man.

"No, I'm Roberts. I work for Mr. Simpson," the man said, introducing himself to me.

"I'm Jeff and this is my friend Bill," I offered with my hand extended to him. Though he was wearing jeans, I had the feeling he would be more comfortable in slacks. I had a feeling for as young as he was, he hadn't worked long for Mr. Simpson. Though he wasn't at least by name a Simpson, he probably was a son of Mr. Simpson's friend. I found him to be friendly, and I didn't see us having any problem with him.

"A pleasure," Roberts said as he shook my hand. Then in turn, he shook Bill's hand and motioned for us to get into the pickup.

We threw our bags into the truck, got ready for whatever he had for us. Roberts got in started the truck, he checked the traffic in his mirrors. With a shrug he pulled away from the curb, and we were on our way. After going around the block, he headed south. Not knowing where we were going, I tried to figure out if we were going to be working on an industrial building or residential one.

"Been out long?" Roberts asked me as he headed south.

"Three days now…," I told him as well as giving him the rest of the story.

He asked, "How about you Bill?"

"I never joined the service… I had enough problems with my wife," Bill told him.

"Both of you have me beat… I've never been in the service or married. I don't know if that makes me any lucky or not," he told us.

"You've got my vote. When, I was your age, I had a wife telling me she didn't need me anymore… I don't know if I pressed my luck," Bill told him.

"You're not that much older than I am," Roberts said, with a questioning tone to his voice.

"I didn't sleep much back then…, and was able to get into more trouble," Bill explained to him.

With a laugh, Roberts replied, "I guess that's why mother made me go to sleep early."

"My mother never had the chance," Bill said in a soft voice. From the way he made the statement it was more to him than to us. Then, before we could comment, he added, "If she had a chance, I probably would have gone out the window… I know, for that's what I did at my grandmother's place."

"What's your excuse Jeff?" He asked me.

"The glory and all of that stuff… Though I'm proud of what I did, I don't know if I would do it again," I answered him.

"I grew up thinking I would go into the service…. Then one night, I caught my father drunk on his ass…," he began to tell us.

"What happened?" I asked, wanting to hear what he had to say.

"Mind you, we weren't poor and my mother was a proud woman. She didn't care what others did at their homes. She had her rules, and that was all there was to it…. This one night, I found dad in the den sitting on the floor with a half bottle of whiskey between his legs. When he heard me come in he looked up at me, and I could see he had been crying," he finally answered. Then, changing lanes, and wiping a tear from his face, he added, "I had never seen him cry before, and it shocked me."

"Did he say anything?" I asked, feeling sorry for him. I found I was jealous of him. I would have given anything to be able to talk to my father.

"Yeah… He said something, in fact, he said a lot… That was after saying over and over that I killed them," he answered.

Bill asked, "What did he mean? Did he tell you what he was talking about?"

"Oh, he told me. He drank another swig out of the bottle first… Then he told me about the orders they got, to clean out the tunnels occupied by the cong guerrillas. He also told me how many miles some of those tunnels went, and how impossible getting the Gooks out of them was… He lost many of his friends because the politicians were giving the orders. They thought they could run the war from Washington… If the politicians weren't bad enough, there were the "Gung Ho" new officers. I can't blame them because they were also following orders. Their orders said they were to go into the tunnels and clean out the cong. The orders were to show us how we should do it… Unfortunately, for them West Point or OCS never taught them the impossibility of cleaning out those tunnels. Many of those young officers didn't come out of the tunnels alive. The death toll got so high they finally canceled the idea of clearing out the tunnels. They finally saw the sad truth, that we were suffering a higher death toll than the enemy's… To this day he feels he was a murderer, which is sad because that's not who he is. If the command had done it the proper way, not as many would have lost their lives. He breaks out into a sweat when he sees someone in a uniform, or an oriental person," he answered. After a pause, he added, "I decided I didn't want to fight in a war where I might be killed out of stupidity."

"There's stupidity all around us… Not just in Vietnam or in the Middle East… Most of the stupidity is with the politicians and the voters," I said, agreeing with his assessment.

"I've heard too many stories such as that…I heard that Johnson and McNamara were in control of the fighting. I also heard they changed their strategies so fast it made it impossible to fight the war as it should be," Bill added.

"War is the shits, at best… A politician getting involved only makes it worse. Then there's the news media. I heard one story about a trooper who was starting his second tour in Vietnam, who said something like "My first tour, I hated the press, and wanted to kill Charlie. Now I hate Charlie, and I want to kill the press." I told him, letting the subject drop. I found the conversation depressing, and I had enough. My aching back wasn't making anything easier. When I heard we would be unloading trucks, I thought I would practice my groaning. I told the two, "I must be getting old."

Bill asked, "Is your back, killing you?"

"You could say that" I answered as I changed my position.

Roberts asked, "Are you going to be able to unload the trucks?"

"That or die," I assured him. As he drove, I found myself lost, and I asked him, "Where are we going?"

"This highway goes to Daly City… but I'll be turning up at the next light. We have a little housing division going in," he answered.

"Never been to Daly City," I replied.

"Me neither… and I haven't worried about it," Bill added.

Roberts asked Bill, "Something against Daly City?"

"No… I would rather be beside my ex-wife without my ex-best friend, being in the same bed," Bill told him.

"Oh, one of those marriages…. I guess it could be worse. My friends don't have anything to take from me," Roberts replied.

"Keep it that way," Bill added as he sat back in his seat.

Though it was only a few more blocks, none of us said anything. Then pulling in through a fenced off area we could see they were building homes. It had been a part of bigger construction projects, but this wasn't that small. I had turned around, and I saw a truck I felt we would be working on. My back began aching as I thought about the total weight the truck was hauling. As I suspected the truck followed us into the construction site. As we entered the site, I could see most of the homes were ready for roofing. Roberts stopped in an area with a lot going on. Out of my open window, I could hear backhoes, hammers pounding and all the other noises in a construction site.

"…Forty-six and fifteen sixteenths," someone shouted out to someone.

"Gotcha," another called back.

"Get those dumpsters, out of there… We need the space for the roofing," someone of authority shouted out to someone.

"I guess we'll be working somewhere around the dumpsters," I commented to Roberts as we both got out of the pick-up.

"From the way it sounds, your guess is right…. Stay here, and I'll find Paul Osborne… You'll be working for him… When you finish unloading the truck, I'll drive you back," he told us.

"Looks like fun…, if you are looking for a broken back," Bill said as he looked around.

"Don't remind me, my back is killing me. I'll make it, but I can think of many jobs I would rather be doing," I confessed to him. We didn't have anything else to do but stand where we were and watch, everyone else work. If anyone were to have asked me, I did feel at home on the site.

"I found him," Roberts said walking up to us.

Behind him was a red-headed man a good foot taller than I was. If that wasn't bad enough, he probably outweighed me by a hundred pounds or more. For as large as he was, I didn't see what they needed us for, he could unload a truck by himself in one armload.

"Paul, these gentlemen are Jeff and Bill… Gentlemen… Paul will be your boss," Roberts said in introducing us.

"Good to meet you," I told the big man as I extended my hand to him.

As he shook my hand he asked, "Ever been on a construction site?"

I hesitated in answering him with his attention diverted by some workers. When he turned back to me, I told him, "With my father being in construction this feels like home to me."

"Then you joined the service, and it has never been the same," he said with a smile.

"You can say that again," I replied.

As he checked out the area, he told us, "I can't have you do anything until they clear some room for you to work in. They should have taken care of this early this morning, but you know how that is… It's only going to take them fifteen to twenty minutes to clear it out of there… I'll come back and get you."

"No problem," Bill assured him.

"I love standing around doing nothing," I told Bill.

With a grin, he asked me, "Would rather be unloading boxcars?"

Other than moving to one side or the other, we didn't do anything for half an hour. It only took them ten minutes to clear out the dumpster area for us. Then a break came along, and it took another fifteen minutes to get the forklifts out of the area. Finally, we saw Paul heading our way. While we waited for him, a trucker moved in closer to the area we would be working in.

"By the way… where did they send you, Afghanistan or Iraq?" Paul asked me.

"Afghanistan," I answered, lying to him.

"It couldn't have been as bad as Vietnam… I know we loved some of the decisions McNamara made. If it wasn't for him, we probably would've won the war," he told us.

I was in the mood for a good story, so I asked, "Like what?"

"The best one is part of his efforts to control our target sights. When he found out how many of our troops it took to monitor the Ho Chi Minh trail he came up with a brilliant idea," he answered.

"And what was this brilliant idea?" I asked. Something told me the end of the story was going to be a good one. As I was listening, I saw trucks with the roofing material. It looked as if they were full of Spanish tile. I found myself praying we didn't have to unload the truck one piece at a time. If that was the plan, I was going to leave.

"He decided what we needed to do was to install listening devices along the trail. I have to say it was a good idea…," he began to tell us, but stopped, to guide a truck that was backing up towards us. He finally added, "They worked great. The men that were staffing them, could make out every sound recorded but one…. Then after much investigation they finally learned what it was."

"What was it?" Bill asked.

"The Viet Cong was pissing on the equipment…. Did it serve their purpose…? No, unless you want to include the laugh the troops got out of it."

"That's funny," Bill replied with a big grin.

"Now with the fun and games, this is what I want you to do… Keep in mind there will be another two or three men to help you…," he explained what he wanted.

I was glad I had put down my registration for forklift experience. I got the job to drive the forklift, as Bill undid the strapping on each row of tiles. Then, once I picked up a load, he guided me to a spot to drop it. Once the stack was on the ground, we would go after another. It was easier than doing it by hand, but it was still going to take us awhile.

"How's your back doing?" Bill asked as he got off my forks and onto the truck.

"Better than it could be," I answered him as I motioned for him to get going.

We worked the rest of the morning and nothing exciting happened. Then lunchtime came, and we hadn't brought anything with us. We found ourselves as hungry as the rest of the men. Unlike them, we had very little money, so we couldn't go after any lunch. Then a roach truck pulled into the yard selling different kinds of food. Most of the workers were buying their lunch from the truck. Bill and I stayed back wishing we could join them. Then seeing the expression on Bill's face, I remembered the money I was holding back.

"What do you think, should we get a bite to eat?" I asked him.

Questioning my offer he asked, "You have money?"

"A little… You can pay me back once we get some money," I offered. It didn't take long for him to get off his ass.

Being impatient, he motioned for me to follow him over to the truck. As he walked ahead of me, he asked, "What are we waiting for?"

"Hungry, are you?" I asked him. I was learning it was fun making some people squirm.

"You know I'm hungry… You ought to go up and down off that truck bed. Then the breakfast we have been getting doesn't do much for you," he answered as we got in behind the rest of the crew.

I had no idea what Bill was thinking about as we waited for our turn to select what we wanted to eat. What concerned me was the choice we would have, and if I could afford it. We both got a couple of Enchiladas, rice and beans with a cola. Sitting down away from rest of the crew, we ate our lunch. Not far from us, there were two men, and we did exchange a few friendly words. Twenty minutes later, we finished our lunch, and we were back unloading the truck.

The afternoon went as it did that morning. Everyone was so busy working we didn't have time to talk. We finished unloading the truck at four o'clock, and I was glad it was over. It had been a long day, but I wanted a few more so I could work up a bankroll. It wasn't long Roberts was loading us into his truck, and we were on our way back.

"I have to say the two of you did a good day's worth of work," Roberts told us as we began to pull out of the yard. Then with a smile, he added, "If you don't mind, we might be calling on your services again."

"You'll have to call us in the next week or two… We should be rich by that time," Bill offered.

"Don't pay any attention to the idiot… Call on us anytime. It felt good doing something," I told him. I wasn't so much worried about getting more work from his company as getting back to the office in time to see Karen. I wanted to get to hear what she wanted to tell me. After I talked to her, I wanted to get our money and get back to the mission.

"The traffic isn't that bad yet thankfully…We should get back before five," Roberts let us know.

"Thanks… Then it's supper and to bed," Bill told him.

"Don't worry too much about rushing… As you know we don't have anyone waiting for us and neither one of us drink," I reminded him. I was anxious to get back, but I didn't want him to think he had to rush.

"Getting back in time to collect your pay is important," he suggested.

"Hurry," I replied with a laugh.

"Aha… I found a glitch in your armor," he commented.

"You've got us there," I replied, as I looked back at Bill.

"You don't hear me arguing, do you?" Bill asked.

Everyone was joking back and forth then the three of us fell into silence. Even with Karen and Jake on my mind, my father's diary was more important. I knew what I was still going to do, was some reading. The diary wasn't large, and I hadn't read as much as I should have. Having a clean change of clothes, I decided I would forgo the pleasure of doing laundry.

"We are almost there. I can let you out anywhere you want," Roberts announced.

"Other than signing our contracts, I can't think of any other place you could drop us off at… So this is fine," I reminded him. Out of the corner of my eye, I could see Bill, trying to find his contract. Mine was in my hand so whenever Robert stopped he could sign it.

"That's right… I almost forgot about that… sorry," he said, as he turned the corner to the office.

As he went around the block to let us off on the side of the office, I looked for Karen. From the outside, I didn't see anyone against the wall, but I hadn't expected to see any. I knew my chances of seeing her were slim at best. As the truck stopped, I looked through the doors of the office, and I couldn't tell if anyone was inside or not.

Not knowing what else to do, I handed Roberts my contract to sign. I told him, "I think I can safely say it was our pleasure."

"I agree," Bill added with a yawn.

"If I don't see the two of you again, I wish you luck with your future," Roberts said as he handed my contract back. Then taking Bill's, he signed it and let us go.

"Thanks again," I shouted out, as he pulled away.

As he turned the corner, he waved, as we headed for the office. As I grabbed the door handle, I prayed Bertha was still there. I gave the door a slight tug, and it opened easily. Then, seeing Bertha smiling, I felt better.

"I had almost given up on you two. I wouldn't have stayed this late if it wasn't for paperwork I had to do and knowing you needed some money," she told us as we walked to the counter.

"Thanks," I managed to get out, as I checked the waiting area for Karen. Not seeing her, I asked Bertha, "Has Karen got back yet?"

She asked, "Her job was only for three hours, so she's come and gone… Is there a problem?"

"No…, she just said she wanted to tell me something this morning as she left," I answered her.

"For six and a half hours after taxes I owe you forty-one dollars and sixty cents each," she told us. Not bothering to look up, she added, "Once you sign the receipt, I'll give you your pay in cash with a copy of the receipt for your records."

"As if we kept records," I replied, thinking the idea was funny.

"I know, but that's the law," she told me.

I wanted to laugh when I heard what I had earned. Back home it wasn't as much as I made in a half hour. I did find it satisfying to get a little cash in my hands. I found myself remembering when I started out, I didn't make forty dollars a day. Laughing to myself, I realized I still wasn't averaging that much a day.

"I can remember paying this much for supper one night with my wife," Bill commented as he took the receipt from her and signed it. Turning back to me, he added, "In fact, this wouldn't pay for a night on the town six months ago."

"How one's life can change…. Then to think how much better you feel being sober," I told him, as I handed my receipt to Bertha.

As she locked the safe she said, "Here you are gentlemen…. See you tomorrow?"

"After I buy a carton of smokes, and pay, Jeff back for lunch, I won't have much left. So…, I'll be back," Bill, answered, as he picked up the cash.

"Same here," I told her as I turned to head for the mission.

"Good, I might have another job for you tomorrow," she told us with a smile.

Turning to Bill I asked him, "I hope you're not being too optimistic?"

"The way my life has been going, anything is an improvement…

We'll see," he replied with an optimistic tone and a shrug. Then leaving the office he suggested, "Maybe we can stop, to buy my smokes and a candy bar…"

"You're in need of some flavor for supper?" I finished for him.

"You've got it," he replied with a laugh. Then, stopping as he pulled his small wade of money out, he confessed, "What I would like to do is to take a woman out to supper. I haven't had the companionship of a woman for a long time."

"One day soon," I assured him. In the back of my mind, I planned to offer him a job with the firm. I wasn't sure how we could use him, but there had to be something he could do. If Ray and I couldn't find him a position somewhere I was sure after I made a few calls, I'd find him something. I knew I could get him something with all the union officials and contractors I knew. My first goal was to find out what happened to my father. Once I found that out, I would see what he could do for Bill. I told him, "I know what you mean… I'm not worried about going to bed with a woman. I would like the chance to share some time with one… Even talking to Karen was a thrill."

"Not worried about going to bed with a woman… Man you are getting old," he replied, with a good hearty laugh. To rub it in, he kept laughing, but it sounded phony.

"Old enough to know what I would like out of life," I told him. If I were to have supper with anyone, it would be Martha. My second choice was to do something with my children.

Then, getting serious, he told me, "Women don't understand that we also need their companionship. A romp in the hay is wonderful but hearing their laugh is something else."

"I know what you are saying… Yeah, and it's from there you gain a friend you appreciate and more," I replied. The subject had been a big part of me since my divorce. With that being the case, I didn't want to go into it any further and needed to change the subject. I asked him, "What are your plans for tonight?"

"I haven't thought much about it… I think the Olympics start tonight. I might watch some of it," he answered. Seeing his reflection in a window he commented, "I could use a change of clothes."

"Maybe next week… If we keep working like we did today," I offered optimistically.

He asked, "What's on your agenda tonight?"

"Washing clothes… and reading the diary," I replied. Thinking of doing my laundry, I knew Martha would have a good laugh. It took her a few years get me to pick up my under shorts, let alone to do laundry. I knew she would enjoy seeing me wash my clothes as I showered.

"We need a life," he commented as we fell into silence.

As we walked back, my spinal column cried out with every step. I didn't let it bother me for it felt good to have some money in my pocket. Though in my real life, I made more in one hour, I was still happy. I knew if I needed bailing out, I could call Martha or Ray. This dumb idea was my idea, and I had to make it on my own. I reminded myself the one and most important object was to learn something about my father. I found it hard to watch everyone around us. People were driving here and there with various expressions on their faces. No matter what their moods were, they had the freedom I was learning to appreciate.

"I'll be right back," Bill announced.

Seeing we were in front of a little store, I knew what he was after. Not having anything else to do I stepped inside myself. I called out to him, "I'm right behind you."

Bill reached down and grabbed a candy bar. Then at the counter, he asked the clerk, "A carton of the cheapest cigarettes you sell."

As he reached under, the counter the clerk answered, "Yes, sir."

I thought he might be reaching for a revolver. I prayed that seeing Bill's money out told him we weren't there to rob him. As this fear ran through my mind, the man laid a carton of cigarettes on the counter. Seeing him set them down where he had, I relaxed a little.

"Twenty-seven thirty-eight," the man told Bill.

"Here you are," Bill replied as he handed him the money. Accepting his change, he walked by me and said, "I have enough to pay you back and a few dollars for lunch tomorrow."

Not replying I picked up a pack of breath mints and laid them down on the counter. I told the man, "That's all I need."

"Eighty-seven cents," the man told me.

"Here," I replied as I counted out the change. Having had the exact change, I picked the Mints up and followed Bill out the door. Once outside I reminded him, "You might not have much left, but you still have more than last night."

"True," he said, agreeing with me. Without any argument, he counted out what his lunch had cost me. Handing it over to me, he said, "Here, we're even."

"Pay me tomorrow, night when we both have more money," I told him.

"Thanks…. Tomorrow night then," he said. With a smile, he put the money back into his pocket.

From the store, it was only another block to the mission. Bill lit up and seemed a little happier as we walked the rest of the way to the mission. Seeing the look on his face, I wondered if I should take up smoking. I was almost willing to try smoking if they could make me that happy. Then, with the memory of trying one as a kid, I decided it wasn't a good idea.

"Well, what is it going to be tonight, fried mush or burnt hot dogs?" Bill asked as we stepped into the mission.

"Burnt water," I answered with a grin of anticipation. Then as a reminder, I told him, "You did have some flavorful enchiladas for lunch."

Smiling he asked, "Thank God... Are you telling me you find it offensive?"

"Don't remind me," I added from the sick memories.

From the barrack's area, a familiar face came out to the lobby area. I greeted the man, "Good to see you again, Charlie."

In return, he asked, "Good evening.... How was the day for you gentlemen?"

"Not bad... Is there a donation pot around here?" I asked,

"Evening Jeff... Bill," Carl said, coming out of his usual hiding place, the dining room.

"Good evening, Carl," I said, greeting him.

"He was just asking about a donation box," Charlie told him.

With an interested look Carl asked, "What donation box?"

"I made some money today and figure you should get at least twenty percent of it," I told him with my honest feelings. I didn't like living off someone and being I was living a lie, I felt it was only right.

"That's not necessary," he assured me.

"No, it's my way," I told him, as I handed him ten dollars.

"Thanks, but you don't have to. We get funds from the state, a couple of foundations, and a private donation," he told us. As he was talking, he held the bill out to me.

"A person named Jake," I added with a smile.

With a questioning look he asked, "How did you learn that?"

"Let me grab a bite, and I'll tell you," I promised him.

"You've got it," he promised as Bill and I went into the dining room.

We were in luck that night with our supper being meat loaf, peas, roll and mashed potatoes. I wasn't a cook, but something told me the meat loaf was mostly bread with artificial flavoring. The same was true with the potatoes with the peas being the only real food on our plates.

"If the meat loaf is bread…, maybe we'll find the meat in the rolls," Bill whispered as we found a table.

"Anything is possible," I answered under my breath.

"Tell me… where did you find out about Jake?" Carl asked as he came to our table and sat his coffee cup down. Then, taking a seat himself, he waited for my answer.

"The manager, at the Polk Street mission the other night," I told him.

"I believe it. Though he's new, he should know not to talk about Jake…. I need to have a talk to him," he said with a look of disgust. Taking a sip of his coffee he added, "Jake has told us that's one of his conditions. If we let anyone know he's contributing any money he'll pull the plug."

"Now that I know this much you might as well as tell the full story," I said pushing to learn more about this elusive man.

"I might as well tell you the rest of the story…, and what I told you the other day was just a pack of lies. Sometime ago I asked him what he wanted me to tell people. He asked me to tell stories such as what I told you…. In telling people what I have, everyone has lost interest in this strange man called Jake," he said with a smile.

"This might be better than the Olympics," Bill said as he lowered his fork.

"Hush," I told him.

"Well, I wasn't around back then, as you know…. From what I have heard he was a resident here, about thirty-five years ago…," he began to tell us. He paused to take a sip of coffee. He then added, "I don't know the details…. From what I have heard, is he drank all of his separation pay and didn't know what else to do…. He arrived here full of doubts, fears and whatever. You know, as you are, a messed up veteran. Between the mission and holding up a sign offering to work. All he ever had was enough money for his booze and cigarettes. Then one day it all changed for him."

"What happened?" I asked. He had gotten my interest, and I wanted to know more. Some of it sounded like my father, but I found it hard to believe that he had become rich enough to help the two missions.

"Maybe I can learn something from hearing about him," Bill said as he pushed his plate to one side.

"Like most of us, he needed to feel as if he belonged. He stayed here first and went over to the place on Polk Street and returned. He finally settled in this place and stayed. From what I understand, he was unusual because he would jump in and help around here when he didn't feel like begging…. From what I have learned, the mission became his family. The administrator back then noted that he thought he had a serious mental problem. There weren't places available when he was in need of a place, as there are now, that might have helped him. The administrator also noticed he was getting worse each day, as if something was eating away at him…. Many men came back feeling so much guilt, they even killed themselves…," he stopped again to sip his coffee.

"What happened that one day?" I asked him. I appreciated the background information, but I wanted the meat. After hearing the best part, I asked about the rest.

Setting his cup down, he continued. He told us, "He was down the street holding up his sign when a man stopped. After talking to Jake, he decided to take him home and let him do some work around his home… Jake did such a good job for the man he came back after him once or twice a week. Then it became a daily affair with picking him up and bringing him back…. As you just offered, he donated twenty percent of whatever he made while he lived here. As with you, no one asked him for the donation but the place was his home. Feeling as he did, he did what he could to help us out financially whenever he could… I think the man's name was Burdock. I might be wrong, but it doesn't matter…He was a financier with a good chunk of money…. Somehow, Jake worked himself into a position where he could give the man some ideas. Mr. Burdock tripled his holdings from the suggestions he had given him. This led Jake to a good-paying position with the man. After a couple of years, the old man died and left everything to Jake…, Lock, stock and barrel."

"And he comes here every month or so," I commented, thinking about that little interesting fact.

"That's great… I wish I could have that kind of luck," Bill said as he shook his head.

"Yes, every month, or two months he comes home to be with his family," Carl answered with a smile. Then, finishing his coffee, he added, "To feel more like his brothers he dresses like a bum… It's when you talk to him; you realize he isn't a bum. You find he's knowledgeable, and an interesting man to talk to."

"The trimmed hair and beard are a giveaway, that he is something other than a homeless person," I replied.

"There is that," Carl said with a grin.

"I'm looking forward to meeting him… I find it interesting with him thinking he knew me. Part of it might be that I look like my father…. He might remember my father and answer some of my questions," I told him once again.

"I can understand your interest…. He might come in before you leave," Carl replied. Then getting up, he announced, "I hate to run, but I promised to take my wife out for a burger."

"Thanks for telling me the story…. It doesn't help my situation any, but it was interesting. We need more men like him," I told him as I got up.

"I wonder if he needs some help around his place," Bill asked as he got up.

Carl told him, "I doubt it… he sold the big place, not having a family or interest in entertaining."

"So, I'll do smaller jobs," Bill said with a grin and a shrub.

"What a guy," I added as I took my dishes to the dirty dish tray area.

"I think it's time for me to lie down and enjoy my candy bar.… Maybe catch some of the games and then a shower," he told me as we walked towards the barracks.

"I hope the mint will take the taste of supper out of my mouth… I just wish it would do something for my indigestion," I replied feeling a belch coming up.

"I have the same problem, and the candy bar probably won't help. I agree that it should taste better than supper, but I would like something better," he said with a grin.

"Well, I think I'll take a shower first, and then I'll lie down and do some reading," I replied. In thinking about everything I remembered I had forgotten my bag, so I went after it.

"Hi," a man said as he came into the dining room.

"Good evening," I returned, surprised someone in the mission had spoken to me. I found it interesting he hadn't added anything to his comment. I found it interesting, and my eyes followed him to the supper line. Then turning back, I caught up with Bill and told him, "Something's wrong.… That guy spoke to me."

"Everyone made mistakes. As an example, I talk to you," he offered.

"You have to remember that you're retarded," I reminded him.

"Thanks," he replied as he went through the lobby. Then passing Charlie, he told him, "Now's it's my turn to relax."

"Have a good night gentleman," Charlie returned.

I got my shower, washed my clothes, bushed my teeth, and I was ready to relax. As I walked into the barracks, Bill pointed at me and began laughing as he pointed at me. I began to worry I had toilet paper hanging from the back of my shorts. Looking between my legs, I didn't see anything. One hand carrying my bag and the other with wet clothes, I couldn't be sure if toilet paper was hanging from my backsides. I asked him, "What's so funny?"

"Those knobby knees of yours," he told me as he continued to laugh.

"Women like them," I said jokingly.

"Blind ones," he replied getting hold of himself.

"Right now a blind one would be fine," I told him as I put my clothes under the mattress. Then before I put my bag under the pillow, I took the diary out. As I lay down, I asked him, "How's the games?"

"Right now, it's only the opening. The games don't start until tomorrow…. So I'm not really into it right now, which is fine. I can't see much more than flashes of the fireworks," he told me.

"Why don't you get closer…? There are plenty of open beds over there?" I suggested to him. I didn't see any sense in straining his eyes, as he must have been doing.

"Too tired to care…. Maybe tomorrow," he said as he rolled over.

I opened the diary and began reading. So much of what I was reading was the same as what I had read before. One passage caught my eye though:

> *I wonder if it's worth fighting the system. Last week I made eighty-two dollars. This week I made twenty-one dollars, so I wonder if it's worth it.*

I knew what he was saying. I had been here three days and hadn't found work yet. Another passage caught my eye and I wanted to cry for my father. The passage read:

> *I've been here for three months. Nothing has changed since I arrived, and I don't know what to do. I'm finding it hard to remember names of different people around here. I'm finding that at times I don't remember my own name… If I had the strength, I would do myself in. I have no future, and my wife and son don't need me. Why do I continue?*

I had the feeling if what I was living wasn't a lie, I might feel the same way as he did. I lie back wondering how many of my roommates felt as he did.

Sitting back up, I read another two pages. Again, he referred to his fears as I had read so many times before. Then he began to write about his frustrations:

> *If Johnson and McNamara had kept their nose out of the war, we could have won it. So many times, we came close to defeating the enemy, but they would call us back. They insisted on picking out our targets on a whim, and that never got us anywhere. We should have been about focusing on the enemy rather than letting him go, to fight a worthless battle. So many times, we had them at the point of submission. They would call us back to a fight a new front a hundred miles away. Then to say we couldn't attack cities in the north was even dumber.*

During the three days in Frisco, I was learning more about Vietnam than I ever knew before. I began to look at the war differently after reading the diary and talking to veterans. I found it hard to believe they could think they could direct the troops from Washington. If Johnson and McNamara had kept their noses out of it and let the command force direct the soldiers the outcome would have been different.

As I closed the diary, I looked up at the ceiling and said quietly, "Sorry dad… I don't know what I can say, but this is a screwed-up world."

CHAPTER SIX

"You sure crapped out early last night," I told Bill, as we sat drinking coffee wondering if we wanted any oatmeal. I had to admit he looked better this morning than most. I wish I had gone to sleep earlier than I had. I felt as if I could go to sleep and catch another eight hours. Instead of going to sleep early, I had sat up and read part of father's diary. What I read was so much information, such as a grown man whining.

"I don't know what happened, I looked over at you, and you were reading. I wasn't able to see the television, so I listened to it…and somewhere during the game I fell asleep," he replied with a smile.

"I wasn't far behind you… I read another ten fifteen pages, and that was all it took," I confessed. After seeing what was on the serving table I asked him, "What do you think…? We might not get any lunch today."

"We have a few dollars yet. I can always pick up a candy bar or something. Right now, I don't feel like eating that crap," he reminded me.

"I know but I hate to part with it…. Tomorrow is Sunday, and I doubt we'll get any work and we may need the money," I told him as I thought it over.

"I forgot about that… I guess I'll force some breakfast down and pray it doesn't come back up," he said as he got up.

On the Serving Line, Bill dipped into the oatmeal. Holding the serving spoon up the oatmeal slid off, and it went "Plop."

As he began to fill his bowl he said, "Just looking at that mess is making me sick…, and you want me to eat it."

"Is there something wrong with the oatmeal?" A man asked from the kitchen.

"It's not the lumps in the clumps…, but I'm tired of oatmeal," Bill told him as he walked back to the table.

"A pampered child…. His mother used to eat it for him," I told the man.

With a confused expression he asked, "What?"

"Don't worry about it," I told him thinking he was short, a few cards in the deck.

We had breakfast and as usual, nothing exciting happened. A couple of guys came into the dining room, grabbed a cup of coffee and left. I found myself thinking no one liked the oatmeal, and I wondered why they bothered to make it. As they passed us, no one spoke to us. I felt better about the silence when I noticed they didn't talk to anyone. A few were chummy with each other, most of them kept to themselves. I settled on the idea they might not have anything against us.

Other than a couple of words, we didn't talk much as we made our way to the day labor office. Like a fool, I kept my eye open for Karen in hopes we could have the chat before anything happened. I was checking every car and looking down every alley. I didn't see her anywhere. I had learned that she had a habit of showing up late. I figured she would do the same that day also. Having given up on seeing her, I kept my attention on what was ahead of me.

As we had the previous morning, we got to the office before anyone else. I turned to Bill and told him, "We have to stop doing this."

He asked, "Why are we getting here too early?"

"Yeah…. We get here before Bertha.

"She has a job," he reminded me.

Hearing the words coming out of his mouth, I felt dumb. The day before I thought we had gotten the job we did because Bertha liked us. Not having looked for a job for many years, I hadn't thought about it. If you want something, you had better be the first one in line. It didn't mean Bertha didn't like us, but it was being first that got us the job. I told him, "You have a point."

"I promise that I'll be sleeping in tomorrow.... I hope we make enough so I can buy a plate of bacon and eggs," he warned me.

"You're making me hungry which I wouldn't think possible after eating that oatmeal," I replied. From his expression, I thought he saw something. When I turned to see, I looked around and saw Bertha pulling into a parking space. At first, I was afraid we had come to the office for nothing. I hadn't thought about the office not being open on Saturdays. Then when we arrived, I saw the sign on the door, and it said they should be open.

"I'm late... Sorry," Bertha said from behind me.

Before I could say anything, I felt her hand with a key in it reach around me into the lock. I was a little embarrassed as I told her, "Sorry for blocking your way."

"That's all right.... My father taught me to work with adversities," she said with a smile.

"His mother said he was a painful birth," Bill told her.

"I'll give you some pain if you're not careful," I told him as I walked inside the office.

"All right, kiddies.... If you don't change your attitude, I might have to rethink my offer of finding you work," she warned us.

"I just aged ten years," Bill told her with a laugh.

"Wow, now he has the IQ of a ten-year-old," I suggested.

"All right..., that's enough of that. If you're not careful I'll log the two of you in as being mentally unstable," Bertha said, motioning for us to leave.

"Was it something we said?" Bill asked me as we went outside.

"Naaa... I don't think so," I told him with a grin.

"Hey Jeff…," I heard someone shout out.

Turning I saw a car pulling up to the curb with a guy at the wheel. Karen had her head out of the passenger window shouting at me. I shouted back to her, "Good morning… I didn't think the two of you would ever show up."

She got out of the car and came running over to me. From the car behind her, the driver was a little too interested in me for my liking. No matter what he thought she gave me a hug and told me, "You'll never believe what happened."

"What?" I asked her.

"Randy came back for me," she shouted out as she let me go.

"Randy?" I asked her since she had never given me a name. I didn't know if he was her brother, or a friend of the father of her daughter.

"He even wants to marry me," she shouted out. Then grabbing my shirtsleeve, she began pulling me towards the car. She gave me a smile, as she added, "I want to introduce you to him."

"All right, I'm coming," I told her as I shook my head, feeling a little funny. Only knowing her a few days, I didn't understand why she felt she must introduce me to him.

"Honey, this is Jeff…. The man who said he would help me," she told him. Then turning back to me, she added, "This is my daughter's father, Randy."

"Glad to meet you Randy…. I wish the two of you luck, and many years of happiness," I told him as I extended my hand out to him.

"Thank you…, and thank you for your offer to help her," he said with a smile. He then reminded her, "Portland's a long way from here."

"I know… I guess we had better get going," she said with a satisfied smile on her face. Then about to get into the car she added, "I almost forgot…. You haven't seen little Alice."

"That's right…, but that's all right you need to get on the road," I told her.

"She's right here in the car seat," she told me as she pointed to the backseat.

I looked between Randy's neck and the door jam and saw a cute little baby girl. I told the two, "You have a beautiful baby there."

"She gets her looks from her mother," Randy said as he looked over at Karen.

"She could do worse," I replied giving him a slap on the arm. Then seeing his questioning look, I added, "She's a beautiful woman in her own right."

"I think so," he assured me.

"You had better get going…. Thanks for coming by and it was a pleasure meeting you, Randy…," I told them as I backed away from the car. Before they pulled away, I reminded then, "If you need any help, give that number a call."

"Thanks," Karen called back to me.

Walking back to the Office, where Bill was, I gave the couple a wave goodbye. I knew there was a smile on my face as they drove off, because I couldn't be happier for them. In ways I wished I had told her more about me, for I could have helped them more. I doubted I would hear anything from them. I had no problem with not helping them, for they needed to earn whatever they wanted on their own to fully appreciate it.

Then, reaching Bill, I told him, "I predict there's trouble ahead…. Something tells me mommy and daddy made him come back for her and his daughter."

"More than likely," he replied.

As with Bill, I felt tired and a nap sounded good to me. Both of us were so tired we didn't talk much. As with the previous morning, I found myself waiting outside. Other than the occasional puff of smoke, it was better than inside so I didn't mind.

Then about an hour later, I realized I was sitting outside alone. Bill had gone back inside to use the restroom. The meat loaf we ate the night before still wasn't sitting well with him. No matter how I tried, I couldn't stop yawning. I had gotten a good night's sleep, but I still felt exhausted. As we stood by the office, I decided I didn't care how tired I was, I wanted another job. I sat down on the cement in hopes my back would quit aching.

"Jeff..., you're up," Bertha called out.

"Right beside you," I answered as I stood up.

"Since I got a good report on the two of you, I have another one," she told me with a smile.

"Good," I said as I got up and brushed myself off. Seeing all the men still waiting, I wondered if I were getting special treatment. Then, remembering her comment about getting a good report on us, I figured that was why.

I hope you don't mind going out of town," she said, handing me a slip of paper. Before I could answer her, she asked me, "Where's that friend of yours?"

I pointed inside the office. Then, seeing his hand on the door about to come out, I motioned for him to join us. As we waited for him, I asked her, "What's this out-of-town business?"

"He has some work at his place in Calistoga," she answered with a questioning look.

"I don't have any problem with it... I guess," I told her. When Bill got to us, I asked him, "The jobs in Calistoga, do you have a problem with that?"

"I don't even know where it is," he replied.

"A little over an hour north of here.... You can go with Jeff again if you want," she told him.

"I would hate to break up a team like ours.... I think I can handle another day with him," he answered her. He warned me, "If you have to do it all, our friendship is over."

"That'll be the day," I told him with a frown.

"Here are your contracts.... Don't forget, it is the same as yesterday. You have to have the contract signed saying you completed the work. Once you return the signed contract, I will pay you. He should be here in thirty minutes... Here's yours Jeff and here is yours Bill. Jeff you should feel thankful you're a veteran. This guy said he wanted a veteran.

It seems he feels all of us should help our service men get back onto their feet," Bertha said with a smile. Then with an even bigger smile, she told Bill, "At least this morning I didn't walk off without giving your contract to you."

"Thank you for that," Bill replied with a bow.

"I'm not sure I can handle a job two days in a row," I commented as I looked at the contract.

"As I told you… Tomorrow, I'm sleeping all day," Bill, added.

"I figured as much after yesterday. Good luck…and it might not be as hard on you as it was yesterday," she said with a smile.

"Yeah…, let me tell you driving a forklift, is hard on a person's back," I answered as I rubbed my back for her.

"Oh, the guy's name is Fred Warner," Bertha said as she walked away.

"Do I need to remind you how old you are," he offered as another excuse.

"I wouldn't go that far," I corrected him.

As Bill lit up his cigarette, my mind went back to Karen and my fears. It made me feel good to see a grin on her face. I had to give Randy credit for coming back and being a man. What worried me was how long the marriage would last. I didn't see a marriage based on a child and a one-night stand lasting long. As a child from a marriage like theirs, I had an idea that might happen. Then I remembered if the marriage didn't work out, she would still be closer to her parents. I felt bad because I enjoyed and appreciated the young woman. I found she only wanted someone to talk to about her problems. She was one of the few that didn't want something out of me, and I will miss her.

"I remember having a look at that gal's husband-to-be… I had such a wonderful dream of their future," Bill told me as he put his cigarette out.

"Like you I have had a few dreams that crashed down on my head," I related to him. I wanted to tell him about Martha and my three kids. I knew if I did, I would have to tell him the rest of the story, so I didn't.

"I'm looking for 08057…, and 58," a man called out from a pickup.

"I think we're having a run, on pickups," I told Bill. I grinned, noticing this one was black, making it different from the other two. I couldn't see much of him through his window, and I got the feeling he was on the thin side. Wearing a baseball cap, I couldn't tell if he was bald or not, but I had a feeling he was. His most distinguishable feature was a snarl on his face. I've seen many men with expressions like his. Men like him made it difficult to get a job done. I didn't care who or what he was as long as he paid us. I shouted out to him, "That's us."

"Get in," he demanded.

"Do we want to do this?" Bill said loud enough for me to hear.

"I was asking myself the same question," I told him in the same low voice. When we got to the Truck, I told Bill, "You can sit in the front seat this time."

"That's all right… You're older, and you deserve the front seat," he told me as he got into the back.

The driver took off from the curb, not saying anything to either of us. Having looked at the contract, I knew the man's name was Fred Warner. Thinking of his name, it reminded me of Fred at the bus depot. Looking at him, there wasn't any comparison between the two of them. I got to thinking that I might start a conversation, as I told him, "I'm Jeff and the one in back is Bill."

"Just call me Fred," he returned. The gruff and to the point way of talking told me he wasn't much for talking.

"So, we're going to Calistoga," I offered.

"Yeah," he answered.

Watching the road as he continued to drive in silence, he turned onto I-80 toward Oakland. I wasn't sure where Calistoga was, but something told me it was around Napa. All I knew about the town was its fame for its wine and hot springs. Never having been to that area, I didn't worry about the route he took. While I have been in the Frisco area, I always relied on cabdrivers. My expectation in getting work was that it would be in the same neighborhood as the Day Labor Office. When I heard we were going out of town worried me. If something went wrong with the job, we could have to walk back to the mission. All we had going for us was that Bertha knew where we were going.

I gave up trying to get him to talk so I laid my head against the window to take a nap. If he didn't want to talk it didn't bother me. I was feeling sleepy so a nap sounded like a good idea. The bumps in the road made it a little hard to nap, but I managed. I woke up hearing Bill snoring in the back. Giving up I sat up straighter, and I saw Fred looking at me. He immediately turned his attention back to the road without saying anything.

After driving a few miles he finally asked, "Iraq?"

"What?" I asked him not sure what he was talking about. I was also a little surprised he had even spoken to me.

He asked, "You're a veteran…, and not one of those make believe protesters, soldier of fortune or mercenary?"

"Trust me…, I'm just a veteran headed for home. I served in Afghanistan…. They mustered out four days ago…," I answered him. As with everyone else, I told him my story, even though it was a lie. From his expression, I didn't think he cared to hear my story.

"Are…, we… there yet?" Bill asked, a little groggy.

"No…, we are still Interstate 80," I answered him, as I turned around to look at him. It was then I noticed a 30-30 Winchester Carbine on a rack over the back window. I found myself wondering if that made Fred a redneck.

"Oh," Bill replied.

"You can go back to sleep if you want. If Bertha's estimate is correct it'll be forty-five to sixty minutes before we get there," I told him.

"I might just do that," he said, yawning.

"I'll wake you when we arrive," I promised him.

Interstate 80 was its usual, bumper to bumper with traffic.

The traffic on the freeway was moving, but not up to the speed limit. From what I could see most of the traffic was truckers, or vacationers loaded down with luggage. Martha and I only took one vacation with our car as packed as some of these were. As we passed one after another, I wondered why I hadn't taken my family on more. Then, as soon as the thought hit me, I knew the answer. Every time, we wanted to go somewhere another job came up. As we drove by the cars full of kids, I found myself wishing I had taken my family on more vacations.

As with Bill, I fell asleep again. I didn't wake up until Fred came to a sudden stop. I couldn't be sure, but from looking at the car ahead of us, he stopped halfway across the crosswalk for a red light. Our driver, undoubtedly caught off guard, had to slam on his brakes. Wondering where we were, I tried to find a sign of some kind. I finally found one and saw we were on country road 29.

"Once we get up into the hills we'll be at my place," Fred announced.

"Sorry about falling asleep.... Yesterday was a long day," I said, apologizing to him.

"Are we there now...? I don't know what's wrong with me," Bill asked once again as he yawned.

From where we had stopped at the light, we didn't go too far, and we turned northeast towards the mountains. I didn't care if he built a cabin or a mansion, I was just wondering what he was building. Where else would you build a cabin other than in the hills? Then, after a few more miles, we began climbing a dirt road, and the ride wasn't that smooth. As we bumped along, I looked around at the scenery. However, though there were dense areas of trees, it wasn't anything like the redwoods. Once we got to the top of the hill, I could see a beautiful landscape of green behind us.

"Not much further," Fred told us.

After a bounce around a couple of clumps of trees, I saw a big hole in the ground. I figured the hole was where the foundation was going. The only problem was that I didn't see any wood around to build forms for the foundation. To make it worse I didn't see any cement or a mixer. I wondered what he wanted us to do. I asked him, "Where's the wood for the forms?"

"While the two of you are cleaning out the trench I'll go back and get the wood," he answered as we got out of the truck. Then, walking over to the trenching, he added, "Later this afternoon, there'll be a cement truck coming up to pour the foundation."

With that, he got back into his truck and drove off. He didn't give us any other explanation or details as to how deep to dig out the trench.

Then as if the man knew we were at a loss in what to do, the truck came to a stop. Having heard it stop I looked up and saw it backing towards us. Fred got out and asked "Something wrong?"

"Ok…, where's the shovel?" Bill asked as he looked around the site.

As with Bill, I didn't see anything other than an empty crate and a wheel barrel. The area was devoid of anything that said construction was going on here. In checking the site out, I saw a trench someone had dug a few weeks earlier. He might have dug it earlier and didn't have time to finish the foundation.

"In the back of the truck," he answered. Not adding anything, he went back to the truck and pulled out the shovels. Then heading back to the cab he added, "I should be back in less than an hour."

As he pulled away from us, I asked Bill, "I wonder why he didn't pick the lumber up on our way here?"

"Good question… I guess we might as well get a start on it," he answered as he grabbed a shovel.

"Hope he picks up some lunch while he's down there," I mentioned as I grabbed my shovel. As I scooped a shovel full of dirt, I noticed how calm the area was. All I could hear were birds in the trees and the rustle of branches from a light breeze.

"I wouldn't mind living up here," Bill commented as he looked out into the valley.

"Yes, it would be nice… I would think he would build something a little bigger," I suggested as I looked at the foundation area. On closer observation I noticed there wasn't any plumbing anywhere. I knew if he brought back some wood, he could run some pipes under the foundation. If that was his plan, we don't have time to do it and make the forms before the cement man came. I told Bill, "Something's wrong."

"What's wrong…? He's building a hunting cabin. For hunting, you don't need anything fancy. Even then, it's large enough for a single man to live in for a while. In time, he could save up enough money to add onto it," he suggested.

"You might be right. He might be planning to expand some time in the future… No matter, I still would think he would make provisions for water and sewer before he built a cabin," I told him as I looked around. Then with a shrug, I began leveling out the trench. I didn't want Fred to get back and not be ready to start building the forms.

I bent to fill my shovel up again, and I heard the crack of a rifle fire. The rifle shot I heard didn't bother me as much as the thud beside me and a puff of dirt. Then, before I could move, I heard the crack of another rifle shot. This time, I heard a "plinking," sound from somewhere. I then realized something had hit my shovel, and I knew it was a bullet. When I hear the bullet, I found I was so scared I didn't know what to do. Out in the open as we were, our choices of hiding places were few. Even if I had a rifle of my own, I would have been too scared to use it. For a brief second the thought of me posing as a veteran came to mind. I asked myself what a veteran would do in a situation as I was in. I couldn't think of anything but messing up my pants. I shouted to Bill, "Someone is shooting at us."

He shouted back to me "What?"

"Get…," I began to tell him to get down, and then I heard the rifle shot and a searing shot of pain. I heard myself screaming, "I've been, hit… Damn it hurts."

I hit the ground as I grabbed my shoulder. As I went down, I saw the empty crate and made my way behind it. In getting there, I let loose of my shoulder, and my hand was full of blood. A knot formed in my stomach, but I kept on going. When I got to the crate, I could feel blood running down my arm. As I looked around the corner of the crate, I didn't see Bill anywhere. I shouted out to him, "Bill… are, you all right?"

"Yeah," he answered softly. As a slug hit the crate he added, "I'm behind the wheel barrel."

I slid back a few inches, and I could see his legs sticking out from the wheel barrel. I asked him, "Have any ideas?"

"Other than sliding down the hill…," he suggested. Another couple of shots brought his suggestion to a halt.

"You killed my son," Fred's voice called out from above us.

"I never knew your son," I called back.

"Maybe not…, but it was men like you that gave my son the idea to join the service," he shouted out to us.

"The man's nuts," Bill said softly.

"And he also has a rifle… I think he's trying to kill us with it," I reminded him.

"Let yourself slide backwards and go over the side…. The further we can get down the hill the less chances, he'll be able to hit us," he suggested.

"I'll try," I whispered back to him. From the way he made his suggestion, it sounded easy, but it wasn't. My shirt came out of my pants and I found dirt, and rocks grinding away at my stomach. As irritating as it was it wasn't as bad as someone shooting at me would be.

He asked, "Are you hit bad?"

"I don't think so," I told him.

"Then let's get out of his range," he said as he began to make his way down the hill.

Not knowing anything else to do, I followed his example. To move my body, I had to use both arms and there wasn't any choice about it. As I moved my arms, lightning bolts of pain shot through my body. Then once I got to the rim of the flat area, gravity began to help. I found myself sliding over rocks, twigs, and I don't know what else. I felt I had lost every ounce of flesh on my face. My arms were also killing me having them pulled over my head. From time to time, I found brush scraping my back and the back of my head. There wasn't a place on me that didn't hurt and my mouth was full of dirt.

From somewhere above us, I could hear more rifle fire. I heard it, but I didn't get to sense any of the shots hitting anywhere around us. I quit sliding when my feet caught a tree root. I laid there, not knowing what else to do other than scream. I bit my tongue and let my body relax a little. Then, lying where I was, I knew I had to bring my arms to my side. When I tried moving my arms, I found I could move my right arm, but my left was another story. I could feel the blood collecting in the fabric of my fatigue sleeve, making a wet feeling. Then as I looked up, I saw a mass of spider webs. I couldn't tell what or how many bugs the web had caught in it but there was a lot. I found myself feeling like I was one of those bugs hanging from the web. Out of reflex, I moved away from the spider web. I knew I should have stayed where I was but spiders, and I have never gotten along very well.

As I moved around, I heard Fred call out to us, "I don't know where you ass's went to, but I'll find you."

I wanted to respond, but I knew better. I had seen enough mysteries on television to know to keep my mouth shut. I couldn't see much with all the trees and brush and that bothered me. I tried to find Bill, but I couldn't see him. When I tried to roll over my shoulder hurt so much I continued to lie on my stomach. I tried to calm myself by lying where I was and listen to what was going on around me.

I heard Fred call out again, "I'm going to get you for killing my son… Your ass…"

I didn't hear all of what he said because of another stab of pain going through me. Not seeing him gave me a chance to see where I was. I was out in the open where Fred might see me. I decided it might be wise to move so Fred couldn't take a shot at me. I have to say my fear was greater than the pain I felt, and I managed to get behind a tree. With the rough bark at my back, I took a deep breath and prayed he hadn't seen me.

I used the tree as a support as I looked around to see what I could do. I didn't see Bill, and that worried me. He had been a couple of feet from me as I slid down the slope, and then he was gone. I wanted to look for him, but I knew I had to protect myself. What I saw below me was acre after acre of trees. I might not have known where I was, but I knew Calistoga was south of me. The trouble was that I knew I would never make it. I realized that I said to myself, "Fred, I guess I'm yours if you want me."

At my feet, I saw a broken limb, and I decided it might be a good club. I managed to slide down the tree trunk to grab it. Then, using the tree again and pushing with my feet, I got back onto my feet. I doubted I could swing it hard enough to do any damage to him. If I couldn't take him out, I would go down trying. As I laughed at the thought, I decided I was going to break his nose.

Trying to get the strength to move on, I heard Fred's truck start up. Hearing it surprised me thinking he might have tried coming down the hill. When I heard his truck start up, I figured he was going back down the hill to catch us there. I silently wished him luck, but I wasn't going down where he would see me. I didn't have any idea what I was going to do, but I wasn't going to give him a target.

Thinking about leaving, I decided it might be the best for me to go on down the hill. As I tried to straighten up again, I heard a crash. Unfortunately, with all the trees around, I wasn't sure where it came from. I prayed it was Fred and his truck. If it was, I was safe, other than being up in the mountains.

I still wondered where Bill had gone. Not knowing where he had gone, I decided to wait where I was for a while. I occupied my time by getting my handkerchief out of my pocket. The problem of wrapping the handkerchief around the wound wasn't half as bad as the pain it caused. It didn't make it feel any better, but I didn't know what else to do. I didn't have any idea how long I stood there, but I finally decided to leave. I had to do something, and staying there wasn't solving anything. It took a little effort, but I managed to push myself off the tree trunk.

I got about twenty feet, and I heard the underbrush moving. I froze not knowing what to do next. Seeing a tree to my left, I headed for it as I tried to keep my left arm stationary. As quickly as I could I ducked behind the tree, feeling the noise was from my right. I tucked my left arm inside my shirt, and I was able to move around easier. As I stood behind the tree, I tried to slow my breathing down. The way my lungs were working, I knew everybody for miles could hear me.

"Jeff…, are you around here," Bill's voice echoed through the trees.

Relaxing a little I answered, "I'm right here."

In a lower voice, he asked, "Where?"

Coming from around the tree, I felt a smile of relief form. I was afraid he hadn't been as lucky as I had been and Fred had killed him. As calmly as I could I told him, "I might have been a little worried… My feet caught a root, and I came to a sudden stop. I looked around for you and didn't see you."

"I'm sorry but I didn't want him to hear me... I went around behind him...," he began to tell me, but I was too excited. I couldn't believe that he would try something that dumb.

Not believing my ears I asked him, "What did you say?"

"We couldn't just stay here... I had to stop him somehow," he said with a big grin.

"Don't stop there, tell me what happened?" I asked, realizing he was right. He hadn't said in so many words, but I knew he had taken care of Fred. With a bullet in me, I wished I could have been the one, to have done him in.

He was laughing when he told me, "I got to the ridge above him, as he got into his truck... I knew I had to do something since his intent seemed to be to kill us. Seeing him get into the truck, I knew I only had one chance to get him. Of course, with him having that rifle kept me from charging him. The only defensive tool I could find was a rock. As he headed down the road, I threw the rock into his windshield."

"So, the crash I heard was him hitting a tree," I replied finding it funny. Then I realized he might be back with his rifle. I asked him slowly, "Is he alive?"

"I don't know... All I know is he drove his truck into a tree. From the steam coming out of his radiator, I would say the truck isn't going anywhere.... Since he wasn't moving, I decided to look for you," he said with a proud smile on his face.

"We better, get up there and see if he is alive or dead," I suggested.

He asked, "I guess you're right... Do you think you can make it?"

"I may need some help going up the hill," I told him.

Our ascent was a little slow with Bill hanging onto me, but we were making it. Then we heard a clap of thunder, and I looked up into the sky. There was a dark cloud above us with more coming our way. I stopped, to get my breath and let the pain subside. I told him, "I hope that isn't a cloud of doom."

"Even if it isn't we don't need any rain right now," he replied. He accentuated his comment by kicking the dirt under our feet. With my nod of yes, he took my right elbow and balanced me.

Not knowing where the truck was, I followed him. As I made the rim, I saw the truck. It looked like it wouldn't take much for it to slide down the hill. As I cleared the rim, I saw Fred stagger out of the truck. He looked up at me with his head covered with blood. He turned sideways as if he was going after his rifle. I managed to find the strength and kicked him in the groin. He fell to his knees uttering a terrible groan.

"Good job… If he had gotten that rifle, we both would be dead now," Bill said, having caught up to me.

"I don't think he likes us… Take his belt and tie him up…, and pull his pants down around his ankles," I suggested. I had seen it done in a movie and didn't see why it wouldn't work.

"What an idea," he replied with a grin on his face. Before Fred came to, he had him tied up and his pants down around his ankles. With a satisfied grin, he asked, "What now, any more ideas?"

"See if he has a cell phone…. We need to call the police," I suggested as I rested on the tire well. My left side was one mass of pain. I didn't mind knowing Fred wasn't feeling any better than I was.

"He's got one," Bill said with a big smile.

"Good… Dial 911…, and get the police up here," I told him.

I watched him dial the number and waited for the number to go through. Then from the expression on his face, I knew it went through. A raindrop hitting me in the face wiped the smile off my face. A sprinkle would be bad enough, so I prayed it wouldn't be a hard rain.

"We need help, up here on the hill…. Yes, a man hired us to help build a cabin…, and he tried to kill us…. Yes, he shot my friend in his upper arm, and he's bleeding bad…. A rifle…. Who's name, mine, or the shooter?" Bill was telling the 911 operator. Then turning to me, he asked me, "What's his full name? She said the caller ID says this, is an unlisted name and number."

"Fred Warner," I answered with a nasty taste in my mouth.

"Ooh…," Fred, muttered as he lay on the ground.

"Shut up before I kick you again… you bastard," I shouted at him.

"His name is Fred Warner…. We captured him…. No, he's not dead, a little uncomfortable, but he's alive…. Where are we?" Bill answered the operator's questions. Again turning to me, he asked me, "Have you any idea where we are?"

"East of twenty nine… We turned onto another paved road that curved around for…," I answered him as the rain picked up.

"…that's about all I can tell you… His pickup isn't drivable… No. He ran into a tree, and the truck is leaning to one side…. Give me a blast of your siren every half-mile or so. When I hear it, I'll let you know where we are by honking the horn of the pickup…Hurry, its beginning to rain and my friend needs medical attention… You don't have to worry about us going anywhere…Thanks," Bill closed the cell phone and gave me a shrug.

"I'm in pain…, and my mouth is full of mud," Fred said as he was squirming on the ground.

"Tough," Bill told him as he came over beside me.

Grinning, he told me as he walked up to me, "I don't think he likes you."

"Trust me the feeling is mutual," I replied as my arm ached. Then it struck me and I told him, "You realized this means another job, we won't get a paycheck for."

I didn't look at my watch being too uncomfortable with the pain in my arm and the rain. I estimated it was a good twenty to thirty minutes, and we heard the first blast of a siren. Bill laid on the horn for a minute, and he waited for another blast of the siren. After four of five repeats, two squad cars came up the hill to us.

As the first officer got out of his car he asked, "What happened here…? Who's the man on the ground?"

The second officer asked, "What are these bums doing up here?"

"He tried to kill us… You'll find his rifle on the front seat," I told him, a little irritated, being in the rain. I didn't need the second officer's remark to make me feel better.

The officer with a disgusted look added, "I asked what you were doing up here."

"He brought us up here to help him set a foundation for a cabin…or what I think is to be a cabin, I answered him. I wanted to ask him why he was treating us like the bad guy. I couldn't figure out his problem with us being the victims.

"Watch your tongue," the first officer told his partner. He then asked, "And he tried to chase you down with the truck, went into a slide, and hit the tree?"

"I find all of this a little funny," the second officer added.

"I can see Jeff, laughing," Bill replied, with irritation in his voice.

I found myself thinking this man wasn't Sherlock Holmes. The rain had just started before we called 911. There wasn't any mud for him to go into a slide. If he had looked at the tire tracks, he would have seen that he just drove off the road. Then, there was this ass of an officer and his smart mouth. As different thoughts were running through my head, I heard another siren, in the distance.

"From up there I threw a rock at his windshield. It surprised him to the point he drove off the road and hit the tree," Bill explained.

"I'm sorry. I'm Officer Mike Hackett," he said introducing himself to us. He then added, "You have to forgive my partner. He doesn't think before he opens his mouth…, but you have to understand the problems we have around here. Vagrants are breaking into everything."

"We may be day laborers, but we're not thieves," Bill assured him. He showed the officer our contract Bertha gave him.

"Like I said, I'm sorry for his mouth," the officer said as he read the contract. Then looking up at Bill, he added, "Looks like everything's in order…. If you don't mind, I would like to make a copy of this. I'll get it back to you before you leave."

"Fine…That's Jeff against the Truck, and I'm Bill," Bill told him, doing our introductions.

"Jim…. Don't touch anything in the truck…. Get it back to the office for the crime lab," the officer shouted out to the other officer. Then as an afterthought, he added, "Get this man cuffed and into the squad car."

"I'm on it, Mike…I just got off from talking to the wrecker," the officer shouted back to him. As he shut the door of his squad car, I saw him pull out a set of handcuffs.

"The ambulance should be here any minute," Officer Hackett assured me. He went on to tell us, "The captain will want to talk to the two of you when we get back to the office."

"I'm anxious to get out of this rain… and off this mountain," I muttered to myself.

"Do you know what they did to me?" Fred shouted out to the officers. Then, feeling the cuffs snap around his wrists, he got a worried look on his face.

"Quit your whining, Jeff… You're not the one that ran up the hill and attacked him," Bill told me with a smile.

"Let's not go there… I got him in the balls at least," I reminded him. As I laughed at Fred and his condition, the ambulance stopped just down the hill from us.

"Ooh…. Be careful," Fred pleaded.

"He might be the one we've been looking for," Officer Hackett told the other officer.

Bill asked him, "What do you mean?"

"There have been a couple of murders over the past few months…. Both men were veterans returning home," Officer Hackett answered him.

"Bring him back to the truck," one of the ambulance attendants suggested to his partner. His partner grabbed a stainless steel case as he headed toward Fred. As Officer Mike took his prisoner to the squad car, he followed them.

The attendant asked me, "Can you walk back to the ambulance?"

"I made it this far… I guess I can make it," I answered him.

Taking my right elbow, he told him, "Let me help you."

"Thanks," I replied as I headed for the ambulance.

With a chuckle the attendant asked, "Couldn't you find something else to do with the day?"

Grinning, I commented "What you want me to make it easy on you?"

"You realized I'm going to be cutting off the one sleeve don't you," he warned me.

"Whatever," I replied. My sleeve was the least of my worries. It did cut my shirt selection of shirts down to one, which was irritating. All I wanted was to get my arm looked at and taken care of. The pain was subsiding, but I knew it would be a problem for a while.

With a concerned look he asked, "Think you can get up into the ambulance?"

"I'll suffer anything to get out of this rain," I told him with a chuckle. He in turn took my right elbow and balanced me as I got into the ambulance. Then inside, I sat on the gurney and waited for him to get in.

From outside I heard Officer Hackett tell someone, "We're ready to leave as soon as you are."

Recognizing the first attendant's voice, I heard him tell the officer, "It shouldn't be too much longer.... The other guy's injury is superficial, but he'll be having a headache for a while."

"Not counting the pain to his family jewels," Officer Hackett reminded him with a chuckle.

"I noticed he was having a problem sitting.... I got the feeling he didn't want to talk about his problem.... I told him the doctor would be checking him out. He could get a blood clot, and then he will have a problem," the attendant told him.

"Thankfully it's not my problem. Once you're on the road, we'll follow you down the hill," Officer Hackett replied.

"You're going to need some stitches, but other than that the bullet didn't do any major damage," my attendant assured me. After finishing with the bandage, he laid me on the gurney. He then announced to his partner, "We're ready to roll, Jim."

"We're on our way," Jim replied as he began to back around.

The trip up the hill was bad enough in Fred's truck but on the Gurney, it was even worse. I didn't think the driver of the ambulance would ever reach the paved road. The bouncing around was bad enough, but the rolling from side to side almost killed me. I could feel every movement during our travel into town. When the ambulance stopped at the entrance to the hospital, I relaxed for a second. I knew the next step was to get me out, and I wasn't ready for that. Then as the backdoors opened, I learned they were taking me in on the gurney, making it a little easier.

"Where are we?" I asked as they began to pull me out.

"Emergency," I attendant answered.

Once outside I saw it was a fair size hospital. As we entered the building, there wasn't any question where I was. Laying my head on the pillow, I went for the ride. As they took me into the hospital, I realized I hadn't seen Bill leave. I asked the attendant, "Where's my friend?"

"They probably took him to the sheriff's office for questioning.… Once they get through talking to your friend, he'll probably come here to interview you," the attendant told me.

I laid on that Gurney for a while with everyone giving me funny looks. After the first half hour, I thought everyone and their uncle had passed by me. One man uttered to someone, "One of those radicals… I guess he got his."

"Now George, don't go assuming again.… You don't know him," a woman told the man.

I could hear a little boy ask as he passed me "Where's mommy at, daddy?"

"She's upstairs with your new baby sister," a man answered him

"A baby sister…," and the little boy's voice trailed off.

"Thank you, Ma'am," I let out without thinking about it. As they went on by, I noticed an orderly coming up toward my feet. He took hold of the gurney and I felt it move.

"Put him into cubicle five," a woman from behind me told the orderly. She then looked at me and asked, "Gang fight I suppose?"

"No, I'm a laborer, and my employer doesn't like veterans.… He thought he would kill me, but he wasn't that good, of a shot," I corrected her.

"I don't believe people can act that way…. There you are protecting us, and this is the thanks you get," she muttered as she wrote on a clipboard.

"I agree with you," I replied.

The noise of a bad wheel on the bed announced my arrival to the cubicle in ER. As most fools, I thought the doctor would be coming in right away. I was wrong, and it took another half hour. As I lay there with no one to talk to I wondered how Bill was faring.

"Open wide," a nurse, told me as she stuck a thermometer into my mouth. Then not being able to say anything, she took my pulse. After writing down my temperature, she asked me for my address and all the other necessary information. I gave her the address of the mission in Frisco, which got me a funny look. With a shrug, she wrote it all down and left.

"Oooooh," someone cried out not far from me. Then with a pause, the same voice told whomever it was working on him, "Easy."

Finally, the doctor came in and began putting my arm back together. There wasn't anything enjoyable about what he did to me. Even with a local anesthetic, I could feel the needle tug at my skin and the thread going through it. With a nurse's help, he bandaged and put my arm in a sling. Once finished, he told me, "It'll be sore for a while but there wasn't that much damage."

"Thanks for the good news… I suspected it would be sore for a while," I told him, glad he was through playing Betsy Ross with my arm.

"Take these for the next couple of days for the pain," he suggested as he handed me a little orange bottle with a couple of pills in it. Then after making a note on a clipboard, he added, "If you feel you need more, just see your doctor."

Taking the bottle from him, I told him, "I doubt I'll take these…. I never have been one to take pills."

"Up to you," he said as he was leaving the cubicle. Then turning back to me, he told me, "The sheriff's on his way."

"Thanks," I told him. I was glad it was over because I wanted to get out of the place. Then, as the curtains closed, I called out to him, "Hey doc."

When he came back through the curtain he asked, "A problem?"

"Could I buy one of those white or green smocks you have around here…? This one is full of blood, missing a sleeve… It's a mess," I asked him.

"Orderly…. Would you get this man a white smock…? An older one if you can find one," he told a passing orderly. Then tuning back to me with a smile, he told me, "The least we can do for a veteran."

"Oh…, before I forget. The bill for this visit…," I gave him a brief explanation of my story and the address of my firm.

"Thanks… For some reason, I thought I could bill the veteran's administration," he told me as he crossed out what he had written down. Then looking back at me, he asked me to repeat my address, which I gave him. With a smile, he added, "That will save administration some problems… As I said the sheriff should be here any minute."

"Thanks again," I told him as I managed to sit up. Lying on my arm was killing me. I found myself thinking about taking one of the pills. Once I was sitting up my arm quit hurting as much as it was, making me feel a little better. Then within minutes, the orderly brought me a clean smock.

"Want some help?" The orderly asked. Then grinning he added, "I haven't heard the full story, but it sounds as if you had a shitty day…. Being an ex-medic from Iraq, I have had my share of problems too."

He carefully removed my sling and helped me unbutton my fatigue top. I tried to act brave and gritted my teeth as he pulled the top over my injured arm. Having forgotten the smock, didn't button up, getting it on was a little more difficult. He tried to get it on me, a couple of different ways, and it didn't work. He finally told me, "There's only one-way of getting it on…, I'll try not to hurt you."

"Thinking about it isn't going to help any… Let's just do it," I told him.

I knew getting the smock on would be worse than taking the fatigue one off. With difficulty, I began to lift my left arm, which he was good enough to help me. As he slipped the smock off my arm, I felt a tear run down my cheek. I tried to smile as I saw the sheriff come into the cubical.

"You look like you could be feeling better," he said as he walked in.

"Thanks," I told the orderly as he went out the curtain.

"My pleasure…, and good luck," he returned as he let the curtain close.

"I'm Sheriff Benson and I have a few questions for you," the sheriff said, greeting me.

"Jeff O'Connor… I figured you might want to know my story…. By the way, where's Bill?" I asked him, with my good hand outstretched to him.

"He's back at the office drinking coffee and making time with my dispatcher," he answered with a smile and shaking my hand carefully.

We got to the discussion about our day with Warner and everything that happened. When he asked me about the drive up from Frisco, I had to tell him I didn't remember anything. I explained to him that Bill, and I, for some reason, slept most of the way. He of course asked me for some form of identification and not thinking about it, I gave him my driver's license. With him having my home address and all, I knew the game was over. I then continued to tell him about Fred shooting me and sliding down the hill. Getting a grin from him, I added that I got my revenge by kicking him. Then swallowing twice, I told him the truth about myself. In telling him, I told him I would prefer he didn't tell Bill or anyone else if possible.

"I understand…. I think. It sounds strange to say the least," he said with a grin as he shook his head. Then standing up he added, "I have one problem… I need the two of you to hang around for a few days. If what we suspect is right, I doubt we will need you to testify. I think the DA can tie a few murders to Mr. Warner… I need to get a statement from you Monday."

"We need a place to stay," I reminded him.

"Sir… I can find you a place, but I can't afford to pay for it," he told me apologetically.

"Bill and I could use a place for the next two nights and some good food… Could I borrow your phone…? I'll make it collect," I asked him.

"I have unlimited calling," he said, taking his cell phone from his belt and handing it to me. As I took it, he added, "Oh, the guy you kicked…"

Taking the phone from him, I asked him, "What about him?"

"His true name is Samuel Warner… Fred was his son," he explained to me.

"I don't understand. He gave the Day Labor office the name of Fred," I replied.

"I suspect he didn't think we would catch him if he used a valid name and address. To tell you the truth, he isn't too bright. I guess he felt justified by using his son's name. The credit card is in his son's and daughter-in-law's name as well as the address he gave the day labor office," he told me.

I found it hard to believe, but I couldn't argue. My first concern was that Bertha wasn't going to pay us. Then, looking at the phone in my hand, I remembered I was going to make a call. I called Ray and told him briefly what had been going on in my life in Frisco. I got him to call one of the hotels in town where we could sleep and eat. With concern in his voice, he agreed to take care of it and recommending I give up on my search. Then, in parting, he promised to call the sheriff back with all the information. I thanked him and let him go about making the arrangements.

Handing the phone back to the sheriff, I told him, "He'll call you back with all the information. Then Bill and I can take a short vacation from the mission and enjoy life once again."

"Thanks for getting me off the hook," he replied with a satisfied smile. Then motioning with his hand, he added, "Let's get out of here."

"I'm for it," I told him as I slid off the gurney. Once my feet hit the floor, I took a deep breath, and I began to follow him. As we left the emergency ward, I asked him, "Do you have any idea where our bags are?"

"Taken care of already…. That was one of your friend's concerns also," he told me.

"Good," I replied happy to hear we hadn't lost them.

CHAPTER SEVEN

Ray got back to me through the sheriff. I learned he had set us up with at the best place in town. Bill asked a few questions, and I told him the city was covering our expenses. He didn't question it but was making plans on what he wanted to eat.

Once we got our room key, we went straight to the coffee shop. The hostess turned her nose at us, but she still seated us. As we looked at our menu's and I noticed a woman walk in with a little girl. The hostess walked them towards our table. As they within a few feet, the woman grabbed the little girl by the shoulder. She made the girl go around the table to avoid getting close to us.

Then, getting to their table the hostess was waiting at, she asked her, "Could we sit somewhere else…? Maybe one of those tables back there…, away from…"

"Yes Ma'am," the hostess answered.

"You realize she didn't want to sit near us don't you?" Bill asked as he looked up from his menu.

"Figured as much," I replied as I continued to look at the menu.

We finally ordered and ate our supper in peace. We got several dirty looks, but no one said anything. Bill ate enough food for two people. When he tried to say two words, he belched three times. With a grin, I told him, "I think it's time for us to leave… You've had enough for one night."

"I had almost forgotten what decent food tasted like. Now, if I could only move," he answered as he wiped his mouth. He belched, patted his belly with a big grin, and told me, "In an hour, or so I'll be ready for some desert."

"You shouldn't have eaten so much. I can sympathize in that we needed something decent to eat… No matter how good it was. I don't want you pacing the floors all-night keeping me awake," I told him.

"Would I do that to my best bud?" He asked when we got to the cashier. Turning to the cashier, I gave her our room key and told her, "Charge it to the room."

"I'll have to check with the front desk," she told me.

"I understand," I replied, wishing we could just leave. My arm was killing me, and I wanted to lie down. When she finally got the authorization, I put a tip on the receipt and pushed it back to her, and as she took it, I told her, "Thank you."

"Thank you sir," she said as she rung up our bill.

That night we didn't do much other than watch television and sleep. The next morning, we went downstairs to the coffee shop again. We went through the same embarrassment as the night before. Bill's mood changed when the waitress brought him his breakfast. He ordered a double order of bacon, eggs, potatoes, and four slices of toast. All he wanted to do after he ate was to take a nap. Once again, he reminded me it was Sunday, and he wasn't doing anything.

Unlike Bill, I couldn't lie around doing nothing, so I decided to go downtown. I just wanted to get out of the room and do some sightseeing. As I walked around downtown, I found myself relaxing for the first time in weeks. It didn't take long, and I began feeling out of place. I found people sidestepping, allowing me to pass them.

"You don't belong here," one woman said as I passed her.

Then a block away, a man and a little boy were coming towards me. When I got closer, the man pointed to me and told his son, "You'll be like him if you don't get an education."

The insults were getting at me, and my arm was hurting. After the third insult, I went back to the room and joined Bill. It wasn't long after I got back that I fell asleep. That morning both of us got enough sleep to last us a month. The rest of the day was watching television and ordering food from room service.

Monday, we ordered breakfast and watched the news. We packed our bags, so we would be ready to go back to Frisco. All we had left to do was clear up the paperwork with the sheriff. Halfway through a movie I realized what time it was. Looking over at the clock on the end table, I saw it was nine thirty. I saw Bill had fallen asleep again, and I wondered where the sheriff was. As I took the diary out to read it, the phone rang.

"Hello," I answered. I don't know why I didn't know it was the sheriff calling. As far as I knew, no one else knew where we were. What he had to tell me wasn't what I wanted to hear. Knowing it was out of my hands, I hung the phone up after talking to him.

As I dropped the receiver, into its cradle, Bill asked, "Who was that, the sheriff?"

"Yes…" I answered him, feeling disappointed.

As he sat on the edge of the bed he asked, "And what did he have to say?"

"Now to find a way home," I muttered as I looked over at Bill. I didn't want to miss Jake, so I wanted to get back in Frisco. I would have liked to extend our stay in Calistoga, but I still had to get back. I just wished I could take our comfortable bed back with us.

The sheriff asked, "How's the arm doing?"

"Not bad… As long as I don't bump against it, use it, or lay on it," I answered with a grin.

With a smile he asked, "I can give you a ride back. I have to go into the Frisco on city business…. Can you be ready in, say fifteen minutes?"

"It will take me two to get upstairs, thirty seconds to grab my bag… I think so," Bill told him.

"I'll grab our bags and check out," I told him as he ran out of the coffee shop.

Our waitress returned and asked us, "May, I get you gentlemen more coffee?"

"No, just the bill… We're leaving your fine establishment, but thanks for everything," I told her. I had expected the sheriff to buy the coffee, but he didn't. I figured it was just as well to add it to the room charges.

"You can pay for it at the cashier," she replied with a questioning look at the sheriff.

I went to the cashier of the coffee shop and then to the checkout counter. Bill met us there and turned in his key card. The sheriff had gone out to get his car and promised to meet us at the entrance. With having everything taken care of, we went out to meet the sheriff.

"I don't know why I'm so excited about getting back," Bill said as we went through the door of the hotel.

"I thought you might be missing the oatmeal," I replied. If that was true, I was going to see if I could get him committed. Then as the sheriff pulled up, I asked him, "Where should we go first…, the day labor office or back to the mission?"

"We owe Bertha an explanation…. If you think you can walk back to the mission," he answered.

"I can make it, if for no other reason than to tell her why he wanted a veteran," I assured him. I let Bill take the backseat behind the security screen.

"Thanks. I thought you might let me sit up front for a change," he replied as he got in.

"A case of age over beauty," I used as an excuse. I wanted to laugh because I knew it was tight in the backseat.

The trip back was uneventful after we told the sheriff what we were out to do. He wished us luck and said he didn't know anyone that got anywhere working as a day laborer. Bill and I told him we understood that, but we still needed money. We pointed out to him if we did a good enough job for someone we might get a permanent job. I found myself surprised the conversation went as well as it did. The sheriff knew the truth about me, and I didn't think I could pull it off. I didn't want Bill to learn the truth about me.

Before we knew it, we were at the day labor office. Bill held the door open for me letting me walk in ahead of him. I walked up to the counter, and Bertha looked up at me giving me a confused and questioning look.

"What the hell…," she began to say but stopped, to look around. Then seeing no one had heard her, she said, "What the heck happened to you?"

I let Bill tell her of our adventures of the previous Saturday. He then ended the story with, "…and how was your weekend?"

"Saturday's rain ruined a few of our plans. Even then it wasn't as bad as yours," she said as she shook her head. With a smile, she offered, "I'm sorry… I have never heard of anything like this happening before… I might be able to make it up to you."

"What can you do…? It wasn't your fault this guy was a whack'o," I told her.

"The two of you were on a job we sent you out on… I have to check, to see if the victim fund has funds available for you. I can also charge your wages to his charge account. I don't know if that will fly, but I should know by tomorrow morning… I hate to make you come back, but I don't know what else to do," she told us.

"We have one other problem…," I began to tell her.

With a questioning look she asked, "What…, there's more?"

"Yes… It turns out the guy used his son's name and credit card," Bill told her.

"That makes it difficult… I'll work out something," she said as she shook her head. She then asked, "Let me have the sheriff's name and the real name of the guy."

I gave her the information and added, "I wish I could tell you more."

"I understand. I'll still see what I can do about getting you your pay…, and hopefully, tomorrow there will be another job for you," she offered.

"With plenty of time on my hands…, I'll be back," Bill, promised her.

"With this arm I can't do anything but walk around… I'll come by in the morning," I told her. Then, before turning to leave, I added, "Thanks… You know you don't have to go through all of this trouble for us."

"It's the least I can do… I do have one other question for you," she told me.

She asked, "Why don't you go to the unemployment office rather than here?"

"I wouldn't feel comfortable going there. I don't have any decent clothes," I answered her.

"I'm about as bad… Then I met this idiot, and here I am," Bill added with a smile.

"I can give you the name of a couple of churches. They'll give you the clothes you need…. The two of you are different from most of my clients. I get the impression the two of you want to make something of yourselves… Most of my clients are only out to make a few bucks for a jug of hooch," she said as she tried to figure us out. Then with a smile she added, "I don't know how to say this…, but thank you."

"You don't have to thank us. We haven't done anything. You're the one deserving the thanks," I assured her. All we had done was to come to her for work. Today was a matter of giving her shit for sending us to Calistoga. From the impression I got from Bill, he was as mystified as I was.

"I don't know…. I got into this job, and day after day it's the same thing. The same men and women keep coming back with the same problem…. Then the two of you come in giving me a feeling that I'm able to help someone… Thanks," she answered with a tear in her eye.

"It's been a long time since anyone has appreciated me…. No, we owe you…. To express my appreciation, I would like to take you and your family out for supper someday," I told her. I let the conversation die, as I followed Bill towards the front door. As I went through the door, I gave Bertha a wave goodbye.

As we left the office, neither one of us said much. I found myself feeling as if I had changed. I had the feeling the events of the past five or six days had changed me. If that was true, I wondered if it was for the good or not. I knew the answer to that question would come with time. I had never felt or had a feeling of self-worth before. Bertha was the first to make me aware of it.

"Steak last night…, and fried cockroaches tonight," Bill replied with a laugh.

"Thanks for ruining a perfect day," I replied as I looked up into the sky.

A young hoodlum asked as we passed him "Did someone hurt the little soldier boy?"

Not thinking about what I was doing, I walked up to the jerk. I grabbed his shirt under his chin with my right arm. Not knowing my own strength, I found I had lifted him off his feet against the wall. As he squirmed, I told him, "One-handed I'm more of a man than you will ever be."

I could see fear in his eyes, and it made me feel good. As my arm weakened, I let him drop to the sidewalk. He didn't even groan, as his body crumpled at my feet. I was about to kick him for luck when I felt Bill's hand grab my right arm.

"Leave him," Bill said softly.

I looked around and saw Bill looking scared. Then seeing him shake his head, I knew I had overstepped the line. I turned to head back down the sidewalk and told him, "I don't know what got into me… That's the closest I've ever come to a fight."

"It's been a rough couple of days," he replied, keeping his hand on my elbow.

"It didn't help my arm out," I told him as I tried to laugh.

"I don't know what's got into you…. You kicked Warner in the groin and now this," he reminded me.

He was right. I had been through enough over the past six days or so.

"What are we going to do, the rest of the day?" Bill asked.

"I'm thinking about having a cup of coffee, lie back and heal. I might even do some reading. If nothing else, I can watch the Olympics…. What about you?" I returned.

"I don't feel like doing anything…. It might be from all the food I ate," he answered.

"You mean I couldn't talk you into a banana split," I told him teasingly.

"I might find room," he answered with a smile.

With a shrug, I reminded him, "You'll have to wait until I get some money."

"You get my hopes up and then drop me like a hot iron," he said, as if I had hurt his feelings. I knew it was a fake expression, so I began laughing as we continued walking back to the mission.

"That was a promise…, you know," I told him. Looking at my watch, I saw it was ten-forty-five. Not that it mattered, it did surprise me that it was as late as it was. I knew it hadn't taken that long to get back to Frisco. I decided our conversation with Bertha took more time than I thought it had.

"I'll hold you to it," he promised.

With a chuckle shared between us, we found ourselves at the doors of the mission. No one greeted us as we entered the lobby. Feeling something was wrong, I walked to the door of the barracks. I found a couple of men were watching television. Looking into the dining room, I didn't see anyone. Usually, Joey or Charlie was in the lobby to greet whoever walked in. As I was looking around, Bill took our bags to the barracks. He then came back out and joined me.

"Nothing going on in there," he told me.

"Let's check out the dining room and kitchen," I suggested.

As Bill went into the dining room, I joined him. In entering the dining room, I heard some noise in the backroom. Looking in that direction, I saw the door and decided to hold off in going back there. I figured they were getting some supplies or something. I motioned to Bill the coffee urn. Seeing he agreed with me, I told him, "We might as well wait out here to see what's going on."

"I guess so… Might as well break into the mission's cuisine early," he replied as he began pouring us some coffee.

"I don't care what your problems are… I'm not putting up with it," Carl's voice came booming out of the backroom.

Then, there was the sound of boxes falling and some shuffling. Bill and I set our cups down and looked at each other. Then Carl's voice came out to us again, "You're fired."

"I'm sorry," a voice I recognized, but I couldn't think of his name shouted back to Carl.

"I'm sorry I hired you…, and to think I trusted you…. Now get out of here," Carl cried out.

"Make me," a male voice told him.

"We had better get back there," I suggested to Bill.

"You won't be much help…, but I might be," he said as he turned around the corner of the counter.

As fast as I could I followed him into the backroom. The place was a wreck with supplies strung all over the place. Then there were the overturned boxes to make it worse. Then something that I didn't expect caught my eye. I saw Joey was about to attack Carl with a baseball bat. I shouted out, "Stop it."

Bill made a flying leap catching Joey off guard. He caught him just above his belt with the bat going one way and the two men another. It took me back a little to see the bat fly in my direction. Then, I saw it was going to land, a few feet to my left. I knew I wasn't in any danger. As I caught my breath, I saw Bill on top, keeping Joey from getting up. With him having him under control, I was able to relax.

"Get the bat," Carl shouted at me.

"I've got it," I told him, as I stooped down and picked it up. With him coming over to me, I handed it to him since I couldn't use it anyway. As he took it from me, I asked him, "What's going on?"

"Long story…. You can let him up now, Bill," he said as he looked around at the mess in the room.

"He might try to attack again," Bill, warned him.

"I doubt it… I now have the baseball bat," Carl said as he punctuated it by pounding the palm of his hand with the bat.

"Good tackle," I told Bill.

"Now get out of here…, and you can keep the stuff in your car… consider it as your last paycheck. Consider yourself lucky because I won't have you prosecuted for the rest of the stuff you stole over the past year…. Now get out of here," Carl shouted at Joey. Again, he punctuated his statement with the bat slapping his palm.

"I'm going," Joey announced with the looked of a whipped dog. Within a few seconds, he was out the door and Carl went over and locked it.

"The first time I met him, I didn't like him…. I had the feeling, he wasn't the type to work here," I told Bill as I reached out to help him up.

"Thanks, but I can make it," he said as he got to his feet.

"Now I know who the guilty one is," Carl said as he began cleaning up the place.

From the doorway a voice asked, "What happened back here?"

Turning around I saw it was the cook. I told him, "I haven't heard everything yet myself… I think it's a long story…." It wasn't my business, so I let the subject drop. Bill and I had done what we could so it was up to Carl now.

"I'll be back in a few minutes to clean this mess up," Carl told him. As he turned, he laid the baseball bat on a shelf and walked out to the dining room.

"I'll buy a cup of our rotten coffee…. With my thanks for saving me, and my apology for the coffee," he said as he turned around to us.

"Come to think of it, we have two cups getting cold out there," Bill, reminded me.

"If we let it cool a little, we could use it for glue," I suggested with a laugh.

"I heard that," Carl said as he handed us our cups. Then, with a smile, he explained to us, "Most of these men drink so much they can't taste the coffee… Because of this little problem we have learned to make it strong."

"I know… I tried cream in it, and it curdled before it reached the Coffee," Bill told him as we went to a table.

"That's enough… I think Carl has a real problem here," I told Bill, knowing he was trying to be funny.

"Not anymore," Carl told us. After he took a sip of his coffee he added, "I appreciate what you did."

"It's been a physical couple of days…. Why not a little more," Bill said as he slapped me on the back.

"One more of those and I'll get the bat," I told him. The shock wave ran down my leg bringing a stream of fire behind it. Then, with a little effort, I smiled at him.

"Looks like you were in the wrong place at the right time," Carl commented.

It didn't take long to tell him about our weekend. In conclusion, I asked him, "I know it's none of our business, but what was all of that about?"

"I guess it won't hurt… I can't match your weekend," he said with a smile. With a nod towards the kitchen, he told us, "We have been missing supplies over the past six months. At first, I have thought it was one of our residents … I then realized most of the men that were here three months ago had left."

"What did you come up with…, or what turned you on to Joey?" I asked him. Off in the storeroom I could hear the cook putting the supplies back on the shelves. From the way it sounded, he wasn't enjoying it even a little.

"Well, we got a large shipment yesterday. I went around and told everyone that I'd be gone, the rest of the day…. Then I waited in the backroom after I went out and through the backdoor," he answered. With a disgusted look, he added, "I didn't have to sit there long…. He finally came back into the storeroom. I got the feeling he was so sure of himself that he just opened the backdoor and didn't even bother to look around. He went about his business without a worry. I watched him selectively picking out this box and then another taking them out to his car. After the third box, I came out of hiding…. It wasn't long before it began to get messy, and you came in…, to my delight."

"And you got your man…. Good work," Bill said, complimenting him.

"I feel so betrayed…. He has worked here long enough that I thought of him as a brother, or part of the family…. I guess I'm getting old," Carl said with a sound of disgust.

A man coming into the dining room and asked, "What's for supper?"

"The only one that knows the answer to that question is John," Carl answered without looking up at the man. As the man walked away from us Carl asked, "What's your plans? It's obvious you won't be working construction for a while."

"That's true…. You sound like a person with something in mind?" I asked him. With Joey gone, I figured he needed someone to cover for his absence.

"You know what I have in mind…, but I'll ask you," he answered with a smile. Then, finishing his coffee, he asked, "Care to take his place? I'll pay you ten dollars an hour."

"I can't say anything but yes… I can't promise more than a month. It depends on what happens, which I'll give you plenty of notice," I told him.

"Bertha's expecting us tomorrow morning," Bill, reminded me.

"That's right, we do have an appointment in the morning," I told Carl, agreeing with Bill.

He asked, "I can get Charlie to come in tomorrow for a while to give you time to do whatever you have to do…. Do you think you can make it back by twelve?"

"I don't see any reason I can't make it…. We should be back by nine," I offered.

"No, noon is fine," he told me with a relieved expression.

My mind went back to the trouble he had with Joey. I began to think about the time it all took place. I couldn't figure out why Joey had come in so early. I asked him, "Why did Joey come in when he did?"

"To cover for me while I was gone," he explained.

"… Joey a few minutes ago. He didn't look too pleased when he drove off," a man said to his friend passing us.

"I guess I could start now and let you go home at a decent time," I offered.

"If you don't mind… I have to get a new lock for the office, and then I'll give you a key," he said a little excited. As he got up, he added, "I'll be back in a few minutes…. The hardware store is just a couple of doors down…. Why don't you go on and tell John not to worry about the mess?"

As he walked out of the dining room, Bill told me, "Sounds like you're set…. Room, board and a paycheck…Now I have to find something for myself…. You sure lucked out with this."

"With my arm being what it is I guess I should feel lucky it worked out this way. I wish it meant a job for you too… I'll catch up with you later… I had better go back and talk to John," I told him as I was getting up.

"The partnership had to end at some point. Since you're busy I think I going to take a shower," he said as he got up.

"Don't use up all the hot water. Come to think of it, as long as it's going to take to get this smock off…. Everyone will be able to take a shower," I added with a laugh.

"See you later," he said as he left.

I don't know why but I felt guilty taking the position at the mission. I knew I should have let someone who really needed a job, take the position. What made it worse was the look on Bill's face as he went to the barracks. It would have been better if Carl could have had two jobs available. I quit worrying about it as I went to the storeroom.

"How's it going," I asked John as I walked into the storeroom. I had never looked at him before, but I found him interesting. He was about six feet or a little more in height. He had blonde wavy hair but there was something even more distinguishable about him. I doubted that he weighed less than two hundred pounds. For the curvature in his spine, I would have bet he had a sunken chest. There was no way anyone could miss him in a crowd.

"This area is off-limits to residents," he told me.

"Carl asked me, to tell you that he'll take care of this mess," I told him. I wanted to tell him I was Joey's replacement, but it wasn't my position. I figured it was up to Carl to tell him I was now an employee. I tried to be friendly by offering, "I've got one good arm, but I'm willing to help."

He asked, "What are you…, Carl's little spy?"

"Just trying to be friendly is all," I told him honestly. He was displaying a familiar attitude I had seen over the past week. I didn't know what his problem was, and I didn't care. I didn't think he was the type to have something against veterans.

As he dropped a can on the floor he asked, "What are you going to tell him now?"

"As I said… Carl wanted me to tell you he would clean the mess up… I guess now that I have relayed the message to you, I'll be leaving," I told him, not wanting to start a fight.

"Jeff, are you in there," I heard Bill call out to me.

"I'm coming," I called back to him. As I turned to go to the dining room, I gave John a slight wave. As I left him with the mess, I wondered how he was going to take me working with him.

"Let's step outside… I need to tell you something I have just learned," he suggested.

"All right," I said, agreeing to go with him. I looked around towards the storeroom and wondered what was going on in there.

As we went outside, two men came inside. There was a slight nod of recognition from the two, but that was about all. Taking it for what it was I felt good. Once I was outside, I looked up and down the street, and I didn't see Carl coming back. Then I turned my attention to Bill. When he stopped, I asked him, "What's the problem?"

"I heard a couple of men watching television talking…," he stopped as a man walked past us. He kept his eye on the man and didn't say anything until he was out of earshot. He went on to tell me, "They said it was strange that Joey got the ax and not John… I didn't want to say anything in fear of causing trouble."

"You mean Joey and John was working together in stealing from the mission?" I asked, not sure that I had understood him correctly. It made sense the two were in it together from the attitude John had just displayed.

"I mean it… John isn't upset at Carl for firing Joey. He's upset because Joey was his means of transportation," Bill told me.

"He was more hostile than upset… He's never said a word to me before. Then he began calling me Carl's spy. I had the feeling if I hadn't gotten out of the storeroom when I did, he would have attacked me," I told him.

He asked, "Might be better if you wait for Carl out here and tell him?"

"Hell no…, I'm not going to run from anyone. In fact, I think I'm going to go in and have another cup of coffee. When Carl comes back, I will tell him what you heard, and then it's up to him," I told him, getting mad.

"You're going to get your opportunity to tell him in a couple of minutes," he warned me.

It wasn't long, and I saw Carl coming down the block with a couple of bags under his arms. Rather than having bought one lock he must have bought a dozen. Not caring, I waited for him to get up to where we were.

With a big smile he asked, "A Union meeting?"

"Not really…," I answered him. I told him what Bill had learned.

"Have you ever had the feeling your world is falling apart…? I feel as if mine is right now…. I guess I had better go in and have a talk to him. He's always done what I asked him to do, though we never have been friends," he said as he headed inside the mission.

I went over and opened the door for him. As he went inside, I told him, "Good luck."

"Thanks…. At least I have enough locks to change all of them out…. I've been meaning to do this for a long-time…. That is, changing the locks out," he replied as he headed for the dining room.

I saw Bill had finished with his cigarette, and I told him, "I think I'll go inside and make sure Carl doesn't get into any more trouble."

"As handicapped as you are I'd better come in with you… There's nothing going on out here anyway," he said, as he threw his cigarette butt into the gutter. When he caught up to me, he added, "And I thought today was going to be boring."

Walking into the dining room, I saw that everything was quiet. I relaxed a little thinking either Carl hadn't talked to John yet or John had taken it well. From my conversation with him, I doubted he took it kindly. With that being, the case, I figured Carl was putting the locks away and hadn't gotten to John yet. Then I heard some noise as if John was still putting stock back on the shelves. Though I thought, I knew what was going on I decided to check.

As I went around the counter, I saw Carl's body sprawled out on the floor. The bag of doorknobs and locks scattered everywhere. He was lying in a pool of blood, and he wasn't moving. I shouted to Bill, "Get a doctor…. Carl's hurt."

He asked, "Is he all right?"

"I don't know, just get an ambulance here," I told him as I bent down to see if Carl was alive.

From behind me a voice asked, "What's going on?"

"I don't know…. It looks like Carl's hurt bad," I answered as I felt for Carl's pulse. It didn't take long to find his pulse, and I could see he was breathing. I didn't like seeing the blood on the back of his head, but he was alive.

"I didn't do it," the voice said behind me.

Turning around I saw it was John speaking to me. I was so upset seeing Carl on the floor I didn't take the time to recognize his voice. I asked him, "You don't have any idea what happened?"

"They're on their way," Bill announced from the pay phone.

One of the residents came into the dining room and asked, "Something wrong in here?"

"I don't know… Carl had an accident," Bill told him.

"I used to be a paramedic… Maybe I can be of help," a man said, running around the counter.

As he came running out of the kitchen John asked, "…hear right? I just mopped this area, because I dropped a jar of mayonnaise,"

"Ooh, my head hurts," Carl muttered as he tried to get up.

"Stay where you are…. You may have a concussion," the resident told him.

"I'm… all…right," Carl managed to get out.

"The medics are on the way," I told him. It surprised me to see so many standing around showing concern. I didn't think any of them cared about anything or anyone. I then asked Carl, "What happened. Do you remember?"

"No," was his only answer.

Outside we could hear a siren telling us the ambulance was here. From the way it looked, he was going to survive, but he still needed to see a doctor.

"At least the ambulance is here," someone announced as if we couldn't hear the siren.

"Sorry I was so rough on you," John said to me. Then with a sheepish look, he added, "If you have time later, I would like to talk to you."

"Sure," I told him as I was looking at Carl. He was my main interest, and John was my last, at the time.

"How's he doing?" Bill asked.

"Better than I feared… If I could only keep him down," I told him.

"You don't have to worry… I'm not going anywhere… I'm just trying to stretch out… Oooh. My head hurts," Carl announced.

As a police officer joined us in the dining room he asked, "What's going on?"

"Over here officer," I called out to him.

"What happened to him," he asked again, seeing Carl on the floor.

From the lobby, I could hear the wheels of a gurney coming through the front door. The first attendant in asked, "Where is the victim?"

"Over here," the officer shouted out to them.

I moved out of their way and went over to where Bill was. I was too interested in Carl to talk to anyone. I had the feeling it was taking them forever to get him on the gurney. It frustrated me not knowing what they were saying. If they had talked more, I would have had an idea why it was taking so long. Instead, they went about their routine not saying anything. I kept telling myself he had a head injury and they had to be careful.

"Is he all right?" One of the residents asked.

"I don't know… They've been working on him for quite a while now," I answered him.

"It's always something," the man replied as he walked over to a friend.

The attendants finally got Carl on the gurney and began to wheel him out to the ambulance. On his way out, he managed to get his keys out of his pocket and gave them to me. His parting words were, "It's in your hands."

"Thanks… I think," I told him wishing I could do something for him. Most of the residents were like me and walked him out to the ambulance. Then as they rolled him inside the ambulance, I called out, "Take care of yourself."

As he was about to leave the officer told me, "The attendant doesn't feel that it's serious. He may have a mild concussion, but they won't know without an x-ray… He was lucky the floor is vinyl and not ceramic. If it had been ceramic his injuries would be much greater."

"Thanks for letting me know," I told him.

"My pleasure…. Watch out for the mayonnaise," he returned with the tip of his hat.

"From assistant to the manager in a little over an hour," Bill said, giving me a bad time.

"Not the way I would want to do it… I don't even have any idea what I'm to do. I don't even know where the office is," I told him as we headed back to the dining room.

"Off from the storeroom," he said unexpectedly.

I asked, "What?"

"The office…. You have to go through the storeroom to get to it. I saw it when I tackled Joey," he explained.

"Maybe, I should give you the keys," I offered.

"I don't think so," he said as he held the door open for me.

"Want some coffee?" I asked him. I could have used a shot, but the coffee was bad enough.

"I'll get you a cup… I know how handicapped you are," he said as he headed for the coffee urn.

"When I get the use of my arm back you are in trouble," I warned him. I realized with all that had gone on I hadn't felt any pain. As I sat at a table, I relaxed, and I could really feel it.

"What now?" Bill asked as he sat the cups down.

"Mind if I have a seat?" John asked, coming up behind Bill.

Bill straightened up as if he was expecting trouble. Waving him to his seat, I told John, "Have a seat."

"Thanks," John said as he gave Bill a concerned look.

"What's on your mind?" I asked him. From the look on his face, I wasn't sure I was ready for it. Being curious, I couldn't help letting him take a seat and tell me what was on his mind.

"First, I would like to apologize for my attitude earlier…, but Joey is my brother-in-law…. Without him, I don't have a job," he explained to us.

"I don't understand… Before you say anything, let me tell you something I have heard. I heard you were in with Joey in stealing the supplies… Understand I'm not accusing you, but just telling you what I have heard. What do you have to say about that?" I asked him.

"I would like to find out who made up that lie… I can't say I haven't taken a loaf of bread home…, but I brought a loaf back. I was afraid Joey was the one that was stealing from the mission. In fact, the other day we had a hot discussion on the subject. I told the bum that without his car, I would have a problem… I don't have any idea why my sister married the bum. I have to say, if it weren't for him, I wouldn't have this job. It doesn't pay much, but without a car, I have had to take whatever.... Now that he's gone, it's all over," he told us.

"What do you mean it's all over...? You are afraid Carl's going to accuse you as an accessory to the thefts?" Bill asked him.

With a long pause, he told us, "I can't cook."

"Tell me something I don't know... I don't know, which is worse around here the coffee or the food," Bill replied.

"Let him explain what he means he can't cook... He's the cook" I told Bill, not understanding it either.

"Joey told me what to put into each dish.... Though I've learned a little over the years, but I'm not a cook," he told us with a look of not knowing what to do.

"I'm with Bill in saying he isn't much of a cook either.... What do we do now, with supper being an hour away?" I asked the two.

"I'll help him," Bill offered.

"Great.... Now we have two in the kitchen that can't cook. I think I'll hunt down some cockroaches and toast them," I replied, wondering what I could do to help. I wasn't the best cook in the world, but I hadn't killed myself on my own cooking.

"I am a chef... I don't know what's in the kitchen, but I'm sure I can put something together," Bill told me.

"I'll be.... I didn't know that" I told him, finding the information surprising. Then, thinking about it, I didn't even know his last name.

"You have a lot to learn about me," he said as he got up. Then, turning to John, he told him, "You know the kitchen better than I do.... We had better get going, or we will have a revolt on our hands."

"All right," John said as he got up to go with Bill.

"Some poached salmon sounds good," I shouted out to the two of them.

As an old man walked up behind me, he asked, "What's this about poached salmon?"

"Just giving them a bad time," I answered as I turned around to look at the man. I didn't remember seeing the old man before, but he looked familiar. His hair was a little long, but not too long, and the same was with his beard. He was wearing a pair of jeans, a tan work shirt, a sweater that was older than I was, and a coat. For as hot as it was outside, I didn't know how he could stand all the clothes he had on.

He asked, "Mind if I get a cup of coffee and join you?"

"On one condition…. You fill my cup up. I'm having a little difficulty with my one arm," I answered as I raised my cup up for him.

"No problem," he said with a grin.

Coming back, he set the cups on the table and took a seat himself. Then, with a concerned look, he asked me, "Who clubbed Carl."

"A jar of mayonnaise," I told him and enjoyed the expression on his face.

Almost coming out of his seat he asked, "What?"

Interrupting us, a man asked, "Carl around?"

"No…, he's at the hospital getting checked out. I haven't heard how he's doing yet," I told him.

"Oh… I needed to talk to him," he replied.

"I can take your name and give him a message…. Or is there something I can do for you?" I asked him, hoping to get rid of him.

He asked, "Think he'll be back tomorrow?"

"I can't tell you… I am hoping he will be," I replied not knowing what else to tell him. From the kitchen, I could hear the sounds of someone, placing pots and pans on the stove. I figured Bill had found something to cook. I found myself wondering what he would be fixing us for supper.

"I'll check back tomorrow then," he said. Not saying anything, he turned around and walked out of the building.

"After slipping on some mayonnaise, he's in the hospital," the old man said, having put it altogether.

"You've got it," I answered. Through the kitchen window, I could see Bill and John were busy enough.

"By the way, they call me Bill," the old man told me.

"I'm Jeff… I'm glad to meet you… Oh, thanks for the coffee," I told him, feeling bad I hadn't thanked him for the coffee sooner.

"I guess I don't have to worry about him then," he said as he picked up his cup and took a swig of coffee.

"I hope we don't have to worry… I'm not looking forward to keeping this job," I told him with a grin.

"No problem…. So you're a veteran," he commented.

"Afghanistan," I told him.

"Fought in Nam," he told me.

"Oh," I replied as I looked around. I never saw Carl do anything but sit where I was, drinking coffee. I figured he did something, and I should be doing it, but I didn't know what.

"One of the saddest times of my life…. We should have won the war," he said. Then holding his cup in front of his face as if he was remembering the experience he fell into silence.

"You were in the infantry?" I asked him. I didn't want to hear his story, but I didn't know what else to do. I knew if I didn't give him a chance to unload, he would sit there forever.

"No, I was a pilot," he told me as he continued holding his cup up in front of himself. Then setting the cup down he added, "So many times I flew over North Vietnam. After you make two or three runs, the terrain becomes familiar. One spot I knew it was one big ammo dump, but I couldn't do anything about it…. It was the same with the ships in the harbor. We knew they were full of ammunition, and I couldn't do anything about them either. Johnson and McNamara were calling the shots. If we had gone in and crushed the Cong, we wouldn't have lost so many of our men. Most of my friends died for nothing."

"Seems that was the case with the entire war," I replied, not having anything to add.

"When I got back home people referred to me as a baby killer…, and many other names," he told me. Then sipping his coffee, he said, "It's like a friend of mine… I guess he was a baby killer. One day coming out of his tent, there was a ten- or eleven-year-old wanting to shine his boots. He didn't see anything wrong and let the kid spit shine his boots…"

"And something tells me there's more," I told him as I cradled my coffee in my hands.

"Yes and this is the part everyone is accused of doing…. After supper, he decided to go for a walk. As any good marine would, he had his rifle, in case something happened… Out of the corner of his eye, he saw a bush tip over and a cong popped up out of the ground. All this friend of mine saw was the rifle in the hands of this individual…," he stopped in mid sentence, to take another sip of his coffee. He set his cup down, and he added, "Without thinking he fires a round at the shooter…. The guy dropped…his rifle went flying. When he went to investigate what he saw, it was the kid who shined his boots earlier."

"That's a shame. I don't understand how any society could allow a child to fight a war," I replied.

As he finished his coffee he asked, "What else was he to do…, let the kid kill him?"

"I know what I would do. I would worry about the ridicule after I shot the shooter," I said to myself.

"He might have saved himself physically…, but he lost his self-respect, self-worth, and everything else that made him the man he once was," he said as he set his cup down and got up. As he left the table he added, "And then they became drunks, with others turning to drugs…. Thankfully, some found themselves again, but many just buried it inside."

"So many came back like that," I told him.

"Too many," the old man replied as he picked up his cup. Then as he took his cup to the dirty dish container, he added, "I'll be seeing you."

"Take it easy," I told him as he left the dining room.

As he was leaving, someone said in greeting the old man, "How's it going…, I didn't think I would be seeing you for a while."

"Wanted to see Carl, but I guess I'm going to have to wait," the old man told him.

"See you the next time you come by," the first guy told him.

Having carried my cup to the dirty dish container, I headed for the kitchen. Then stopping, I realized I knew who the old man was. It took the conversation between him and the man bumping into him. I realized who he was and went running after him. I found myself muttering, "You're Jake's friend, Phil."

"Did Phil go in there?" I asked a man coming out of the barracks.

"I didn't know he was around," he answered as he pushed past me.

"Thanks," I muttered as I went out the front door. Looking up and down the street all I could see were several cars going by. Out in the lead was a semi-expensive car, I found it hard to believe would be in this area. Then, looking up and down the sidewalk, there were a few people; none were Phil. I couldn't see him and I asked myself, "Why are you so stupid…. He could have told me where I can find Jake."

I didn't know what else to do, so I went back inside again. Since I didn't catch him, I figured I would check on supper. Not having had any lunch, I was getting hungry. My stomach was at the point I would have been willing to bite into the meat loaf from the week before. Then, remembering Bill was supposedly a chef, I felt there might be hope of a decent meal in the old mission that night. As I walked into the kitchen I asked, "What's for supper."

"A surprise," Bill answered.

If I were to believe my nose, I would bet we're having spaghetti. Walking over a little closer I saw I was right. Looking over at John, I told him, "It's a shame he's in your way."

"I think you have that backwards… I'm in his way. I'm thinking about bringing my family down for supper," John told me with a big smile.

"I promised John I would write out some of my recipes for him," Bill said. As we were talking, he took a spoon, dipped it into the sauce, and tasted it. From the smile on his face, he approved of it.

"I'm looking forward to supper… And I hope it's soon," I told them.

"Bill says all that's left is cooking the spaghetti," John told me.

"There might not be any left by that time… If John keeps sampling as he has been," Bill warned me.

"You've had enough," I told John, and I turned around to go into the dining room.

As I was leaving, I heard Bill tell John, "We should have made more. By making, twice what you need you can freeze it…? Then you won't have t…"

Once out into the dining room I saw men waiting for supper. I had a feeling the aroma coming out of the kitchen got their attention. Everyone had a big smile on their face as their attention was on the kitchen. I wondered how often this scene had happened in past years. I knew they were in for a treat.

"Smells good and not like garbage," one man said as I passed him,

"I don't think Bill or John will disappoint us," I assured him.

"I hope it's almost ready…I am" a second one said as I passed by him.

"Almost," I told him and then I went to the coffee urn and poured myself another cup of coffee. As I was about to pick up my cup, I noticed one of the residents coming towards me.

He asked, "How is Carl?"

"I haven't heard… You know how ER is. We might not hear anything for another eight hours," I told him.

"I hope he's not hurt bad," he replied as he went in order to join everyone else.

Bill and John finally brought supper out and put it on the line.

There wasn't a scrap of spaghetti left after everyone had their fill. After supper, everyone was in a talkative mood. I didn't know if it was the food or Joey's absence that made the change. It was clear everyone liked the meal that Bill had prepared. While everyone was still in the dining room, I announced, "I would be willing to help wash dishes, but I only have one arm right now… I'm looking for volunteers."

"If supper is that good every night you can count on me," one of the older men announced.

"Me too," another man said, standing up.

"John," I shouted out to my kitchen crew.

"Yes," John answered coming out into the dining room.

"You have some volunteers to wash dishes," I told him.

"What did I just hear?" Bill asked as he came out of the kitchen.

A round of applause greeted him and then the chanting started, "More…, more…, more…"

With John joining in by clapping, Bill beamed from ear to ear. Being who he was he bowed with a shit-eating grin on his face. No one refused to take care of their own dishes. With John telling him he had everything under control, Bill came over and had a cup of coffee with me.

"The spaghetti reminded me of my mother's cooking," a man said, slapping Bill on the back.

One of the residents asked Bill, "Are you going to be working with John now?"

"I don't know," Bill told the man.

"Something tells me you might have a job here," I warned him.

"It was fun… I doubt Carl can afford the two of us," he replied.

"I talked to John about that accusation," Bill told me.

"And…, did you learn anything interesting?" I asked him.

"Nothing concrete, but he may not have helped Joey…. His values don't match someone's that would do something like stealing from a mission," he answered.

"I hope you're right… We'll have to leave it up to Carl though," I replied.

Looking around I couldn't get over the number of degenerates, there were. I could understand people suffering from hard times and needing help. Most of these men aren't worried about improving themselves. They don't even go to the day labor office to find work. All they do is wander the streets, go through trash bins, and beg for money. To some degree, I understand it's from the rejection they feel from society. I also know the root of their problems goes deeper than society's rejection of them. Society's rejection is a crutch; they use it to justify their lives. I found myself wondering if my father was like these men.

With a feeling of disgust, I laid on my cot praying for a good night's sleep. As I drifted off, I told myself it hadn't been all bad.

CHAPTER EIGHT

After supper, they invited us to watch the Olympics with them in the barracks. I wasn't much for the Olympics, but it was different from what I was used to watch on television. Spending some time with them, I learned most were interesting men. Everyone was talking about the meal Bill had fixed. Hearing about the meal and the game began to get old to me. I left everyone in the barracks and went to Carl's office. Looking around the office, I found an answering machine with a message on it. Not knowing if I should play it or not, I went ahead just in case it was important.

> *"Jeff... I'm Carl's wife, and I thought I would let you know he's alright. He is home resting right now and should be in tomorrow morning.... If you have any questions, please call 537-9648.... Thanks*

I couldn't have been happier to hear he was all right. I erased the message and saw there was a second message. I left the message on the machine for Carl to play. After thinking about it, I pushed play. The message said:

> *I thought I would let you know you haven't seen the last of me.*

I didn't have to give this message any thought for I knew it was from Joey. Hearing the tone of his voice, I was a little worried. I knew people made idle threats, but this one worried me. I didn't want to leave the message on the machine, but I knew I had to. I felt sorry for Carl having problems such as this one.

The desk only had a few pieces of paper lying on it. I noticed a couple of pieces of paper on the desk that caught my attention. I knew they weren't any of my business, so I left them where they were. As I looked around, I didn't see anything that would give me an idea of what I should be doing. All I knew was a man coming in order to take over the night shift. Not knowing the man, I had no idea how he would react to me. I had heard from Bill his name was Mike and decided I would wait for him. I closed up the office and went out to the dining room for another cup of coffee to wait for him.

John finally left, excited about supper, and the rest of the residents went to the barracks to watch the games. Everyone left me alone to drink my coffee. I finished my coffee and decided it might be a good time to read more of the diary. As I entered the barracks, I noticed how quiet everyone was. Rather than going back to the dining room, I decided to read in bed. I opened the diary and began reading it when I heard an announcer say:

> "*…and he now has won his tenth gold metal. He is the most…*"

I found myself wondering what it would be like to be the most decorated Olympian in history. Feeling proud of the win, I headed to the dining room again.

"You're not watching the games?" Bill asked as I was about to go through the door.

"Don't think so… I have a job to do," I called back to him.

"Be that way," he returned as he turned back to the television.

Sitting at the table, I took a sip of my coffee and opened the diary. I didn't bother to find where I had left off but just opened it. The top of the first page that caught my eye, I read:

> *I know I can never go to my wife and son and be what they need from me. After seeing the woman with her dead child cradled in her arms in a village near the Cambodian border. The child's face was almost gone as was her right*

arm. The mother in tears sat on the ground rocking her daughter back and forth. I can't get her and the others out of my mind. I know I will think of them every time I look at my son. I don't think I could do that to him or myself.

I will never know if I were the responsible person or not. All I know is when they attacked us, we did what we had to, to defend ourselves. When the enemy takes refuge in a village, the villagers pay the price.

I wish I had gone to Canada and avoided the draft. What I grew up thinking about wars was not what it was like. If I were the type, playing ball with my son would be fun… I know I couldn't handle it, and my son would pay the price. It might be better if he never knows me.

"Hello," a voice called out from the lobby.

"In here," I returned. Having a job to fulfil, I got up to see who was in the lobby.

"A man told me I might find a bed here," a young man told me as I got to the lobby.

What greeted me was a man in his mid teens. I found it hard to believe someone as young as this kid wouldn't be in the confines of his home. I wanted to help the kid with whatever problem he had. The problem was this wasn't the right place. I felt sorry for him, seeing the bruises on his face and arms. I motioned for him to follow me into the dining room. Before I did anything, I wanted to learn who he was and why he was here.

Once seated, I asked him, "What's your name?"

"Gary Townsend," he answered as he looked around the lobby.

"I'm Jeff O'Connor…. What brings you here?" I asked him.

One of the residents went over to get a cup of coffee. As he poured his coffee he asked, "A new member to our little group?"

"Yes," I answered then turning my attention back to Gary.

"My stepfather is a drunk... When he is drinking, I pay for it with beatings. Tired of it and decided I would take off on my own. I thought I would find a job and then get a place to live... No one will give me a job. I don't have enough money to eat or get a place to sleep. Now I don't know what to do...," he finally answered me.

"Where are you from?" I asked. In hearing his story, it explained his bruises.

"Oakland," he answered. Then looking around he asked, "Could I have a cup of coffee?"

"Help yourself... I'll get Bill, and he might find something in the kitchen," I offered him.

"That would be great," he replied as he got up.

"I'll be right back," I told him, as I headed for the barracks. As I got up, I saw the kid pouring himself a cup of coffee. Then picking up the sugar container, he poured five or six spoonful into his cup. The idea of that much sugar almost made me sick. Shaking the thought off, I went in order to get Bill.

"Bill, could you give me a hand?" I called out to him.

"Yeah," he answered as he got up.

Reaching me, I motioned for him to follow me. Then as we entered the dining room, I told him, "Gary hasn't had supper yet.... See if you can find something for him if you would. Then maybe find one of the beds near ours."

In a hushed voice, he asked, "What are you going to be doing?"

"Make a phone call," I answered him in a low voice. Then reaching Gary, I told him, "Gary, this is Bill.... He is a mean chef. If you had gotten here a little earlier, you would have tasted the best spaghetti in the world... I know there aren't any leftovers from supper, but he'll find something and a bed for you."

"Thanks," he replied with a smile.

"Follow me Gary.... We don't have much of a selection, but I think I know what I can fix you," Bill told him.

"I'm hungry," Gary warned him.

As the two of them went back to the kitchen, I went to the office to call social services. In ways, I felt I was betraying the kid, but the mission wasn't a good place for him. I felt he needed to be in school and a place where he could get the care he deserved.

I left him in the dining room to call the police from the office phone. It didn't take long to learn there wasn't anything they could do as late as it was. They did offer to send a patrol car over and pick up the kid. When I asked what they would do with him, they told me they would put him in a cell. I didn't like that idea and told him I would take care of him for the night. I could see Gary was happy where he was, and I didn't see where one night would hurt. With the call made, I went back out to the dining room. Then when I got out there, I found him bringing out some food for himself. Reaching the table before them, I replied, "That was fast."

"I'm good," Bill said with a big smile.

"Tastes great," Gary, said as he stuffed his mouth.

"Where's Carl?" Mike asked, coming up to us.

"Hi… Carl let Joey go and…," I began telling him the events of the day. While telling him the full story, I had moved us to another table. I didn't think the kid needed to hear us talk about him. I told him about Gary and my phone call about him. I asked him to keep an eye on the kid. I didn't want the kid to take off before the proper authorities interviewed him. I decided to turn the place over to him and hit the sack.

"If no one minds, I'm going to bed," I told Bill and his new friend.

"He's almost done and then we'll be joining you," Bill told me.

I picked up the diary and went into the barracks. I didn't mind that everyone was still watching the Olympics. As tired as I was, I doubted the television would keep me awake. I tucked the diary back into my bag and got ready for a shower. As I got myself ready, the words of my father came back to me. I wondered how I would feel if I had been in his shoes.

When I had taken my shower, I crawled into bed and fell asleep. I woke up with Bill snoring, and I remembered he wanted me to wake him. I rocked him and told him, "It's that time."

He woke up, but I wasn't sure if he was fully awake. He asked, "What?"

"You said you wanted me to wake you up," I reminded him. As we talked, I saw Gary was sleeping on the other side of him. I found myself happy he hadn't taken off in the middle of the night.

"Oh yeah… I want to fix the oatmeal this morning," he said, remembering what he wanted to do.

"What again was it, you wanted to do?" I asked him, needing a cup of coffee.

"Make the oatmeal myself…, to make a change, add a little maple syrup in it," he answered as he pulled his pants on.

"Sounds interesting… I think I'll join you and have a cup of coffee," I told him. Thankfully, I had started to dress a few minutes before he did. My arm was hurting so bad it took a while to get my shirt on.

Walking into the kitchen, we caught Mike making the oatmeal. Bill told him, "If you don't mind, I'll make it."

"I usually make it," Mike said, looking as if his authority was in question.

"I know… I just want to do something different this morning for the guys…. Tomorrow, you can make it," Bill explained to him.

"If Jeff doesn't mind… I don't like making it anyway. My mother can tell you how much I hate the stuff," he said with a smile.

"I can tell," Bill replied with a chuckle.

"I don't care for oatmeal myself…. Though in the position that I'm in right now, I can't be choosy," I told Mike as I went back out to the dining room for some coffee. Then thinking of Bill, I poured him a cup and took it into him.

I spent the next twenty minutes talking to Mike. I didn't learn anything from him other than a respect for John. He had to agree John wasn't much of a cook, but he was trying. He also felt the man was honest. Then our conversation ended with Bill bringing out the oatmeal.

I went ahead and helped myself and took a seat at the table. In spooning it up, I had to say the consistency was better than I had seen so far at the mission. No matter what the consistency of it was, it was still oatmeal. After taking the first bite, I told Mike, "You should try it… There's a hint of maple to it."

"Thanks…. I'll take your word for it," he said, going back to the lobby.

"Are you ready for our walk over to see Bertha?" I asked as I turned back to Bill.

"Let me finish getting dressed, and then I'll be ready…. I can use the money," he answered as he finished his bowl. Then finishing his coffee, he added "To tell you the truth I don't care for oatmeal either…. My grandparents didn't eat anything else. I think oatmeal is what drove me out onto my own. By the way how is your shoulder?"

"Hi…. What are you two doing?" Gary asked, sounding as if he was half-awake.

"Just finished breakfast…. With you sleeping as well as you was. I thought I would let you sleep for awhile longer," I told him.

"It's there yet… At least when I put my shirt on, I felt it," I answered him as I went back to Gary.

Back at the table, I talked to Gary about his home life. As with Bill and I, he had lost his mother at an early age in an accident. It sounded as if his father blamed himself for her death. I told him he couldn't stay at the mission. Having forgotten that idea, we talked about his future. I reminded him Social Services were there to help kids like him. He agreed he couldn't exist on his own, and they might be the answer. He told me he didn't care what happened, as long as he didn't have to go home. I knew he would leave home again if they made him go back. It surprised me when he said he didn't mind talking to Social Services. He was a little surprised, but he understood I had to do it.

It wasn't long, and we were on our way. Having Gary with us made the walk a little more interesting. The kid had a sense of humor that I found amusing. He also noticed things I would never have noticed, making humorous comments about them.

"A great day for a walk," Bill said, looking up into the sky.

"You might want to rethink that idea…. There are pigeons around, and I don't think you want to get an eye full," Gary warned him.

"Good point, Gary," Bill said as he brought his head down and covering it with his hands.

"And they say the newer generation is dumb," I told him, laughing at the two of them.

I found myself wishing my kids were with me. I couldn't remember the last time we had laughed at anything. Other than the night before I left for Frisco, Martha and I never took time to enjoy anything together. I knew she and the kids did, but I wasn't part of that picture. I found myself wondering if I needed to change. I knew the answer, and I made a silent promise I would change. I knew if I were to change, it would have to be for me and not everyone else.

"Look at the back of those Jeeps…," Gary, said watching the traffic pass us.

Bill asked him "What about them?"

"Don't they look like their butts are hiked up into the air," he answered with a laugh.

"Never noticed that before," I replied.

"He'll get through life all right… Those with a sense of humor can get over humps the rest of us can't," Bill added with a smile.

"Unlike you and I," I suggested.

"Well, you do have a tendency to take everything seriously," he answered.

With a curious look, Gary asked the two of us "Are you two brothers?"

"I have many problems, but that's not one of them… We've only known each other for a week now…. Why do you ask?" I asked him. I have to admit we had become friends without any trouble.

"Just the thought of the idea makes me want to take another shower," Bill told him.

All the rest of the way we didn't say much. I would have bet from the look on his face that he was thinking about Gary's question. He looked as if the thought had made him sick to his stomach. I found it interesting we had become so close. In the years, Ray and I had known each other we hadn't gotten half as close.

"I would offer you a penny for your thoughts, but I don't have one," Bill told me.

"Don't give me that…. I know you have money. Not much, maybe, but you have a few dollars…. I was just thinking about some people I know," I told him. Then seeing the office ahead of us, I added, "I would like to run by one of those churches and see if I can get some different clothes. I'm getting tired of wearing the same fatigue shirt."

"I can't get it on or off too easy with this arm the way it is… in another couple of days, I shouldn't have any problem, but until then I would like a different shirt," I explained to him. Then, thinking about Gary, I added with a nod toward the kid, "We can go to the church after we get back."

Bill asked, "Not a bad idea…. I could use a change myself… What's wrong with the smock?"

I didn't bother to answer him. I did go on to ask him "There's a florist around here isn't there?"

"I believe you're right. I think it's in the next block…. Maybe two doors up from the corner," Bill answered with a questioning look.

"Give me a dollar," I told him as I held my good handout.

He asked, "What for?"

"I think we owe Bertha a rose," I told him as I waited for the dollar.

"All right…, but I think we owe her more than that," he answered as he fished out a dollar bill.

"I know, but we don't have enough money," I replied as I took the dollar from him. With the money in my pocket, I left them and headed for the florist. It didn't take long to buy the rose, and I met them back at the corner. I told them, "I guess we can see her now."

As we got to the office, Gary asked, "Who are all of those people?"

"Men like us that need a job," I explained to him.

"You have a job," Gary reminded me.

"He didn't have one until yesterday afternoon," Bill told him.

"Well, you are the cook…, so you have a job," Gary said, confirming Bill's position.

"No, I was just helping out… I haven't worked there for long. Even at that it's only been part-time," Bill clarified for him.

"Oh," Gary said, in deep thought.

As we entered the office, I explained to Gary, "This is an office where people get part-time jobs."

I let the two of them walk ahead of me. I kept the rose behind my back so Bertha couldn't see it.

"Running a little late this morning," Bertha said as we walked up to the counter.

"Had a few problems last night…," I told her the condensed version of the night. Then, before she could say anything, I held out the rose for her. As she took it, I told her, "This is for being so helpful."

"You didn't have to do that," she replied, as she smelled it.

"Yes we do," Bill told her as he grinned at me.

"I don't know about the two of you…but thank you. I sure would like to know how you two can get into the messes you get into," she said with the same big smile. As she talked to us, she pulled some papers out of a stack. Then looking at the papers she told us, "I have it worked out so I can pay you for two days."

"Two days? I don't understand the contract was for one-day…, not two. Even then, the job wasn't with the guy you thought it was," Bill asked, not expecting two days to pay.

She then asked him, "The two of you were there for two days, weren't you? After that there's nothing left for the two of you to worry about. Everything about his credentials was checked out so it's going through. The money's coming out of a special fund, so his daughter-in-law won't have to pay for it either."

"Didn't anyone teach you not to argue with a woman? All you're supposed to do is say thanks," I reminded him. I turned back to Bertha and asked her, "Where do I sign?"

"Right here," she told me showing the line for me to sign. She asked, "Who's the little one…, one of your kids?"

"No…, no…. He came into the mission looking for a bed last night. Once we leave here, we are going to see if we can help him out," I explained to her. Then looking at the form, I noticed it was different from the last one we signed. Trusting her, I went ahead and signed it.

"Want a smart little boy… Gary could use a good home," Bill told her. As he waited to sign for his money he added, "And as Jeff said…, thanks."

"You're welcome. I wouldn't mind taking him home, but my husband would accuse me of doing something I didn't do… I don't think so. I don't have room for the three I have now. Sign here, Bill," she answered him as she gave him a form to sign.

"That's one-hundred-two dollars and forty cents for each of you," she told us as she counted it out to us.

"Been a long time since I've seen that much money… Thank you, Bertha," Bill said as he held it in his hands.

"Yes, thank you…. You didn't have to go through all that trouble you know," I told her.

"The two of you, earned it and then some… I talked to the sheriff in Calistoga, and he told me a little more… about Warner," she said, stopping as if she caught herself.

"Whatever… I didn't have any problem with the sheriff. Without asking him, he gave us a ride back to town … I hate taking money from a woman and running off. Still, we have to get Gary back to the mission. I promise…. You haven't seen the last of us," I told her.

She asked, "So you're not going to keep the job as assistant manager?"

"I doubt I'm much good for anything else right now. My bum arm shouldn't keep me from stopping by to say hi," I answered her with a wink.

"It's too late to get a job today, so I'll be back in the morning," Bill told her. Then with a hand on Gary's back, they headed outside.

"Thanks again…, for everything," I told her as I gave her a salute.

Interrupting us, a woman asked, "What time is it?"

"My pleasure gentlemen…," she replied as we turned to leave. She turned to the woman and told her, "There's a clock on the wall…. It's 8:17"

"This is the richest I've been for weeks," Bill said with a big grin. With his money in one hand, he reached to get his wallet. With a surprised look, he said, "My wallet's missing. I wonder what I did with it."

"I don't know what to tell you," I told him.

"There wasn't anything but my ID and photos in it… I don't know what's wrong with me," he said as he looked around the floor. Not seeing it on the floor, he threw his hands up in defeat. As he slipped the money into his front pocket he added, "I guess that's what God made pockets for."

As he held the door open, I reminded him, "Have you forgotten something?"

"Are you accusing me of forgetting that I owe you a couple of bucks…? I can't believe you would think that after all we've been through. You of all people accusing me of stiffing you," he said as he made a hurt expression with his lower lip stuck out.

"I would never say that of you," I assured him with a smile. Before he could respond I suggested, "Maybe you can hold it for me… or be my banker…. Knowing my luck someone will rob me."

"Hell, I thought I had earned it by opening all the doors I have been doing lately," he replied still with his lower lip hanging out. Then with a grin he added, "I hadn't forgotten, and I don't mind hanging onto the money, I owe you… If I spend it let me apologize now."

"I understand," I replied.

"Do the two of you do anything but talk? I thought we were going after some doughnuts," Gary asked, as he headed down the sidewalk towards the mission.

"He told us," Bill shouted back to me as he tried to catch up to the kid.

"I'll catch up to you guys," I shouted to him. Gary was laughing as he ran backward keeping just ahead of Bill.

"Look fellows…, someone has wounded the veteran," one of the men standing against the wall, commented as I passed him.

"I bet he got a purple heart for it," another added with a chuckle.

I automatically came up with several responses I could have made, but I didn't. I was feeling good about everything, and fighting would have spoiled it all. It wasn't worth starting a fight over, and I continued with my effort to catch up with the other two. Gary's future was my main concern; after that I didn't care one-way or the other. I had a feeling he was a good kid who needed a little attention. We hadn't known him but a few hours. I had a feeling if he had a chance, he would go places.

"You are getting old?" Bill asked, waiting for me to catch up to them.

"It's not age… It's not easy to run with this arm of mine in a sling," I reminded him. Then reaching out and roughing up Gary's hair, I asked him, "Feel like a doughnut?"

"I don't know about him, But I would love a doughnut," Bill replied.

"Me too," Gary answered excitedly.

"That little convenience store I think has doughnuts," I suggested.

"You don't have to wait long…. The stores at the next corner," Bill told Gary.

As I ate one of my doughnuts, we headed back to the mission. When we got there, I stood at the door, afraid to go in. Having seen an official car parked in front of the mission, I knew who was waiting for us. Though Gary was agreeable to the idea of going with Social Services, I didn't know if I liked the idea. I wished I could have done something for him myself. I knew I would have to go through them anyway. Then the legal battles with his father would take a while. I knew there wasn't much of anything else I could do. Sucking in a breath, I opened the door and went inside. To my surprise, Carl met me with a smile and big bandage wrapped around his head.

"What are you doing here…, you should be home taking it easy?" I asked him as I came into the room. Then, seeing the expression on his face, I added, "Don't get me wrong, I'm glad to see you."

"Better to get headaches here than at home," he answered with a smile. With a solemn look, he told me, "I don't know what's going on…, but there are a couple of people waiting for you in the dining room."

I heard the front door open. When I turned around, I saw Bill and Gary walk into the shelter. I asked Bill, "Would you mind waiting out here for a minute or two?"

"I can handle that…. What do you think Gary?" Bill asked.

"I guess so…, I have to use the bathroom though," he answered with a grin.

As I went into the Dining room, I heard Bill ask him, "Do you know where it is?"

"I think I can find it," Gary answered as he left.

As I walked up to the woman she asked, "Mr. O'Connor?"

"Yes, and good morning to you both," I replied as I extended my hand to the man with her.

"This is Officer Joe Morgan, and I'm Ms. Alice Anderson, from Social Services," she said as we shook hands. As she released my hand, she asked me, "Where's the boy?"

"He's in the restroom right now. He should be out shortly," I answered her. Ms. Anderson was a medium height woman who looked as if she had eaten one too many desserts. She wasn't fat but was on the heavy side with straight auburn hair. Officer Morgan looked to be about the same weight, making him too large for the police force in a suit. His most distinguished feature was his shiny bald head. Both looked to be in their mid forties. I forgot about them as I looked to see if Gary was in the lobby, and I couldn't see him. Stepping back, I asked Bill, "He hasn't come out, I take it?"

"Not yet," he answered. With a glance towards the barracks, he added, "If he doesn't come out in a minute, I'll go in and get him."

"Thanks," I replied as I went back into the dining room. Sitting, I told them, "I guess we wait."

"He probably went out the back door," Officer Anderson replied as he looked around the dining room.

Time dragged on forever as I sat there. As I turned to see if Bill was in the lobby, Carl came over to me.

"We have a problem… He…," he told me once he stooped to my level.

"He went out the backdoor," I said, finishing for him.

"Yep," he said as he stood up.

"Damn," I replied as I got up myself.

"He took off?" Officer Anderson asked.

"Looks like it," I answered as I went to the lobby. Reaching the Lobby, I saw Bill coming back towards me. I asked him, "You didn't find him?"

"I'm sorry, but no… I went out back, and I didn't see him. I even walked to both ends of the alley, and I didn't find him."

"No point standing around here… We have two other calls," Ms. Anderson told her companion.

"I'm sorry… I got the impression he was eager to have a place to go to… I guess I could have tied him down," I said apologetically.

"It's not your fault…. Morgan should have gone to the restroom with him," she said, giving the Officer a stern look.

With an indignant expression on his face, Officer Morgan replied lamely, "I didn't know."

"Let's go," she told him as she headed for the front door.

Not knowing what else to do I followed them. Both Carl and Bill looked sick about it all. I had a feeling I knew how they felt. They didn't see any need to follow him into the restroom, so they didn't. I told them, "It wasn't your fault."

"We're sorry… I would have bet anything he wasn't going to run," Bill told her as he opened the door for her.

"It happens more times than I would like to count," she said, not saying thanks, good-bye, or anything else.

To our surprise, we found Gary standing against the Social Service car. With a smile he told us, "I couldn't let Jeff and Bill get into trouble."

"I'll be…. This is a first," Ms Anderson said. Turning her head around towards me, she gave me a questioning look. Then turning back to Gary, she told him, "They wouldn't have been in trouble."

"Disappointed maybe…, but it's your life. Our concern is not what we want, but to help you," I added, knowing there was a grin on my face.

"That goes for us also," Ms. Anderson, told him. As she got into the car, she told us, "Thank you gentlemen."

"You know where you can find us, if you feel the need to talk," Bill offered.

"Good luck, Gary," I added, feeling proud of him.

"Bye…, and thanks for everything," he said, giving Bill and me a hug.

We stood there and watched the car pull away. Once again, I felt honored being able to do something right. Now, if I could change my life, I would be happy. When the car got out of sight, we went back into the Mission.

"Here's hoping his life will be better than it could have been," Bill said, looking back in the direction the car had gone.

"Yeah…. Not having a father might not be that bad if he was the type that beat me," I replied as he closed the door.

"I agree," he added.

"Other than harboring a teenager, what else has been going on?" Carl asked with a smile.

"We beat a dog to death and roasted him for supper…. Then we attacked the Bedbugs," Bill offered.

"Forgive me gentlemen, but I need to take care of some important business," I told them as I went to the restroom.

Heading back to talk to Carl, I wondered what he was going to say about the previous night. We didn't have any problems, but it was a little different from a usual night, such as us housing Gary. With all the possibilities going through my head, I saw something on the floor, under Bill's bed. As I got closer, I saw it was a wallet. Not seeing anyone around, I could have let him come after it. I decided I would be a good guy, and I picked it up. It slipped out of my hands and fell to the floor again. As I reached down to pick it up, I saw a picture of a bearded man on a driver's license. In the inside compartment, I saw a touch of green that surprised me. What surprised me more is what I read. Closing it, I decided to give it to Bill later.

"You're not sloshing when you take a step," Bill noted as I walked up to them.

"I have to admit I feel better," I replied as I looked at their coffee. Turning towards the coffee urn, I told him, "With you owing me so much, you could've gotten me a cup."

"Oh yes…. Like this one," he replied as he took it off the seat next to him.

"You amaze me… Thanks," I said, sitting next to him.

"Well…. Tell me how you saw last night," Carl asked.

"Just a boring night," he said with a smile. Then heading into the dining room, he got his usual cup of coffee. Then sitting, he added with a smile, "I understand supper was memorable."

"I can tell you there weren't any leftovers…. It was even enjoyable," I told him.

As he raised his coffee to his lips he asked, "Sounds as if we need another cook…. Are you applying for the job Bill?"

"I wouldn't want to see John lose his job. You might get me to help out," Bill told him.

"Let me think about it…. With what I know of John's ties to Joey, I don't know if I want to keep him," Carl told us.

Bill and I gave him our evaluation of John. After discussing the problem, I told him about the phone message and Gary. I then told him, "Oh, there was one more message."

He asked, "Who?"

"That friend of Jake's.... He called for you," I told him.

"I know. He called me once he left here. He said you two talked for a while," he told me.

"It was more me listening and him talking," I told him.

"Whatever you did or said…, impressed him," he replied with a smile.

Bill asked, "Are we going to make that run?"

I asked Carl "Do I have time?"

"Hey Carl…, I like your head scarf," one man shouted out from the lobby.

"Thanks Jerry… I wore it just for you," Carl called back to him.

As he looked at the two of us, he asked, "Time to do what?"

"Time to go to the church…, wherever it may be for a change of clothes," I answered.

"Sure, it's around the corner and down two blocks," he told us.

"We'll be back as soon as we can," I assured him as I got up. Bill having not gotten up yet, I asked him, "Are you coming?"

"I don't know… I've become fond of these clothes… What the hell, I guess I can go see what they have…, I'm particular about what I wear," he answered with a smile.

"You're particular…? You can't even spell the word" I replied as I waited for him to put his cup in the dirty dish container.

"I wonder if they have a tux, my size," he said, coming to the door where I was waiting.

Not understanding, I asked him "To cook in?"

"Of course…. Give this place a touch of class," he answered with a smile.

"Get out of here," Carl said, waving us out with a smile.

As the door closed, I heard him tell Mike, "Two mental cases that…."

"I think he loves us," Bill said as we made the corner.

"That worries me," I replied. Feeling the wallet in my back pocket, I had many questions for him. I didn't feel walking the streets or the mission was the place for a serious conversation. I began to look around to find a place we could stop at and talk about things. I looked up and saw a bar but decided against it. After what he had told me about his drinking, I didn't want to cause him a problem. I still needed a park or somewhere private for what I wanted to talk to him about.

"Why are you so quiet?" Bill asked as we walked along.

"Thinking," I answered him as I looked up and down the street. Not far ahead of us, I saw a little sign that said café. I figured after we got a change we could stop there and have some pie and coffee. Then turning to Bill, I commented "It shouldn't be much further."

"Nope…. Another half block maybe," he said, agreeing with me.

He asked, "I have been meaning to ask you about your father's diary… How's it going?"

"Sad, interesting, informative…. I have a little feeling I know what he went though. I would never have gained the feeling I have if I hadn't walked in my father's footsteps," I told him.

"If you don't mind, I would like to read a little of it," he said, sounding serious.

"I don't have any problems with that," I assured him. Thinking of the picture in my pocket, I asked him, "Want to see a picture of him?"

He answered "Sure…why not?"

I reached into my pocket and pulled out the small envelope that contained my father's picture and my ID. Taking it out of the envelope my father's eyes were looking up at me. With a grin, I handed it to him to look at.

"He looks a lot like you," he replied as he handed the picture back to me. With a grin, he added, "Another two doors and I think we have found the place…. At supper I can show off my new tux."

"In your dreams," I replied as we took the last few steps.

"It's my dream… I can wear anything I want," he added.

"If you hear someone knocking…. It won't be me," I told him as we got to the door of the church. It wasn't a big place, and I didn't care. I just wanted a pair of jeans and a shirt or two. I was willing to make a donation to offset what I took.

The helpers running the clothing store were friendly and helpful. We got what we needed, and I offered them ten dollars for their trouble. To my surprise, they wouldn't take any money from me. With a heartfelt thank you, Bill and I headed back to the mission. He didn't know it, but we had one more stop to make.

"Back to the salt mines," he said, tossing his bag in the air. With a grin, he added, "I wish I could find my wallet… I can't believe I lost it."

"You'll find it…. We haven't been too many places," I replied. Seeing the café ahead of us, I told him, "I think I'm going to buy you a cup of coffee and a piece of pie."

"I know you have a few dollars, but can you afford it?" He asked.

"You forget. I have a full-time job now," I reminded him.

"It's your money," he answered, when we were a couple of doors away from the café.

"Let's go in and see what they have to offer," I suggested.

"Old age before beauty," he told me as he held the door open for me.

"Thank you," I extended to him.

After ordering, we were sitting there feeling worthwhile. For the first time since taking Martha out to supper, I was buying something to eat in a restaurant. I felt a little out of place, but as I looked at the other customers, I realized we weren't too bad. The first clue was the waitress came to the table as if we were all right.

He took a bite of his apple pie and asked, "Why do I have this feeling there's more to this coffee and pie?"

"You used to wear a beard, didn't you?" I asked him playfully.

As if he had caught on, he asked, "For a while…. Why do you ask?"

"I thought I saw a picture of you," I told him.

Sitting back in his chair a blank expression came down his face. He didn't say anything, but he stared at me as if he was waiting for something. I was nice and made him wait. With me not saying anything, he began to get nervous. He finally asked me, "You found my wallet?"

"And in it.... I didn't count it, but it looked like money.... In fact, a lot more money than I have seen in a while.... Mr. William O'Connor," I answered him. He looked like he wanted to crawl under-the-table. The look of a kid having stolen a sucker was on his face. I finally reached into my rear pocket and pulled out his wallet. As I passed it to him, I told him, "I think it's time we had a little talk."

"My grandmother's going to be, pissed..., and I have never met her," he said with an irritated tone to his voice.

"What grandmother?" I asked him, not understanding.

"You know the days of flower power are over," a man said, passing our table.

"It sure is... I'm just a few days late," I shouted out to him. Turning back to Bill, I asked him, "Well?"

"My grandmother.... Your grandmother... our grandmother," he blurted out.

"I know my mother only had one child..., and that's me. Is it safe for me to assume you're my half brother?" I asked him.

"That's what our grandmother told me," He answered.

I sat back in my chair in shock hearing what he had just told me. I found my head spinning with everything that had happened in the past two weeks. As the shock subsided, I found more questions popping up in my head. Leaning towards him, I asked him, "Tell me your story...? I take it, you know mine."

"Not all of it... I got a call the same day you left. This woman introduced herself as being the mother of my father... After a few questions, I realized she was who she told me she was. To say I was in shock would be an understatement...," he began to tell me.

"I can see that.... Then she told you about my crazy stunt," I added for him.

"If I had been anyone else, I might have done the same… Like you I have always wondered about my father as you have. She got my interest when she told me what you were going to do. All she had done was ask me to keep an eye on you… Then I told my manager I was taking some time off, and I came to the mission, and the rest is history," he said with a smile.

"No…, no…, no. You don't get off that easy. Where do you live and what do you do?" I asked him. I had a feeling, I knew the answer, but I wanted to hear it from him.

"I've lived here all my life…. I'm a chef who owns his own restaurant. I'm married to a wonderful woman named Teri and Jacob is my one-year-old son. Oh, did I mention I have two cocker spaniels," he answered with a smile.

"That's what I was afraid you were going to tell me…. What do we do now?" I asked more to myself than him. Allowing the waitress to fill my cup, I added, "We can't continue this charade."

He asked, "Have you learned all that you wanted to?"

"Not really… I have a few more questions," I answered. I had a lot more questions. The first one was why I was doing what I was. I had an idea how he lived, but that was all. I had learned more about the Vietnam War than I had ever wanted to know. I also had experienced some of the ridicule he must have felt. The problem as I saw it was that I didn't have a year or five years to get to know what his life was like. If I didn't do anything else I wanted to find out what happened to him. My only clue was Jake and his friend Phil. Not knowing what else to do, I told him, "I guess we keep it up a little longer."

With a stupid grin, he asked me, "Can we go out once in a while and have a good breakfast…? I'll buy."

"Give me back the seven dollars you owe me," I told him with my hand out. As I laughed at him, I added, "Sounds like a good idea. I still would like to meet Jake and see if he can tell me what happened to our father. Once I find that out, I can put him to rest."

He asked, "Sounds like a plan…. Tell me about our grandmother?"

I gave him a description of her. I explained she was a stubborn woman who stuck by her convictions. Thinking back to my first few years with her, I told him a few stories. I had already told him about her giving me the diary, so I didn't have to tell him that again. Then it hit me, and I told him, "Now I know what she was going to tell me when I finished the diary."

With a questioning look he asked, "What's that?"

"She was going to tell me about you," I explained.

"I'm surprised, she didn't tell you…and me sooner. I would have liked to have known I had a brother," he said with a tear in his eye. Then wiping his eyes, he grinned and added "I guess the secret she was holding back from me is the diary."

"As I said earlier, you can read it any time you want," I told him.

"I might just start tonight…, if you don't mind, brother," he said.

"No, I don't mind. As brothers we've have already had some major experiences in the past week or so. I doubt if there's many brothers who can match what we've been through," I reminded him with a chuckle as I thought about it.

"I could have done without the bullets. Are we ready to go…? I have supper to fix," he reminded me as he got up from the table.

"Don't forget who has a bullet hole in him," I reminded him as I got up.

"I have a funny feeling you'll remind me of that for a long time," he said, letting me pick up the tab. Then, to rub it in, I told him, "And who do you think picked the tab up in Calistoga?"

"I was wondering about that… Thanks," he said, continuing to let me catch the tab. With a chuckle, he reminded me, "You offered."

"Brother… I do get even," I replied. I went back and laid two dollars on the table. Catching up to him, I told him, "What are you waiting for? We have jobs to do."

"Yes, brother of mine," he said mimicking me.

"I hope you don't mind, but I like the idea of having a brother," I told him as we left the café.

"I like it myself…. It might be wise to keep that information to ourselves at the mission," he suggested.

On our way back to the mission, we did nothing but talk. He told me about his mother's death and a brief history of his life as a child. In turn, I told him about my life as an orphan, and I think he had a better life. In seriousness, he invited me to his home before I left the area. He wanted me to meet his family as well as them meet me.

We finally got back to the mission and found a couple of trucks in front. Curious we picked up our pace and ran into the building. Seeing Carl, I told him, "Sorry it took us so long…, what's going on outside?"

"A surprise," Carl answered with a sly grin.

"Someone's in the Kitchen" Bill announced.

"Oh, you won't have to worry about supper," Carl told him. Then seeing Bill's disappointed look, he added, "I am going to hire you full-time. You can teach John how to cook."

"Thank you… I'm looking forward to working with John. I have a feeling he wants to learn," Bill said with a wink to me.

"Now tell us… What's going on?" I asked Carl again.

"One of our sponsors is treating all of us to steaks," he answered.

Carl never told me, but I had the feeling Jake picked up the tab. I didn't care if he did or not, the steaks and baked potatoes tasted good. I got the feeling everyone enjoyed their supper. I found the steak wasn't as good as the cheesecake. I was wishing Martha were there to enjoy it with me.

Later, that evening I found Bill propped against the wall watching television. Not interested in the program everyone was watching, I read our fathers diary. Skimming the pages, I was in hope of finding something about Bill in it. It took me a while but finally I found something interesting:

> *I did it again. A group of us went to a friend's party. There were a little pot and booze available. Everyone was having a good time. To make the evening even better I met a beauty of a woman. We shared a joint and danced the night away. We finally found an empty bedroom and had our own party.*

A few months later Susan looked me up and gave me the bad news. She told me she was two months along. It blew me away hearing her news. I first questioned her if she thought the child was mine. She assured me she hadn't seen anyone after that one night at the party. I couldn't argue, and I wanted to make it right by her. We got into her car and headed to Tahoe, and a justice of the peace married us. There are those that can marry, but others that should never think about it. All we had in common was the joint we shared. With that one joint, we were to have a child. I saw her occasionally before I left, but I never lived with her. Our son was the cutest baby I have ever seen. In playing with him my memories of that woman and her daughter in Vietnam never came to me. I found myself feeling guilty for not going back to Janis and getting to know my first son.

If I were to think before I did something rather than afterwards, maybe I wouldn't be such an ass. People wonder why I don't socialize any more than I do. My son William is a good example of why I don't. It irritates me that I don't know my first son's name. I hope someday both of my boys will forgive a stupid old man.

"Here…. You wanted to read the diary. Try the right-hand page," I told Bill as I handed the diary to him.

CHAPTER NINE

"It's that time," I announced as I shook Bill awake.

"What," he asked as he rolled over.

"Oatmeal time," I added as I got up to go to the restroom. When I came back into the barracks, I found he was still asleep. With a chuckle, I returned to the restroom, for a glass of water. Then taking back to his bedside, I let the water drip onto his face.

"Go away.... Peg and I are having too much fun," he replied with a snort.

Dumping the full glass on him, I told him, "Get your ass out of that bed.... You have some men waiting for their oatmeal."

"All right.... I'm getting up," he finally answered.

As he rose from the cot, I got the feeling, he wanted to kill me. I politely backed away from him and asked him, "I think I'll get some coffee..., do you want some?"

As he hung one leg over the side of the bed he asked, "Do you want to wear it?"

"I'll leave now," I said, leaving the room. I found myself laughing remembering wanting a brother, who I could pull pranks on. I remembered having woken my grandmother as I had done to him, and she almost killed me. As I looked at him, I had a feeling that I was lucky to have survived, and as my reward, I laughed like hell.

Entering the dining room, I saw Mike sitting alone. He had a couple of books and papers in front of him. I found myself thinking how unobservant I had been over the previous two weeks. I hadn't realized that he was putting in more than eight hours a day at the mission. Then seeing how young he was I wondered why he was working so many hours. I thought I would go over and ask him.

With my cup of coffee, I walked over to his table. As I approached him, I asked him, "Mind if I join you?"

"No.... Have a seat," he answered. With a smile, he pushed some of the papers to one side.

"Hope I'm not bothering you.... You seem to be busy," I told him.

"No..., I'm just getting caught up on some homework," he answered.

Surprised by his answer I asked, "Homework...? you mean you're a college student?"

"Morning," Bill said, greeting Mike and giving me a dirty look.

"What did you do to make him mad?" Mike asked as he looked back at Bill.

"Woke him up with some water in his face... I knew the men would be getting up soon and wanting breakfast," I answered.

"I would have gotten it," he said, turning back to me.

"I know... I just wanted to be mean to someone. What's this studying you're doing?" I asked.

"Oh, yeah.... I feel as if I've been going to college forever. Working your way through takes a while...," he said. He cut his answer short when one of the men walked into the dining room. Then turning back to me, he added, "...I'm trying to get a teaching degree in mathematics.... If that's not enough I'm getting information on a book about my father."

"Are you saying your father lived here?" I asked him. The idea of another orphan looking for his father intrigued me.

"Oh, he wasn't like most of these men.... He lived here for a while when he got out of the service. He had never had any goals other than joining the service. Then after two tours in Vietnam, he decided the service wasn't for him.... Then he found this place," he told me.

"What happened?" I asked, finding a need to hear the rest of the story.

Laughing, he told me, "He got into the wrong crowd; drinking, smoking, and all of that…. He even got into some petty stuff and served three days here and there in jail. Then he ended up here, and his life changed."

I asked him "How did his life change?"

"Well…. Needing money, he began panhandling. Then, coming back here, he found the men disgusting, and it frightened him. He found himself becoming like the men around him. To fight it, he went back to school and got his high school diploma. He was here during that time of his life. In being around these men he went on to college and got his degree in psychology with the intent of helping people like them."

I went on to ask him "Did he reach his goal?"

With a grin, he answered, "Yes…, and became successful in his field. He's now teaching at the university."

"Why don't you live at home…? Even better than that, why isn't your father helping you?" I asked. If his father was that important, he should be helping his son.

"He wanted to help me…. Like him I'm stubborn and want to make my own way no matter what it takes. Then, living here off and on gives me material for the book I want to write. I have a feeling a man can make something of himself no matter what happens. My father is a good example, and I think people need to know he did it…, and they can do it also."

"That's a commendable thought… It's nice to see a man proud of his father," I told him as I drank my coffee.

He asked me, "What about your father?"

"He was also a guest here…," I answered, and I told him rest of the story.

"That's during the same time my father was here," he said excitedly.

"They must have known each other then," I commented. Excitement began to run through me thinking he might have known mine. I asked him, "Are you going to be seeing your father in the next day or two?"

"With this being my day off, we're having supper together tonight. Then after supper I'll be going to my apartment," he answered.

I reached into my pocket and pulled out the picture of my father. Handing it to him, I asked him, "If you would, see if he recognizes this man."

As he looked at the picture he asked, "Your father, I take it?"

"That's him," I answered.

"What's going on?" Bill asked as he walked up to the table.

Not wanting the full story to come out, I answered, "Mike's father was here the same time my father was here.... I'm letting him take my father's picture to his to see if he recognizes him."

"That's interesting," Bill replied. Then sitting beside me, he asked, "Where's Mike's father now?"

I gave him a shortened version of Mike and his father's story. I could see Bill's interest in the possibilities grow. With a shrug I told him, "Might turn into nothing, but I have to explore every avenue."

"I can understand that.... Maybe something will come of it," Bill replied.

"If you don't mind, I think I had better be off to school," Mike said as he gathered his materials.

"I think I can handle this," I assured him with a gesture of my hand to the empty room.

"Only with my help," Bill told him as he got up and headed for the coffee urn.

"Don't forget the picture," I reminded Mike as I handed it to him.

"Won't... I was going to slip it into my pocket. I'm sure my father is going to be as excited seeing it as you are him seeing it. He's always wondering what happened to the men here," he assured me.

"If you find any teachers over there for Jeff..., send them by," Bill told him as he took his seat.

"See you in a couple of days," Mike said as he left us to our own conversation.

"The oatmeal is waiting," Bill told me.

"Think I'll pass this morning," I told him as I thought of the possibilities in Mike's father.

"I wonder if he remembers dad." Bill said as he brought his cup to his lips.

As an old man walked past us, he asked Bill "Maple or plain?"

"A surprise," Bill answered. Then turning to me, he told him, "I slipped a little applesauce into it this morning."

"Getting fancy," I answered, complimenting him. Then, thinking about his question about Mike's father, I added, "We might not learn anything from Mike's father, but it can't hurt to meet with him."

"It's better than doing nothing," he said, agreeing with me. Then, reaching into his pocket, he pulled his hand out and asked, "Have some change…? I think I should call Bertha and tell her I won't be looking for a job."

"That's nice of you…, but you are getting expensive," I said as I got up to pull some change out for him. Then, noticing what he was wearing, I looked at what I was wearing. I told him, "You know what? I think it's time to get rid of these fatigues."

"Whatever… You're a big boy now," he said as he headed for the payphone.

Going into the barracks, I saw most of the men getting dressed for breakfast. Right behind me was the man from the dining room with a big smile on his face. I moved to one side to let him by.

The man announced, "You should try out the oatmeal this morning… I haven't had a breakfast like that since I was a kid."

"We're coming," one man told him as he looked around at the others.

I went over to my cot and began to undress. As I took the fatigues off, I put them into my bag. Pulling a pair of jeans and a shirt out of the bag, I found my mood improving. I didn't normally wear jeans, but it was more acceptable than the fatigues I had been wearing. Feeling better, I began thinking about going for a walk in the neighborhood and see if the people would treat me differently. Tucking my bag under the cot, I went back out to the dining room.

Bill looked up from a newspaper and smiled at me. Then setting the paper down, he told me, "If you were to get rid of the sling you would look human."

"Thanks," I replied. Thinking about his comment about the sling, I looked at it. My arm wasn't anything like it had been, and I wondered if I could get away without it. I realized my arm was a little stiff as I slid my arm out of it, but it didn't feel that bad. It didn't hurt so I decided I could do without the sling. I saw Bill look at me, and I asked him, "Is that better?"

"Now put it around your head and it will be an improvement," he answered as he finished reading the paper.

As I took a seat I asked, "What's your problem?"

"I need to visit my wife and son," he said.

"Why don't you leave?" I asked him. I went through the same problem when Martha and I first separated. I took a while before I could accept the idea of sleeping alone. I hadn't gotten to the point where I liked it, but I did accept it.

"I can't.... Even though I promised grandma I would look after you, I want to find the same answers," he told me.

"I'll let you know what I find out," I told him. He had another place to go to, and I understood that. I wished I could go somewhere other than the mission myself.

"I want to be here if there's any excitement," he explained.

"Go home for the night and come back in the morning," I suggested.

"I might do that.... My mother-in-law is there and my wife might like seeing me," he answered as he folded the paper up.

"Good morning gentlemen," Carl said, coming from the storeroom.

"Good morning," I said, offering him a seat at our table.

"I have to say those steaks were good," Bill, commented as Carl took a seat.

As I got up, I asked him "Want a cup of coffee?"

"Yeah…. Black," he answered. Then turning back to Bill, he added, "They were good."

Carrying two cups of coffee took me a minute or two. My left hand and arm couldn't manage the weight. I transferred the second cup into my other hand and was able to get back to the table. I sat the cups down and commented, "I have to agree supper was great last night."

"We have Jeff to thank for the steaks," Carl told us with a grin.

Not understanding, I asked him "Me…? How did I have anything to do with us getting steak for supper?"

"No idea… All I know is that it had something to do with you impressing Jake's friend…. He phoned and told me the crew was coming over. For some reason, he thought you needed a good supper to build up your hopes," he answered. Then, after sipping his coffee he added, "Thanks for the coffee… I would like to be the first to say you look better out of the fatigues."

"Thanks…. I owe you for telling me where the church's donation room was. Yes, I think I have worn them long enough," I said agreeing with him. Then with Bill grinning, I added, "I'm thinking about walking around the block. The attitude I got wearing the fatigues wasn't the best. I think I'll see if there is a change with me wearing this."

Bill asked me "Want me to come as your bodyguard?"

"Sure…. My arm isn't that good yet," I answered. Then turning to Carl, I told him, "We won't be long…. If you talk to Jake or his friend, tell them thanks… but I didn't deserve it."

"No problem…. I was planning to be here all-day anyway. Enjoy your walk," he said with a wave.

As he got up Bill asked him "Come to think of it…, was your wife mad at you?"

With a confused look Carl asked, "What do you mean?"

"Well, we have heard about her, but haven't ever seen her... I thought she might have come and had a steak with you last night. I know they had more than enough," Bill explained to him.

"To tell you the truth, she doesn't feel comfortable around you misfits," he answered.

"Jeff, did you hear that...? We're misfits," Bill said with a grin.

I asked him "And you think she's wrong?"

"No.... But not bad enough to miss a steak supper," Bill said.

"I would think after this many years I would have...," Carl began to tell us.

I interrupted him by telling him, "You don't have to explain... and he's only giving you a bad time."

"Yeah," Bill added with a wave to him.

"Boy, you know how to hurt a guy," I told him.

"I guess I wasn't thinking. I just thought his wife would have been here..., and with her not showing up I thought I would ask," he explained.

"Oh well, how about breakfast..., and I mean a real breakfast?" I asked him. I was hoping that he would forget my financial status.

"That sounds great. I'll even pick up the tab," he said, ruining my fun.

"Damn you.... I was going to stick you with the tab. With you offering to buy it takes the fun out of it," I replied as I dragged him along.

We only had to go back towards Mission and Fremont. I remembered the night that I walked to the mission, passing a couple of coffee shops that looked clean. I was looking forward to a good breakfast. The last one we had was in Calistoga, and I was in need of another. With the good food we have had, my taste buds wanted something other than oatmeal.

Our walk and breakfast didn't bring about a single stare or comment. A couple of women glanced our way, but that was about it. Even with the women, they weren't anything I would have looked at, so it wasn't worth it. We finished our breakfast and headed back to the mission. The only noticeable thing was that it was a nice day. As the young kid had mentioned the previous morning, the pigeons and gulls were out. It wasn't advisable to look up into the sky.

"How was your walk?" Carl asked us as we came through the front door.

"A couple of old ugly women checked Jeff out," Bill told him.

"They were checking Bill out, but they didn't want to be obvious," I added. Looking around I didn't see anyone, I asked him, "Anything happening around here?"

"As if you were a mind reader, I got a call," he answered.

"If you don't mind, I need to sit at a table…. My arm is killing me, and I don't want to wear that damn sling," I told him as I walked into the dining room.

He followed me into the room and told me, "Like I said I had a call from Jake."

I asked him "Did you give him my message?"

"Yes, and he said it was his problem," Carl answered. Then with a big smile he added, "It looks as if you won't have to wait until he comes back."

"What are you talking about?" I asked him.

"He's sending a car over tomorrow morning to pick you up. For some reason, he wants to talk to you… I have to warn you I gave him your name, and that you were looking for information about your father," he answered.

"No…, that's all right. In fact, that's great, I won't have to beat around the bush," I told him. With Bill sitting beside him, I could see him giving me a thumbs up.

"The place is yours. I have to make a few calls, and then the accountant is coming to go over the books for the state," Carl said as he got up.

"Better you than me," I told him as I motioned for him to go to his office.

"I wonder if I can go with you," Bill said.

"You go, or I stay here…. I don't see any problem. If nothing else, we'll tell whoever picks us up that we're brothers…. It will be the truth meaning you want information as much as I do," I suggested to him.

The rest of the day nothing happened worth mentioning. I did enjoy sitting back and having conversations with a couple of the residents. Each one of them asked if there was another surprise supper the preceding night. I had to be honest and told them Bill and John would be fixing our supper. Hearing that Bill was going to work in the kitchen took a load off my mind.

"Good afternoon," John said, coming into the dining room.

As he took a seat across from me, I asked him "How's it going?"

"All right, I guess… I talked to Carl last night," he told me.

"Oh…, what did he have to say?" I asked, not sure if it was about Bill's cooking.

"I guess it was good news…. He said Bill would be working with me, and I know I will learn a lot from him. On the other side of the coin, it doesn't mean Carl won't fire me in the next couple of days," he answered, a little nervous.

"Trust me… Bill doesn't want your job…. In fact, he only consented to work in the kitchen if Carl kept you on," I told him. A smile replaced the nervous expression he had when he heard what I had to say. I asked him, "Do you like to cook?"

"Yes…, I would like to become a chef someday," he said with a grin.

"You may get a surprise one day… I can't say anymore, but be patient, watch and learn," I suggested to him. I didn't know, but I thought Bill might take him to his restaurant and teach him how to cook. I figured I might have to plant the idea in his head, but he would.

"Hey, John… We're not getting supper cooked with you out there," Bill called out from the kitchen.

"I'd better get back there," he said, excusing himself.

"Remember… be patient, watch and learn," I said, reminding him.

"I will," he replied with the same smile as he headed for the kitchen.

I got up and followed him into the kitchen. Holding the door for John, I asked, "What's for supper?"

"Not steak," John answered. He was busy twisting and turning as he grabbed and placed pans on the stove.

"I'll let you two have your fun," I told them.

As I left them to their work, I heard Bill tell John, "…some rice and vegetables out."

Back out in the dining room Carl was coming from his office. I asked him, "Any more from Jake?"

"No. He normally calls every other month and sometimes longer…. In fact, I've heard more from him in the past week than I do in a year… Come to think of it, most of my conversations with him has been when he came by as a homeless person."

"Strange… I guess he can do whatever he wants. Some play poker and he comes here," I commented.

"That's about right," he replied with a smile. He then turned back to me and asked, "What are your feelings about visiting him?"

"Other than going somewhere I can't get back from… I'm looking forward to it," I told him.

"Well, I have to get out of here. With my wife having missed the steaks last night, I have to take her out tonight," he told me with a smile.

"And since you ate steak, you have to settle with soup," I added.

"Something, like that," he said as he headed for the front door. Turning back to me, he told me, "Charlie will be in later…. Once he gets here, your time is your own. See you in the morning."

"You too," I called back to him. Hearing the door close, I wondered what I was going to do with my free time. I would have rather gone to a movie or something, but I knew that was out of the question. All I had left was to go down the street with Bill and have a cup of coffee. Once I got back, I could read the diary. It didn't sound like an exciting night, but I didn't have much choice. Giving up the thought of a night off, I picked up the paper and read a few articles.

Tired of reading, I went over to the payphone. I dialed my calling card number and then Martha's phone number. I realized I was missing her as bad as Bill was missing his wife. I also owed it to my kids to let them know I was all right. I waited, and the phone rang four times without an answer. When the voice mail beeped, I left a message "I thought I would let you and the kids know I'm all right…. I miss you, and I'll call you later."

Hanging the phone up, an aroma hit me from the kitchen. Taking a deep breath, the aroma gave a message I couldn't believe. I headed for the kitchen to see if I was right. As I opened the door, the aroma was stronger. I asked the two men, "Chinese?"

"Doesn't that sound like it would be a good change…? I found some chicken but not enough to feed everyone. I tried to come up with a way to stretch it out so I thought… Chinese was a logical solution," he asked.

"Well Frisco's known for its Chinese cuisine," I replied as I shook my head in disbelief.

"Just trying to be fashionable," he said, giving me a smile.

"The food these guys have been getting has spoiled them… If Bill ever leaves, Carl will have a revolt on his hands," John added as he checked on a pot of rice. Taking a bite into his mouth, he nodded his head with a smile. He then put the lid back on and announced, "It's ready."

I looked at my watch and saw it was five-thirty. Feeling good about their job, I told them, "I'll tell them supper's ready."

"It'll be out shortly," Bill, told me.

As I stepped into the dining room, I heard someone ask, "Is Jeff around?"

"I'm right here," I answered. I turned around, and I saw it was Mike. Behind him, there was a man I didn't recognize. Unlike the men, I had been living with, he had on light gray slacks, jacket and white shirt, but no tie. With his white hair, I figured him in his late fifties or early sixties. I had to chuckle, knowing it was his father.

"Jeff this is my father Robert Kelly… Dad this is Jeff," Mike said, introducing the two of us.

"Jeff O'Connor, sir… A pleasure to meet you," I said with my hand out to him. As a resident passed me, I told him, "Let everyone know supper is ready."

"Right," the man answered.

"Jeff O'Connor is a name I'll never forget," Mr. Kelly told me as he shook my hand.

Off in the lobby Charlie was watching every move we made. I could see he wanted to ask questions, but he knew better. I turned back to Mike and his father and asked him, "What can I do for you? I wasn't expecting you to come here…. From what you said earlier the two of you were going out to supper."

"We'll still have supper, but this is a chance in a lifetime… I had to come and meet you," Mr. Kelly told me. Looking over at his son, he asked him, "What do you think of taking him to supper with us?"

"I don't have any problem with that," Mike answered with an understanding smile.

As he turned back to me, he asked, "What do you say?"

"I do have one request…, which I'll explain later," I told him.

Smiling, he asked, "What's that…, take everyone here with us?"

"No just one… Bill," I told him. With Bill being my brother, I didn't see any reason he couldn't be part of this find. Both of us were free for the evening with supper made and Charlie being here.

"Fine," he answered with a questioning look to his son.

"I'll be right back," I told them. I didn't worry about my arm hurting, and I let it swing as I ran to the kitchen. Going through the door, I found myself clutching my arm. It was hurting from one end to the other. I shouted to Bill, "Let John finish whatever there is to do…. We have to take off for a while."

He asked, "Calm down… What's going on?"

"Get out of here and you'll find out," I told him.

"Trust me, I can handle it," John assured him.

"I guess nothing can go wrong now… I've cooked everything already, and you can serve it anytime you want…. John, it's all yours,"

Bill told him as he took off his apron. Then as he pushed the door open he asked, "What's going on?"

"Mike's father is out there, and he's taking us out to supper.... Probably, for a burger and fries, so he can get some information," I answered.

With him pushing me to one side, he asked me, "What are we waiting for?"

"You…, you fool," I replied as I held my arm, trying to keep up with them. Mike and his father were smiling as we got to them.

Mr. Kelly asked, "Are we ready?"

"We're as ready as we'll ever be," I told him.

"Wish I had something better on than this… It's a case of a limited wardrobe," Bill told Mr. Kelly.

"I know just the place…. It's across town, but you'll fit right in," Mr. Kelly told him as we walked out the front door.

Bill and I took the backseat as the Kelly's got into the front. As Mr. Kelly started the engine and pulled out from the curb, he pulled into the lane, telling us, "I have never been as surprised as when Mike showed me your father's picture."

"Our father's picture," I corrected him.

Mike had a questioning look on his face. He asked, "Are you telling me the two of you are brothers?"

"It's a long story…, but we just realized we were brothers yesterday," Bill added with a smile.

"This is getting more and more interesting," Mr. Kelly said as he kept his eyes on traffic.

Traffic was a little hectic so there wasn't much talking going on. I looked over at Bill, and he had a worried look on his face. I asked him, "What's wrong?"

"We'll see," he answered, as he continued to look out the window. Then after we had traveled, a few blocks he asked, "What restaurant are we going to?"

"A place I haven't been to in a year or two… I don't know why because it's always been my favorite place," he answered.

"What's the name of it?" Bill asked.

"Ironically it's called…," Mr. Kelly started to tell him.

"Let me guess… It's Billy's," Bill offered as he interrupted him.

"How did you guess?" Mike asked.

"A wild guess… I guess I'm buying supper," Bill replied.

"That doesn't mean what I think it does, does it?" I asked him.

"Oh no, it was my invite," Mr. Kelly told him.

After a little pause and a shrug, Bill told him, "But it's my restaurant. I can't have supper there without picking up the bill."

Mr. Kelly turned around for a second and told us, "Honestly. I didn't know…. We can go somewhere else."

"That's all right…. I've been missing the place anyway," Bill assured him as he slid into the seat. Then, seeing me silently laughing, he swung a mock punch at me.

"I'm sorry, but I think it's ironic," I said apologetically to him.

"What are you saying?" Mr. Kelly asked.

"Such as running into people that knew our father…. Then I learn a man I had just met at the mission is my brother. With all of that, why not go to Bill's restaurant," I answered him. Then glancing over at Bill, I added, "It all fits."

"I guess it does," Mike added.

As we drove along, I found I had a good idea where we were. I got the feeling that Bill's place was near the Wharf. Thinking back, I couldn't remember a place called Billy's but I had gone to the wharf. I wasn't aware of any restaurants off the wharf.

"Will I get to meet your wife?" I asked Bill. With him taking time to watch over me, it made sense, she might be running the place. Slapping his knee, I added, "I now wish I was a little more dressed up than I am. I wasn't too worried before."

"Trust me it doesn't matter," he assured me.

I wasn't sure what he meant, but I sat back and waited for us to arrive. It wasn't long, and I could make out the wharf area. Mr. Kelly made a left and went around a block. He pulled into a parking lot, and I knew we had arrived. With a grin and another slap on Bill's knee I announced, "I think we have arrived."

"That we have," Mr. Kelly said with a smile.

I got out, and I looked around. All the people coming and going out to the place impressed me. Men were wearing shorts, jeans, or slacks, allowing me to fit right in. I asked Bill, "Will we find your wife without searching?"

"You mean is she gorgeous…. Yes, she is," he answered with a smile.

"What does she see in you?" I asked as he held the door open for us.

"A chance to go out to eat for nothing," he answered with a smile.

"I knew it had to be something," I replied as I walked past him. It wasn't hard to spot his wife. She was holding four menus in her hands. Looking up, she saw Bill and her body froze. I walked over to her and told her, "Hi Teri. I'm Jeff, Bill's half-brother."

Limply, she held her hand out and said, "I'm glad to meet you… I didn't expect to see him for a while."

"I suggested for him to come home for a night…. Then Mr. Kelly invited us out to supper…," I began to tell her. I stopped talking when I saw her attention being on Bill and not me. I wasn't much for women with black hair, but Bill's wife was different. She was every inch as beautiful as Martha was. I couldn't wait for the two of them to be in the same room.

"Hi, Hon," she said greeting her husband, ignoring me.

"Next," someone shouted out.

"Don't think so buddy…, some things are not on the Menu," Bill told the guy as he let his wife go.

"It was just an idea," the man said with a grin to his friends.

"Teri…. Why don't you join us and let Mary cover for you," Bill suggested.

"I guess she could…. If you think it's all right," she told him as she motioned to someone to join her. She then turned to the customers gathered in the entryway and told them, "We'll be right with you."

"Better be… I'm picking up the tab," he told her as he smiled at all of us. Then, turning to Mr. Kelly, he asked him, "Do you mind, Mr. Kelly?"

"I don't see any reason not to invite her," he answered with a smile.

"Yes, Mrs. O'Connor," a young girl said coming up to Teri.

"Mary, the boss is giving me a dinner break…. Take over for me would you," Teri told her as she handed the young woman the menus. She then told her, "We'll take table fifteen."

"Yes Mrs. O'Connor," Mary said with a smile. Then turning to the customers, she asked "How many in your party?"

Shaking her head, Teri picked up four more menus. With them in her hands, she followed us to the table. As we walked through the dining room, I saw they were doing good business. Of the two or three dozen tables, only three were empty. From the looks on the customers' faces everyone was enjoying their experience in Billy's. I commented to Bill, "Looks like you're doing all right here."

"We're managing…. I think it's Teri's charm that brings them in," he said, turning back to me with a smile.

"I can understand that…. I've eaten your cooking," I replied.

"The two of you even sound like brothers," Teri said as she took the seat Bill was holding for her.

Bill introduced his wife to Mike and his father. Then, with the waiter coming to our table, I was glad to see Bill order a Martini. As I sat back, I ordered my usual Seven and Seven. I nudged him and asked him, "I thought you were on the wagon?"

"Like you, I've been playing a part," he answered with a smile.

It wasn't long, and he offered a few choices that weren't on the menu. Mr. Kelly declined in favor of his favorite. Mike followed suit in ordering the same as his father. Bill, Teri, and I had Beef Wellington. I figured that if he was picking up the tab, I was going to have a good meal. We had settled down to talk when our drinks arrived.

"Could Teri see the picture of our father?" Bill asked.

"I'm sorry… I meant to give it back to Jeff…. Here, you are Ma'am," Mr. Kelly said pulling the picture out of his jacket.

"He sure looks like Jeff back then," Teri comments.

"As Mike can tell you. I didn't know how to react when I saw you lying on that bed…. You looked so much like your father it was scary. When I heard his son was at the mission, it was even a bigger shock…, now I find there are two boys. I sense there's an interesting story here," he told her. Then, sipping his drink, he looked at me.

"I would like to hear this story," Mike said, looking at Bill and me.

Bill and I looked at each other, and I got the feeling it was up to me to tell them our story. I started by saying, "With me being I'm the older of the two of us…, and the one that started it all, I guess it's up to me. It began about two and a half weeks ago when…,"

"You should have seen the expression on Bill's face when his grandmother called him. Just talking to her was a big enough surprise…. With the mouthpiece of the phone covered, he was screaming with excitement. Then she told him he had a brother…that he almost lost it. Thankfully, he was standing next to a chair when he dropped," Teri told us.

"It wasn't that I had a brother…, as much as learning, that I was the youngest. All my life I've been the king. Now I had an older brother making me the pipsqueak in the family," Bill added.

"And you make for a good pipsqueak," I assured him.

"I'm not sure if I'm ready for this banter," Teri replied with a big smile. From the look on her face, she was happy. She leaned over and gave her husband a kiss on the cheek.

Two weeks at the mission and I felt I had left the normal world. Now being where I was, I found the hustle and bustle of the place exciting. The problem was this was an important get-together and everything going on around me was distracting. To keep with the program, I asked Mr. Kelly, "Please…. Tell us about our father."

"No problem… I owe him, for who and what I am today…," he began telling us. Then with the waiter setting our orders in front of us, he stopped his narration. Once the waiter moved around the table he added, "As I was about to say. When I got to the mission..., I have to say I had my share of problems. As with my friends, I had come back feeling proud of what we tried to do in Vietnam.... To be honest, I wasn't proud of everything I did or was a part of that happened in Nam. There were many memories I needed to forget. I got back to Frisco expecting everyone to be proud of us, and we would be accepted as heroes... When I stepped out into the real world, I found that wasn't the case. If I had an idea what I was going to do with my life, it might not have been so bad. The rejections kept those memories of the war part of my everyday life. There was no way of putting them to the back of my mind. I couldn't find work or anyone that would have anything to do with me. The only ones I could associate with were other veterans with the same problem. Those with families and jobs waiting for them didn't have it as bad... You have to believe in Nam, we did what they ordered us to do and nothing else. The mission was the only place there was for a person as messed up as I was. That's when I met your father...." He paused to take a bite of his meal.

Like everyone else, my interest was more in his story than eating. Our meal was getting cold, and our drinks were melting. I followed his example, cut into my Beef Wellington, and took a taste of it.

"That's as good, if not better than I remembered," Mr. Kelly said with a satisfied look.

"I'll let my kitchen know that sir," Bill said with a smile of pride.

"Thank God, he didn't come last night," I heard Teri say softly to him.

"The best I've ever had.... Beef Wellington, is Martha's favorite dish," I added.

"Tell us rest of the story," Mike told his father.

"All right.... As I was saying, I got to the mission in rough shape... Now I don't mean to scare you, but your dad was in rougher shape than I was. It didn't take much to make him mad. I got to the point I would move if he got anywhere near me...," he said, starting again. As he paused, he looked down at his plate and took another bite of his steak.

I lost my interest in eating when I heard what he had to tell us. With tears forming in my eyes, I was glued to his every word. I found a knot in my stomach that I couldn't get rid of. I didn't want to hear that my father was so bad people would run from him. As different thoughts came to mind, the worst was thinking my mother might have been better off without him.

"As I was saying he wasn't anyone I wanted any part of. I felt I had enough problems as a dozen people, and I didn't need his…. I don't remember what happened, but I found myself talking to him…. As days went by, our conversations became to go into more personal things. Then over a few months, we finally became friends. I learned he had a lot of guilt he couldn't shake off. If I knew, then what I know now I might have been some help to him…. The last time I talked to him was thirty some years ago; he thanked me for helping him. I have no idea what I said or did, but he was thankful… I think that, in reality, I was the one that benefited the most from that friendship," he told us as he went back to his supper.

"We had better start eating before it gets too cold to enjoy," Teri suggested.

"Sorry about being so long winded," Mr. Kelly said apologetically.

"Don't get me wrong…. I want to hear the rest of the story. I was just thinking of the food….Sorry," Teri said with an apologetic look.

"If I were paying for this meal, I might be concerned about it. With Bill doing the paying for it, I'll take whatever I can get… and there'll be other meals," I added with a smile to Bill.

"Not after I get my hands on you," he added with a phony grin.

"Anyway, as I was saying…. I think I got the best out of the deal… It didn't take long for me to learn he had a brilliant mind. Looking back, I think that was his biggest problem. He felt everything should go his way, or it didn't happen… I guess you could say he thought out of the box. His thinking process left no room for anyone else…. One of his brilliant ideas was to get me back in school. He kept harping that I didn't want to become like him and the others. I told him he had to find some way of changing himself. I suggested for him to call himself "J." I also suggested for him not to tell anyone he had been in the service. To all of that I added that he shouldn't talk to other vets about Nam," he told us.

"I thought the men that I knew at the mission had problems.... Your father seemed as many as all of them put together," Mike commented.

In a shortened version Mike told me as much. I had finally got to the point where I could eat and listen while he told the story. I had a feeling there was more to the story, but there wasn't time. I was waiting to hear what happened to my father after the mission.

As he wiped his mouth, Mr. Kelly told us, "He began to change when he decided he wasn't going to talk about Nam. When he decided to go by "J," he became a new person. Then with a name change, came a constant smile and a sense of focus. He began getting work and had a positive outlook on life. He would come back from his job laughing about what happened that day. I was going to night school and trying to find work during the day. We didn't get to see much of each other until I got my high school diploma," he told us with a big grin.

"I take it was then that you went to college," Bill said, sipping his drink.

The waiter asked, "Can I get you anything else?"

"Another drink.... My wine found an empty bottom," I said being the first to answer.

Bill asked me, "No dessert?"

"No room," I replied.

Everyone else placed their orders, and Mr. Kelly went on with his story, "As I was saying, I had gotten my diploma. Once I had it, I thought I could go out and get a job.... Then your father jumped all over me and said I needed to get a college degree. I laughed at him and continued to look for work. The more I looked the more disappointed I became. One interviewer said I should get a college degree, and I might have a better chance in finding a job..., and Jeff had been saying that all along. At his suggestion of using the GI bill, I went off to college."

I asked, "What about our father?"

"Well during that last couple of months of the summer I didn't see much of him. From what he told me he was happy with the job that he had. He never told me much about it, and I knew he didn't like me asking questions, about his life… Before I went off to college, we sat up all-night talking about various subjects.Our main topic of discussion was how we had changed each other. He convinced me to go into medicine. That night we parted with a handshake, and a thank you…. One summer I rode down with a friend at Berkley to see him. I found he had moved out of the mission some months earlier, and no one knew where to… I have always wondered what happened to him. I would like to thank him for the life he gave me. If it wasn't for him, I wouldn't have the son I have," he said finishing his story.

"Damn," I muttered.

He asked, "What…. Did I say something wrong?"

"No… Just I was in hopes you could tell us what happened to him," I replied, with a feeling of disappointment. I prayed Jake wouldn't pan out as Mr. Kelly had.

"I'm sorry…. At least I have gotten to know he has two successful sons. I have enjoyed this evening. I haven't told anyone this story for a long time. If you ever do find your father, tell him I would like to see him," he told us. Then, reaching for his wallet, he pulled out a business card and handed it to me. With a smile, he added, "If you see him give him my card."

"Rest assured if I ever do find him, I'll give this to him," I promised him as I put the card in my pocket.

He asked, "What's your plan now?"

"I think it's time to pull the plug…. It was a neat idea, and I have learned a lot about him. I have also learned I have a brother, and that is something I didn't expect. Even more important, I have learned more than I thought I would, and it wasn't about him. I've learned even more about myself…. I need to see my ex-wife and my kids. I don't know if we'll ever get back together again, but at least I can be a better father to my kids," I answered.

He asked, "So you're headed home?"

"I also had the pleasure of hearing from a grandmother I have never known," Bill added.

"I do have one appointment tomorrow…, and then I'll be leaving," I replied as I sat back and downed my drink. I knew I had gotten to the point I didn't care if I found or learned anymore about my father. I wanted to go home to see Martha and my kids. Even more than that, I wanted to talk to Martha. I wanted to tell her what an ass I had been and apologize.

"Let's get you home," he offered as he got up.

"Stay where you are and enjoy your son…. Teri can take us back," Bill told him as he rose from the table.

"You're not coming home?" Teri asked with a surprised look on her face.

"A commitment is a commitment. Now that I've gotten to know my brother, I feel a greater need to go the distance even if it's only for one more day," he reminded her. With a concerned look, he added, "I may not see my brother for a while."

"Oh, you'll be seeing me…. I'm going to need some help to get home," I replied.

"I guess I could loan you the fifty dollars for bus fare," he offered.

"Thanks… I'll call Martha or Ray and have one of them book me a flight," I told him.

"Thanks for supper," Mr. Kelly said, standing up offering his hand to us.

"Thank you…. I learned something tonight about our father," I replied as I shook his hand.

"Yes, thanks and it was my pleasure…. Come back any time and your meal is on the house… A friend of dad's is part of our family," Bill told him.

"Thank you," he said with a smile.

"Let's go," I suggested. Teri drove us back in silence. She looked at her husband and then back at me. I finally got my tongue out of my ass and told her, "Bill is a lucky man…. Thank you for letting him come to my aid… He might not have stopped a bullet, but he was there."

"A bullet…? I haven't heard about that," she screamed out.

"Big mouth," Bill said. Then turning to his wife, he promised her, "Tomorrow night I'll tell you all about it."

"I'm not sure if I'm going to let you spend another night at that place," she told him.

"It didn't happen there," he told her.

We finally got back and I was glad. Even though the cot wasn't comfortable, it was mine. Charlie greeted me with a smile as I walked into the place.

"Have a message for you," he said handing me a slip of paper.

"Thanks," I replied, taking it from him. The number on it belonged to Martha's cell phone. Fear began to run through me seeing the number. There had to be a problem with one of our kids. I couldn't imagine her calling for any other reason. I ran to the pay phone and dialed her number.

I found everything going through my mind as I waited for her to answer. The worst was that something had happened to one of the kids. At first, I thought she might have been returning my call, but she would have done that on the house phone. With her using her cell phone, it worried me. Finally, she answered, "What's up…. Yes, I'm all right. I need to see you and have a little talk with you…. No this isn't the time and place for what I need to discuss with you…. What do you mean in the morning?"

"What?" I shouted out feeling embarrassed about my outburst, I looked around to see if anyone saw me. Then back to the phone, I asked her, "Did I hear you right…, that you're here in Frisco…? Oh, my God…. I love you. I have so much to tell you and the kids…I would love to, but it's getting late…"

I told her about Jake and my need to see him. I told her I would see her the following afternoon, and I had a surprise for her. She kept bugging me and I finally told her, "I have a brother… Oh, so she told you… I guess, it isn't a surprise then. At least, we might be able to spend some time in town and visit with them…. All right, I'll see you tomorrow and give the kids my love."

"What was that all about?" Bill asked from a table behind me.

"Martha and the kids are in town," I told him. I wasn't sure if he had heard any of the conversation so I added, "I told her that we might be able to come over and get to know each other."

"Of course," he returned with a smile.

"I told her a little about you and our meeting with Jake in the morning. I explained why we want to see him, and that I wanted to see her also. I promised I would call her when we get back… It's a little too late now," I told him.

"This is going to be better than I could have hoped for," he replied as he got up go to our cots.

I hadn't told him I had offered his home to my family to stay at for a week or so. As I remembered it, I should have told him, but after hemming and hawing around, I couldn't tell him. I decided that Martha, my kids and I would stay at a hotel and visit Bill and his family when we could. To my delight, he said we didn't have to get a hotel room, and that we could stay at his place. He said it would give us more time to visit. I went to sleep that night feeling happy for the first time since I arrived at the mission. For the first time in weeks, everything was going right, or at least I thought it was.

CHAPTER TEN

"Jeff…. Get up" a voice said.

I heard the voice off in the dark reaches of my mind, and I thought it was a nightmare. I woke a little and knew I was tossing and turning trying to shake it.

"Jeff…we have a problem" the voice said.

This time I knew it wasn't a dream. I figured it was Bill playing a practical joke, and I slowly opened my eyes trying to get up the energy to punch him. Once I had my eyes open, I saw Jay standing beside my cot. He offered to fill in on the night shift for us. I hadn't foreseen any problems, so I didn't worry. I asked, "What's going on?"

"We have a problem…. I've called the police all ready," he answered.

I sat up and asked, "What's wrong?"

I looked around, and I didn't see Bill in his cot. I was thinking Jay had woken him first. I looked at the clock on the wall, and it said 1:30 AM.

"I found Cory dead in the bathroom…. He was stabbed," Jay finally answered.

I didn't get to say anything before I heard sirens. What he had told me took me back a little, but I knew I didn't have time to ask questions. I told him "I had better get some pants on…. You had better take care of Frisco's finest."

"All right" he replied as he turned to go out front.

As I rummaged around for my pants, I tried to remember who Cory was. Then as I found my pants, I remembered a man moving in the day before and a brief introduction. I felt better having remembered him, but now as to what happened to Bill. I prayed nothing had happened to him as I finished zipping up my pants.

I went out front to the entry area and Jay was talking to a couple of officers. As I came through the door, he turned and motioned for me to join them.

"This is Jeff O'Connor our Assistant Manager," Jay said in introducing me to the officers.

"Good morning" as I offered my hand.

"This is Lieutenant Osborne and Sergeant Franks," Jay told me.

Neither officer took my hand, but they did nod their heads at me. I told everyone "I had better give Carl, a call."

Lieutenant Osborne asked, "Carl is the manager?"

"Jay knows more about what has gone on around her for the past few hours than I do," I answered. To my surprise, neither officer seemed to object when I walked off.

I found myself looking around the Dining room in hopes that Bill was there. I didn't see him, so I grabbed the phone and gave Carl a call. The phone rang a number of times before he answered. When he finally did, and heard the news, he had a number of questions once I got him awake, but I didn't know that much myself. I hung up with the knowledge he was on his way. I turned around and went back to Jay and the officers.

Jay was saying, "...wake them up for you."

"I bet it will be a waste of time" the Sergeant replied.

"You might as well wake them, so we can get it over with," the Lieutenant said. Before Jay could go into the dorm he asked, "And where is the body…. I need to check that area out first?"

"Through the dorm in the restroom" Jay told him.

"Make sure no one goes back there," the Lieutenant told Officer Franks.

"Carl will be here in a few minutes," I told the three. Jay nodded his head in understanding but the officers just went on their way. I found myself thinking, 'Yeah, why worry about what happens in a Shelter… We're nothing but bums.'

Before I could get very far a couple of men with a gurney came inside. The gurney was bouncing around making enough noise to wake the dead. On top of it laid a body bag. The look on the two men's faces was similar to zombies, and I wanted to laugh. They didn't smile or show any expression, but their blank eyes told me what they wanted. I didn't say anything to them, but I did point the way for them. They automatically went through the door not saying thank your or anything.

As the last one went through the door I muttered, "I don't mind…. I'll shut the door for you."

In the other room, I could hear men grumbling. I knew how they felt having to get up out of a sound sleep. If they had thought about it as much as I had, they would have realized they probably wouldn't be getting to sleep any time soon. If I could have had my wish, I would have liked to have taken a nap, with what Bill and I had going on later that day. Though I felt sorry for the man, I had my own problems. One of the things I was looking forward to was seeing my wife and kids. There was also the meeting with our father's friend that I was beginning to feel apprehensive about doing. Though I had gone through a lot of work to find him, I knew in my heart that he wasn't the man I was looking for.

I wanted to go in back and see what was going on, but I wasn't interested. I had seen enough crime shows and had seen their interpretations to have an idea. I went back into the dining room and checked the coffeepot. To my surprise, there was some left, and I poured myself a cup. When I saw Jay walk in shaking his head I asked, "Want a cup… I think there's enough?"

"I'll get it and make a pot…. I have a feeling, we'll need it before this is, over" he replied looking disgusted.

I asked him, "What's wrong?"

"It's just their attitudes. They don't seem upset or really care a man was stabbed," he answered. Not adding anything he unplugged the coffeepot and poured himself a cup.

"Keep in mind they think of us as worthless bums… and then they see murders every day. I would find it hard for them not to be cold to all of it. If they didn't feel that way they would go nuts," I added.

"I know but it's just the idea. Cory might have been on the skids and old, but he was alive…and I feel sorry for him," he said going into the kitchen.

"He wasn't that old. I believe he was telling Carl and me he had just turned fifty-nine last month" I said correcting him. I wanted to laugh because Jay was in his twenties as I did at that age anyone over fifty was old.

"He sure looked older than that," he said giving me a smile.

"I know…between a rough life and turning gray at a young age makes it hard to judge a person's age" I added.

I looked around and almost felt lost as well as being worried about Bill. I hadn't known him long but him being gone wasn't something I was used to. Then the memory of him saying he had a drinking problem came to mind. I looked up at the clock, saw it was almost 2:00 AM, and wondered if he was going to be coming in with booze on his breath. With it being closing time for the bars, he should be getting back soon. I shrugged my shoulders and decided he must have gone home to his wife. I felt a warm feeling thinking that it sounded like a good idea. With that thought, I wondered if Martha and I would ever get back together.

I heard the kitchen door open, but my attention was on the dorm area. I could see a couple of men walking around and a few sitting on their cots. From what I could see, they weren't any happier than I was being woken up as they had been. I wanted to shout out 'What's your problem you don't have a job to go to," but I didn't.

"This ought to hold us for a couple of hours," Jay announced as he came back into the dining area.

"I'm thrilled" I replied as I watched him plug in the coffeepot.

He picked up his cup and came over to join me at a table. As he sat down, I asked "Have you seen Bill?"

"I saw him a couple of hours ago as I went to the restroom as he was coming out here," he answered.

I asked, "Did he say anything to you?"

"Just that he couldn't sleep is all he told me. I didn't watch to see where he went," he said.

While we talked, the Sergeant went outside. He didn't even look in our general direction. It wasn't long before he came back inside, and he wasn't carrying anything special. As soon as he came in a man in a suit walked in carrying a case. I figured he was an investigator to take pictures and collect evidence. I didn't care as long as he would be done quickly so I could go back to sleep. I was about to open my mouth when Carl walked in.

He looked around and when he saw us, he came to the table. He asked, "Well what's happening?"

"I don't know much more than you do. Now Jay here has at least seen the body," I answered.

He turned and headed to the coffeepot. On his way over to it, he asked, "Well Jay what do you know?"

"I went to take a dump and found Cory slumped in the corner by the sinks. I called the police and woke Jeff up…the officers had me wake everyone up and told me they would get back to me," Jay answered.

"And I'm sure they are doing a crack job as they always do…and I was having such a sweet dream" Carl replied as he came back to us.

"And Bill's is missing" I added.

As he took a seat, he gave me a questioning look. I shrugged my shoulders and added, "I don't have any idea where he went. I know he was looking forward to going home, but he decided not to."

"I hope he wasn't involved with Cory" Carl replied.

"Wouldn't that make things interesting" I replied with a shiver. I hadn't known him that long so I couldn't say for sure what he was capable of doing. I didn't see any reason he would have killed the man, and it didn't seem to fit what I knew of him. My thoughts didn't get far for I saw the Lieutenant come into the room.

"I don't think we will be here much longer," he told us. He turned and walked back to the dorm.

"That was short and sweet," Carl said turning to watch the Lieutenant walk away.

I asked, "As we were questioning…. They are doing what kind of job?"

Before he could say anything, the front door opened. Three officers in uniforms wearing helmets and carrying batons walked it. They looked at us and around the dining room. Jay pointed to the dorm, and they turned and went in that direction.

"A talkative bunch" Jay replied as he turned back to us.

"Maybe they don't have anything worth saying," I suggested. As the words left my mouth, I heard the kitchen door open. Since everyone who would be going in and out of there was sitting at the table it startled me. I turned and saw Bill rubbing his eyes as he came towards us.

He asked, "What's going on out here?"

I asked, "A better question is, where have, you have been hiding?"

"I couldn't sleep so I thought I would write out some recipes for John. I went into the office to get some paper and sat at the desk and fell asleep," he answered with a yawn. He sat down and looked like he was going back to sleep.

I asked, "Want some coffee?"

He asked, "Do I have to…I would rather go back to sleep?"

As I got him some coffee, the other two filled him in. I didn't hurry to get back to the table because I didn't want to listen to it again. Like him, I wanted to go to sleep, and I didn't really care about anything else. What was going to happen later was my only interest.

"I think it might be time to move…It's getting too exciting for me around here," Bill said as I set his coffee down.

"I can't disagree with that idea. Right now, I would rather be with Martha yelling at me," I replied as I sat down.

"I would rather be with my wife hearing how she has missed me," he added with a smile.

"Both of you can take a flying leap" Carl commented.

I looked up, and I saw the coroner men taking the body out. I nodded to everyone that something was going on. I told them, "Hopefully it won't be much longer."

"That depends on them questioning everyone," Jay reminded me.

"Wake me when it's my turn," Bill told us as he laid his head on the table.

We talked for a while, but it was apparent none of us had anything worth saying. Carl finally got up and walked over to the door of the dorm. He turned and shrugged his shoulders as he came back to the table.

He sat down still shaking his head. He finally told us, "They talking to the kid in the corner."

Jay asked, "He's Chris isn't he?"

"I think so" I replied. In the short time, I had been there, men had come and gone. Only a few of them had I taken the time to get to know well enough to remember their names.

"If it's the kid I'm thinking his name is Chris," Bill added.

"Yes he's Chris…I'm not sure, but I think him and Cory were friends" Carl confirmed.

We sat there for a while longer not saying much. There was some scuffling around in the dorm but with that, many men in one room it wasn't surprising. Jay got bored, and he got up and looked through the doors. He didn't turn around, but he waived us over to where he was. I managed to get up, and I walked over to see what had excited him.

I looked through the door not sure what I was looking for. I looked towards the corner after Carl had said they were talking to the kid. What I found were the two helmeted cops were putting handcuffs on him. I told Jay, "I guess they found their man."

"Looks like it" he replied.

"We better go back to the table and wait to see what happens," I suggested.

As we went back to the table, I could hear movement behind us. I turned, and the two cops were taking the kid outside.

"I can't believe the kid killed Cory," Carl uttered.

"You never know now days" Bill replied as he watched them go out the door.

Everyone stood up to wait to see what was going to happen next. It wasn't long before the Lieutenant and Sergeant come out from the dorm.

"I wish all of my cases were that easy," the Lieutenant said walking up to us. He turned to the Sergeant and told him, "I'll be out in a minute."

Carl asked, "What's going on with Chris?"

"Funny thing about him…I looked over the body, and I didn't see anything I didn't expect. He was just an older man like many that someone felt a need to kill…" he began telling us. He looked back towards the dorm and then to us. He added, "I went out to begin interviewing the men, and I decided to start with him…"

I asked, "And he confessed right then?"

He laughed before he answered. He told us, "He was sitting in the center of the bed muttering…. I hope you're happy now mom. I had a good idea what he meant, but I needed more."

"He must have been bloody," Jay suggested.

"No but that would have made it easier. We looked around, and the Sergeant found a bloody knife under the bed," he answered.

"And he did it to get even for him leaving his mother" Bill suggested.

"That's it, in a nutshell," the Lieutenant, answered. He saluted us, and he turned and left us to talk among ourselves.

Bill nudged me and asked, "Give you any idea's what you could do to your father?"

"I doubt he would be worth killing," I answered. In the back of my mind, I was asking myself the same question. Though the idea had some merit I knew it wasn't worth it. If I had been him, I might have ended up just like him so who was I to judge.

"Let's hit the sack, morning is going to be coming soon," I suggested to Bill.

He asked with a frown, "It isn't here already?"

"I'm going to try to get a couple of minutes," I told him as I went into the dorm.

CHAPTER

ELEVEN

"Time to rise," I announced as I shook Bill awake. With each push, I felt my muscles cry. I knew if I had gotten a couple of hours sleep, I wouldn't have felt so bad.

I'm awake… I haven't slept all night, as you know. The memories of the last two weeks kept flashing through my head as well as Cory being killed," he told me as he sat up.

"I had the same problem so don't cry on my shoulders" I replied. I got a little sleep, but not as much as I would have liked to. As we talked, about the events of Cory's death, I could hear others in the dorm also talking about it. It was sad that someone would go to that extreme. I reached down to get a shoe for Bill, and I noticed my arm wasn't hurting any more.

"You know I was a little worried last night when I didn't find you in your cot," I told him. As I watched him tie his shoes I added, "I almost thought you killed the old man."

"Thanks, I like you to" he replied with a smile.

"If I could, I would be going back to bed," I told him.

"I'm with you on that score," he answered. Then, rubbing his eyes, he told me, "You know as I went to sleep, and I got to thinking our father had a serious mental problem or was he just an ass. He didn't realize or care what he had… I think our grandmother agreed back then with that thought. Then, for some reason, she felt it was time for us to meet."

"So you think she set this up," I suggested.

"I don't think she did. I know she did…. She had a good idea what you would do once she gave you the diary. She also had a good idea you wouldn't ever find our father…. Not wanting this to go to waste. She set this up, so we could meet each other. One of these days, I'm going to go down to LA and thank her. If it wasn't for her, I would never have met you," he told me with a smile.

"All you have to do is come down to LA… I think she would like to meet you," I assured him. Getting dressed, I reminded him, "Breakfast time…. You know, I think you might be right. She always had the special ability to know when to do something."

"I know…. Give me a minute," he said.

"I'll get some coffee," I offered. I began thinking about what she was going to tell me after I read the diary. I had a feeling she had known I had a brother for quite a while. Since she knew the secret, she was waiting for me to learn about my father first. Then, when I decided to go to Frisco, it made it simpler for her.

"Thanks…. I knew there was a good point in having a brother who understands," he said.

The morning grew long as we waited for whoever was coming to pick us up. After Bill made the oatmeal, there was nothing but one cup of coffee after another. In my excitement, I forgot we were to work around the place. Before either one of us could leave I had to talk to Carl. If need be, I would hang around until he got someone to take my place. As with Bill, I wasn't sure what he could do. He had John, but he wasn't much of a cook.

"Your ride hasn't shown up, yet I take it," Carl said, coming into the dining room.

"Not yet," I answered him with a wave. Then as he went to the coffeepot, I told him, "We have something we need to talk to you about."

"Oh," he replied as he poured coffee into his cup. Coming over to our table he asked, "What's up…? You're leaving me?"

"Well… in a…" I told him the truth. It was interesting to see the look of expectation that came over his face.

"I expected something like this…. Neither one of you should take up acting," he said with a grin.

Bill asked him "What do you mean?"

"Let's see…. The men around here don't worry about their personal hygiene…. Jeff supposedly got into this mess somehow. It didn't take me long to see he's too headstrong to sit around and do nothing. You, Bill, are good enough cook, that you could go anywhere and get a job. Neither one of you had a buyable story…. It was just a piece here and there that didn't fit," he answered, still with a smile.

"I'm sorry about the deception. We don't plan to leave you stranded. I'll hang around until you find someone…. I can't speak for my brother, but I doubt he will walk out on you either," I assured him.

"I can pop over in the morning and set John up for supper. If he's willing, I'll take him to my place and teach him how to cook on his days off…. If that doesn't work out, we can try it over lunch hour," Bill offered.

"Not that I have anything against you Jeff, I already have someone over at the other place waiting to come in…. That lets you off the hook. Bill…, I can't speak for John, but I would appreciate anything you can do for the next few days at least. If John's willing to learn from you, I'll keep him around…, as long as you don't give him any ideas of gourmet meals," Carl said with a snicker.

"I promise, just wholesome home-cooked meals," Bill said, assuring him.

"Then I don't see any problem…. I am really glad that you found each other. It's a story worth writing about, and I'm glad I was here to see it come together. I hope this meeting with Jake pans out for the two of you," Carl said saluting us with his cup. Then, setting his cup down, he smiled and told us, "I have to say meeting the two of you will be a memory I will never forget. I wish I could be around to see what happens next."

"You'll be seeing Bill, but I will still keep in touch with you…. As an idea, we could set up a fundraiser to help the mission," I suggested.

"Hey, brother…. That sounds like a good idea. We could meet here two or three weeks from now," Bill suggested with excitement.

"We can talk about that later… I think your ride just pulled up," Carl said as he pointed through a crack in the blinds.

"We might as well meet him outside," I suggested.

"I guess so…. The sooner we get this over with, the sooner I meet your wife," Bill said, picking up my cup and putting it away.

I heard Phil ask Mike, "Is Jeff O'Connor around?"

"Right here Phil," I told him from around the door jam. Later, when I saw Jake, I wanted to laugh, thinking Phil, and he were twins. The two of them were wearing the same slacks, shirts, and shoes. He didn't have his three or four layers of clothes. He had on a pair of slacks, high polished shoes, sport shirt, and wearing glasses. I got the impression the masquerade was over. I found it funny when one of the residents walked past Phil and didn't recognize him.

"We should be on our way…. Jake likes to be punctual," he said, motioning for me to follow him.

"My brother will be right here," I told him.

"I'm right behind you," Bill said.

"I don't understand…, but it's all right," Phil said, holding the door for us.

"See you two later," Carl shouted out.

"We'll be back," Bill called out to him.

"Take the back seat," Phil almost ordered.

"All right," I answered as I walked around to the other side of the car. I saw Bill give me a funny look with a nod to Phil. I didn't have any problem sitting with Bill, but it was strange. Normally, one passenger would get into the front and the third or fourth in the backseat. Not letting it get to me, I opened the door, sat, and waited for us to get to Jake's place.

As Phil drove off, Bill's hands were on his lap. When he saw me look at him, he turned his palms up suggesting he wanted to know what was going on. I replied with a shrug off my shoulders because I didn't know.

I found Phil's attitude strange when I thought about our meeting a couple of days back. The two of us had a long conversation. I found it strange that he wasn't saying anything.

"Where does Jake live?" I asked Phil, to verify where we were going.

"Just west of Marin City," he answered.

"About fifteen miles North of Frisco on the other side of the Golden Gate," Bill updated me.

"Oh," I replied, with only the Golden Gate making any sense to me.

It wasn't long, and we approached the 101-highway entrance where we headed west to the bridge tollbooth. With him in the outside lane heading north, I could see Alcatraz with all of its history. I could see the remains of the prison and found it hard to believe it was a sanctuary for birds at one time. I also knew if we went far enough on highway 101, we would be in the Redwoods. I had always wanted to see them but hadn't taken the time. If I were right, I thought if we went south, far enough we would find the Hearst Castle, which was another place I had meant to visit.

At the speed we were going, it didn't take long to cross the bridge, and I saw a sign for Marin City. I couldn't see anything objectionable about the area, but we were on the freeway. Phil turned off on the Donahue Street exit and headed west a few blocks. He pulled up in front of a moderate-sized home. It wasn't as big as Martha's or my place, but it was big enough. I found it hard to believe a man living in the area he did, would give as much money as he was to the missions.

"I'll take you in to meet with Jake," Phil said as he got out of the car.

"Thanks," I replied as I opened the door to get out. As I got out, thoughts of what I wanted to tell and ask Jake came to mind. Then Bill got out, and I decided to improvise. I knew down deep that I didn't need to know everything I thought I did. Over the past few days, I had also learned what I had missed out from a father wouldn't do my any good now. Talking to him was more to end the journey and nothing but that.

With hesitation Bill asked, "Are we ready?"

"I am," I answered, wondering if he felt the same way I did.

With Bill at my side, we followed Phil into the house. Phil told us, "To the right… He'll be in the Den."

With a shrug to Bill, I motioned my head, to the right. Eight feet from the front door was another door. I stopped in front of it and looked back at Phil. He motioned for me to knock which I did.

"Enter," a voice came through the door.

Once I had the door open I found Jake looking up at me. He stood with his hand out to greet. I enjoyed the surprised expression on his face when he saw Bill, walk in behind me. I casually announced, "This is my brother William O'Connor."

"I was expecting you, Jeff, but not a brother," Jake said, sounding, a little cold. He motioned for us to take the two chairs in front of his desk.

"With Bill also interested in learning about our father, I thought it only right to bring him with me," I explained to the man. I found it interesting the two men must have bought their clothes at "Twins are Us." As I looked around the room, I saw the walls were solid shelves. From the way it looked, there wasn't any room for one more book. The room I estimated was twenty by twenty. I figured the house went deeper than its width, having a den this size in it. On his desk was a gold lamp that would have been brass if it were in my house. The rug under my feet was oriental, and it looked expensive. After buying one for Martha, I had an idea what they were worth.

"That's fine… It's a pleasure to meet the two of you. Jeff was a good but troubled friend of mine in the old days," he said as he shook our hands. He sat back in his leather chair and told us, "When I saw you that first morning I thought I was looking at your father. I have to admit you took me back a little… I almost thought he had returned. Then realizing how many years it had been, I knew it wasn't him."

"No, just his son," I replied.

As we were talking, he was sitting with both elbows on the arms of his chair, with his hands cupped in front of his mouth. As he talked through his fingers, he asked, "What can I do for you?"

His question surprised me a little with him setting up the meeting. It wasn't as if I didn't want to talk to him, for I did. I finally answered, "I.... I mean we, would like to learn everything we can about our father."

"I can give you some information I guess.... As I said it's been a longtime," he said. As the words were out of his mouth, he reached down and opened a drawer in his desk. Then he pulled out a file folder and opened it up. As he pulled some papers out, he told us, "I don't know anything after nineteen-seventy-eight. To the best of my knowledge, he died. I'm not sure why I even kept these notes, but I did. Now with the two of you here, I'm glad I did."

Not knowing what to say, I kept my mouth shut. Again, it was a meeting of his calling, and I wanted to see what he had to offer. I found the time span between the death of our father, and grandmother received the diary interesting. I also found it interesting that in Jake pulling the papers out of his desk, as if this was a business transaction.

"You have to understand as long ago as we are talking about… I only remember him telling me about one son born about the same time as he went to war…. Now mind you, he wasn't thinking clearly back then. It took a while, but he did get hold of himself and became successful. As I go through these notes, I see he did set up two trust funds. There's one for you, Jeff, and the other for your brother, William. It seems his banker was to send money as support for the two of you. He also set it up so you would get a scholarship to go to any college of your choice."

"You were his financial adviser?" Bill asked, finally saying something.

"Oh no, he didn't need any advice. The best way of explaining his financial position is to say he had a diversified portfolio. No one told him what to do, but I have made a few suggestions over the years," he answered.

"He had left the mission by seventy-eight," I replied trying to keep it all straight. I didn't know what Bill was thinking, but I had always wondered where my grandmother had gotten the money. When my grandfather died, he left a ten-thousand dollar life insurance policy, but that wouldn't have been enough money. The scholarship, I remembered the application came in the mail. As a senior in high school, I was wondering how I would get to college. Then, one afternoon the application came, we filled it out and sent it back. It was a matter of two weeks, and we learned I got the scholarship.

"The latter half," he said. He ended the interview by closing the file and putting it away. He then asked me, "Out of curiosity what has gone on in your life, Jeff?"

"Went to college, married, became a partner in a consulting firm, and had three children. My ex-wife and I have one girl and two boys," I answered him, feeling it was necessary to go into detail.

He asked, "What about you, Bill?"

"The same as my brother; I went to college, married the first woman I dated, opened a restaurant, and I have a one-year-old son. In fact, if you're ever in the wharf area, come to Billy's, and I'll buy you supper," Bill told him.

"I guess that's it… Phil will take you to wherever you would like to go," he told us. He made it clear the meeting was over and motioned for us to leave.

"You can't tell us any more about our father?" I asked him as I rose. As he rose, he smiled and added, "I wish I could have been more help in finding your father…. Remember all you've gone through wasn't for nothing. The two of you found each other."

"Yes, there's that, but I still wish we had found our father," I replied. I wanted to laugh as I answered him. I found the meeting with Jake proved my suspicions were right. I was also glad I didn't waste my time asking him the questions I thought I should. Now, after hearing what he had to say, I didn't need answers to my question.

Before he could answer, Phil came into the room. With a solemn expression, he told us, "This way gentleman."

I was about to turn to leave, but I remembered something I thought he might like. I reached into my pocket and pulled out Mr. Kelly's business card. I told Jake, "You might as well as put this in your file…. Mr. Kelly was in hopes of seeing our father someday."

"Our wives are waiting," Bill said, helping me to get out of there.

"Yeah…. I want to see my kids," I said, agreeing it was time to leave.

Phil asked, "Where to?"

"Back to the mission.... I think Bill needs to talk to John," I told him.

"Almost forgot about John," Bill said as he got into the car.

The trip back was as exciting as the trip to Jake's place. For some reason, I found the meeting informative and interesting. Though I was a little frustrated with him, I still found it went about how I had expected it to. I also found it interesting Phil didn't say a word when he let us out at the mission.

"By the way.... Why did you give Kelly's card to him?" Bill asked me.

"What did Mr. Kelly say his wish was?" I asked him as a reminder.

"He wanted to see our father again," he answered.

"So, I did what he asked... I gave our father the card," I told him.

"What?" Bill asked, not understanding.

"Think about it... Is it that hard to see changing his name from Jeff to Jake? Jake isn't that far removed from "J." What I see in Jake is how I see our father, arrogant, self-centered, too uncaring, and the same age. Jake is also knowledgeable about his financial status... What are the chances of two men bumping into us that would know our father?" I answered him.

"Wish you had some proof," he said, not agreeing with me.

"I'll get it for you..., but what difference does it make? So, you want to take Teri and your son to visit him?" I asked him.

"I don't care if he is my father.... I've had enough of him and everything else. I've done all right with or without his help. All I need at my age is to be a good husband and father," he answered.

"I feel if nothing else, our father whoever his is or isn't, has given us something... and I don't mean money to get us started. A minister or any book couldn't teach us what he has.... The first time I get a drink in my hands, I'm going to toast him," I told him.

"I'll drink to that, brother," Bill replied with a slap on my back.

Bill helped John with getting supper started and left him to finish. John also agreed he would like to come to Billy's and learn how to cook. Bill told him if he liked cooking, he would help him through a culinary school.

Both of us forgot our bags, for some reason, and I was afraid someone might have taken them. When I went into the barracks, they were where we had left them. In shaking my bag, I could tell the diary was still in it. I called Martha and told her how to find us once I had my bag packed. As I held it, I wondered why I was keeping any of it. I decided to keep all of it as I had everything else I had owned in my life.

As I headed to the front door, I felt a tear run down my cheek. I felt relieved that I would be out of the place. I was also sad that I would be leaving my brother behind. It didn't matter that I could come up and see him anytime I wanted or not. I was about to end another chapter of my life. As I grabbed the doorknob, I knew Carl and Bill were on the sidewalk waiting for me. Then, saying good-bye and thanks to Carl, I joined Bill on the sidewalk.

I picked my bag up and told Bill, "I think I need some new duds."

"Don't look at me to argue," he answered.

"How do you feel about the past two weeks?" I asked him.

"Not like I thought I would… I am happy, but I do feel disappointed …, and I'm not talking just about getting to know you. I'm referring to finding our father," he answered.

Over the next few days Martha, the kids and I stayed at Bill and Teri's place. I have to say it was a beautiful place with a wonderful view of the city. What made it special was that our two families would get to know each other. My brother even tried to make a pool player out of me. Then, one night we had a joint birthday party just for the hell of it. Bill invited some friends over, and we didn't go to bed until two or three in the morning. The night before I was to take my family home, I dug out the diary. I turned to the last page and was glad I hadn't read it.

At breakfast the following morning, I handed Bill the diary. As he took it, I told him, "It's yours…. Why don't you read the last page to everyone?"

From the look on his face, he didn't look like he wanted to. I watched Teri as he opened the diary and turned to the last page. He swallowed hard, and began to read:

August 31, 1978
I Jeff A. O'Connor pronounce myself dead
November 1, 1978
My new name is
Jake A. Allison

"Tell me you didn't read this before now," Bill said, looking over at me.

"Last night before I went to sleep…, was the first time," I answered. Then with a smile toward Martha, I added, "If I had I wouldn't have tried walking in our father's footsteps…, and I wouldn't be the man I am today."

"That's sad when someone feels they have to do something like that" Martha replied.

"What's your thinking about it all?" Bill asked.

"I don't know… I have to say I learned, a lot about what veterans have to go through…. Not too far back he talks about a battle he was in. He says they went in once without the Medi-Vac group. A friend of his had to lie in his own blood dying. With each burst of gunfire, he would shutter. Then when a helicopter came over, he would grin thinking help was on the way. A frown would appear when a machine gun on the chopper would go off telling him it wasn't a Medi-Vac chopper. This nineteen-year-oldfriend of our father died not getting the medical attention he needed…. All of this was because someone in DC didn't think the troops needed the support. It's no wonder he felt as he did. I'm surprised that most people don't appreciate our men and women in uniform," I answered. I looked at the diary in his hands and thought about what I had read and seen. I finally added, "I can see where the lack of acceptance messed him up. Everyone needs to feel appreciated, and I doubt he ever felt as if he was… I think he had many problems before he went to war…. When he got back, the rejection broke the proverbial back of the camel."

"I think I agree… I also feel sorry for the men coming back from war. I just don't understand what people are thinking…. If it weren't for our armed services, we wouldn't have the country we have…. I don't know if they treated dad differently or not. I doubt it would have made any difference," he replied as he looked at the last page of the diary.

"There's an interesting story he tells just before that," I told him. I didn't have to hear him read it. I remembered it only too well:

Bill began reading:

> *I just got back from the funeral of a friend. I didn't know him personally, but he was a friend and a brother in arms. I went to the funeral with a friend.*
>
> *As I walked around listening to others, I heard a story of Joe's last days, on this world. From what I heard has made me decide not to me anymore.*
>
> *They sent Joe to Viet Name before we were actively involved in the conflict as they call it. This was back in the days of Eisenhower. His position was, called an "Advisor" to the South Vietnam army. His real job was to make friends with Mayor's of different villages. These Mayors were opposed to our way of thinking. Once he had made friends with them, he was to assassinate them. Then one day he was walking through a village and a mortar shell hit twenty-five feet from him. The blast picked him up and threw him fifty feet. The impact crushed all of his organs.*
>
> *Oh, he got a medical discharge, but he didn't get any help with medical problems. He didn't get recognition for what he did in the service. All his discharge papers say about his tour of duty as having only gone through basic training. Unlike mine that says the bases I had been at and my service in Nam. He didn't say anything other than him, going to boot camp. The time he spent in Nam couldn't be listed because we weren't officially there. In the end, the Army wasn't supporting him in any way. The American public had no use for him.*

He ended up dying in a rooming house alone. The last few months of his life was a life of fear from his stay in Nam. Anytime at college someone began typing he went into a rage, thinking it was machine-gun fire. The only ones at his funeral service were fellow vets that knew of him. In passing he died alone not loved or appreciated by the service or his country.

I want out of anything that ties me to that part of my life.

After he read the piece, he sat the diary down. He looked over at me and shook his head.

"I have never been in his position, but I would also find it sad but I don't think I would give up" I commented.

"I agree. My life has been rough at times, but I can't see giving up as he did," Bill replied.

"Maybe now that he knows a little about you, things will change" Martha suggested.

"We'll see as time goes on" I replied feeling doubtful about it.

CHAPTER TWELVE

One year, three days later:

By this time, eight months had gone by since Martha, and I had remarried. Bill and his family had been to our place several times. He had also met his grandmother and had taken her to Frisco, which surprised me. To make it even stranger, my partner and I had become friends. He even talked me into playing a round of golf and I found that I enjoyed it. I knew that my trying to find my father had turned my life around one hundred and eighty degrees. To my delight, she was happy with the new me as were the kids.

Then a day I never expected to come met me head on. I received an envelope by messenger at my firm's office. When I opened it, I found an article, letter, and six round-trip tickets to San Francisco. With the tickets was a newspaper clipping with a heading that read:

MULTIMILLIONAIRE DIES IN HIS SLEEP AT THE AGE OF 65

I didn't have to read the article to feel sad. After I got back home from my search for my father, I had a dream. The dream was that the two of us would get to know each other. After reading the heading, I knew that dream had died. I found the article interesting in that it gave the history of my father's business venture. It should have irritated me, but I wasn't, in that it didn't list his survivors. I set the clipping down and called my brother.

He told me he had just read the same article and was about to call me. I told him what I had received, and he suggested I read it. When I opened the letter, I saw Phil had signed it. The letter said I was to bring my family and my grandmother. It also said someone would meet me at the hotel the following morning. In relating this information to Bill, he told me they also had reservations at the same hotel. With a few words, we agreed to meet each other that night.

It took us most of the morning to get the kids and grandmother ready for our trip. On the plane, none of us said much, and it seemed the other passengers respected my loss by not saying anything. The plane finally made it to the Frisco airport where we got off, and I got a rental car. For the first time, in my memories, I didn't look at the surroundings, but drove straight to the hotel. After giving the valet the keys to the car, we checked in and went to our room. As I checked us in the clerk gave me a note from Bill suggesting we meet for supper.

Later Martha and I ordered supper in for the kids, and grandma joined us as we made our way to the restaurant. Walking into the dining room, I saw Bill and once he saw me, he stood up to greet me.

"Now we're back to where we were a year ago. We didn't have a father then, and we don't have one now," he said giving me a hug when I got to the table.

"Yep, most of our lives, we didn't even know our father was alive, let alone know him" I added as we let go of each other.

"He was nothing but a disappointment" grandma added as she took her seat.

Our wives greeted each other with expressions of sorrow. Then Martha turned to Bill and asked him "You never saw him but that one time, did you?"

"No… I left messages asking to see him, but he never returned my calls" he answered her.

"Not surprising. He didn't take the time to see you when you were growing up" grandmother added.

All of us turned to her as Martha asked her "I understand how you feel but is this the time to be so negative?"

"What difference does it make? He could have been there for his boys…. He did help bring them into the world," she answered as she picked up her menu.

"We did all right without him, and he did pay for our college education," I told her.

"That's not the point a boy needs his father to show him how to be a man" she added.

"I find it hard to talk about the dead," Martha told her.

"That's all right," I told my wife as I patted her on the hand.

Bill looked up from his menu and told us "Phil came by the restaurant a week ago. I saw him walk in, as I was escorting some customers to a table. I let one of my waitresses seat them as I made my way to greet him. Then before I could get to him, he turned around and left."

"That's about the time the article said father died" I commented.

Bill's wife Teri added, "I've been wondering about that. I have a feeling your father might have wanted to see Bill, for some reason, and sent Phil over."

Bill asked, "Then why didn't he talk to me?"

"He doesn't have any use for the two of you…. You boy's might be perceived as complications to him" she answered.

"He might have been the reason your father didn't have anything to do with you two" Martha suggested.

A waiter walked up to the table and asked, "Can I take your order?"

"I'll have a…" Bill began giving his drink order. The rest of us then gave him our drink orders as we began looking at the menu seriously. The waiter returned with our drinks, and we ordered our meals.

As the waiter left us grandmother announced, "I guess I was wrong in keeping the diary so long. In saying that I know if I had to do it again, I would do the same thing."

With a feeling of irritation, I asked her "Why…didn't you think I needed to know my father?"

"He didn't seem to want to know you so why confuse you," she answered. As she looked around, I think she saw the questions on everyone's faces as I did. As she sat her drink down, she added, "If I had the answers to the questions you would have asked I might have let you have it sooner, but I didn't."

Bill asked her "Then why did you give it to Jeff when you did?"

After a minute of silence, she answered him. She said, "With Jeff, feeling as he did I thought he might feel better knowing he was as bad off as his father… It also gave me an opportunity to get the two of you together."

Bill didn't stop there and went on to ask her "How long did you know about me?"

Grandmother opened her purse and pulled out a piece of paper. She looked at the piece in her hands and then back at us. With hesitation, she handed the paper to him.

As Bill took it from her, he asked her "What's this?"

"Read it…I received it in the mail about when you were born," she told him.

Not realizing it, I asked, "You what?"

Everyone at the table looked at me, grandmother and then back to Bill. No one added anything but waited for him to say something. We were also interested in hearing what was on the piece of paper she had given him.

"It says…. Dear mother, I thought I would let you know you have another grandson. Then it gives my mother's name and address" he tells us as he hands it back to grandmother. He didn't say anything else as he got up and walked away.

Terri looking worried asked him "Where are you going?"

"I need a minute to think…. I'll be back," he told her as he walked out of the dining room.

As Bill walked away the waiter returned to our table, with his arms filled with plates. As he sat them down, he said "Here are your meals."

Martha asks, "I wonder what's wrong?"

"I don't know," I answered as I looked over at grandmother.

"I should go and see what's wrong with him," Teri said looking towards the entrance Bill had gone through.

"He might have gone to the restroom" grandmother suggested as she poked at her supper.

"I doubt it…, he usually says that's where he's going" Teri replied as she looked around the table.

"Let him work it out" I suggested. I had an idea what was going through his head. I had an idea the same things were going through his head as it did mine when she gave me the diary.

No one even looked at their meal nor said much. I had the feeling everyone in the restaurant was looking at us, and I wanted to leave. After what seemed like an hour, Bill finally returned and sat at the table. I wanted to ask him what was on his mind but thought better of it.

After he straightened his napkin across his lap, Bill told grandmother "So you didn't care enough about me to see or call me."

"I wanted to…but I didn't know what to say or do," she finally answered. Then looking around she got up and announced, "I don't think I'm hungry. I'm going to my room."

"So, you were as full of hatred as he was and didn't bother," Bill commented with a tear in his eyes.

The four of us picked at our meal and silently agreed we didn't feel like eating. Martha and I left Bill and his wife in the lobby and they joined us shortly as we went to the bar to have a drink. I didn't finish mine wondering how the kids were doing. I also wanted to see what grandmother was up to. I felt sorry for Bill and irritated with her, but I felt I owed her a little understanding.

As I was about to cross the lobby, the elevator doors opened. Two paramedics came out pushing a gurney with grandma on it.

I cried out, "What happened…she's my grandmother?"

"Possible stroke" the lead attendant answered.

As I patted her hand as they went by I asked, "Where are you taking her?"

"General Hospital" the attendant answered not stopping.

I wanted to tell her I loved her, but I remembered Martha, Bill and his wife were still in the lounge. I looked back at Grandma as they were putting her into the ambulance. I looked towards the lounge not sure what to do. I finally ran into the lounge.

Bill was just getting up when he saw me. He asked, "What's wrong?"

"They're taking her to the hospital," I told them.

Martha came over and wrapped her arm around me. She asked, "What happened?"

"They think she might have had a stroke...I've got to get to the hospital" I told her pulling away from her.

"I'll go with you...I also love her," she said in a firm voice.

"I'll watch the kids," Teri offered.

"I'll drive" Bill said as he headed out of the lounge.

"Thanks Teri...We're in 10...0...," Martha began telling her.

"I know which room they're in" Teri replied as she ushered us out of the lobby.

"I'll get the car," Bill said as he ran to the valet.

Martha said something, but I had no idea what it was. The thought of having lost my mother, now my father I had just found in the past year ran through my mind. I wasn't in any mood to lose the only parent I really knew. Grandma had her problems, but I loved her still. If given the chance, she would accept Bill as her grandson. I looked into the sky and prayed, "Please God, give her the chance."

I didn't have any idea how long it took or when Martha and I got into the car. I vaguely remember seeing buildings go by as Bill drove to the hospital. He dropped us off at the emergency entrance, and we ran inside. I tried to take control, but I heard Martha ask about Grandma.

The nurse at the desk checked in back and told us, "They are with her right now. As soon as I learn something I'll let you know."

"Thank you," Martha said ushering me to a seat.

"I knew I should have gone after her," I muttered.

"It isn't your fault…She's getting old and this is something you, and I have talked about a number of times," she said as we sat down.

"All of this had to have been hard on her and her heart just couldn't take it" I muttered.

"But there isn't anything you could have done. She wanted to come as much as you wanted her. She's just getting old…be thankful she wasn't home alone. As it is she now has a chance to make it," she told me.

"I pray you're…" I began to say but Bill came running in.

He asked, "How is she?"

"We don't know yet…they're working with her," I told him.

The three of us just sat there waiting. I finally got tired and got up to walk around. I was wishing I was like Bill and could go out for a smoke.

"I'm going outside" he said coming up to me.

"I'll join you" I replied following him outside. I had signaled Martha where we were going, and she waved us on.

"I never saw this coming…I wish I had kept my mouth shut" Bill said as he lit his cigarette.

I wanted to say something, but I knew if I did, I would have another problem. I thought I understood how he felt, but it was grandma dying inside. After some thought I told him, "I don't understand her either. She has always kept things from me, and I just grew up accepting it… Now this has brought all of it back to me, and I don't know what to say. I love her but her keeping us apart wasn't right."

Like me, he didn't say anything. I watched him light up another and looked back into the emergency room. I saw Martha shrug her shoulders as if she was wondering what was going on between Bill and I. I shrugged back trying to let her know there wasn't anything to report.

As Bill was putting out his cigarette, I saw a man in a white coat walk up to Martha. I told Bill, "I believe the doctor is talking to Martha."

"Let's get in there and find out what's happening," he said heading for the door.

As we walked up the doctor was saying, "…anxiety attack. We'll keep her overnight, but I don't think there is anything to worry about."

I asked him, "Can we see her?"

"She's in cubicle seven…. Don't be long because they'll be taking her upstairs soon. I would like to see her get some sleep. It might be easier if only one of you go in at a time," he answered.

"You go in first," Martha suggested.

"That might be a good idea. If she's up to it, then I'll go in later" Bill replied. He turned as if he was going to go back outside, but he stopped and took a seat.

"I'll stay out here with Bill," Martha said as she gave me a kiss. Then releasing me, she added, "Give her my love."

"I will," I promised. I went through the emergency-room doors and looked around. In the center of the room was a large desk with nurses and doctors going from behind it. The curtained off cubicles circled around the desk with their numbers over each opening. I spotted cubicle seven and headed straight for it. To my surprise, no one took notice of me.

I got to the opening and hesitated, not sure if I should go in. I listened for a minute, and I didn't hear anything. As I stood there, I wasn't sure what I was going to say when I saw her. I wanted to yell at her that being where we were, was bad enough. Then with the attitude, she had taken with her grandson was unforgivable. I let different thoughts run through my mind, and I still didn't know what to say. I finally just opened the curtain and walked in.

"Hi," she said with tired eyes.

Her face was whiter than I ever remembered seeing it. Her overall appearance took me back a little, and I was afraid to say anything. I finally got out, "How are you feeling?"

"I've felt better but the doctor has given me a sedative," she answered as her eyelids drooped.

"I won't stay long…. We were worried about you. The ambulance attendant said you might have had a stroke," I told her.

"It isn't my time…. It just that everything got to me" she replied. She laid there not adding anything, and I didn't bother her. She finally opened her eyes and smiled. She added, "I guess your brother is outside."

"Yes," I told her.

"Tell him I'm sorry but I don't think I can stay awake much longer," she told me.

"I think he'll understand" I assured her.

"And give Martha my love… I know I have to change. He isn't a bad boy it's me that did him wrong…I don't know if I can change after all these…," she said, but she fell asleep not finishing her thought.

I took a seat and sat there for a couple of minutes. I didn't want to leave and have her wake up to find that I had left.

As the nurse walked in, she gave me an interested look. Then she looked at her patient and checked her vitals. She made a few notes on her clipboard and turned back to me. She then said, "You can leave if you want. I doubt she'll wake up until sometime in the morning."

"Thanks…my wife and brother are waiting outside. If anything happens to her, you can reach me at…," I went on to give her my contact information. As I was about to leave, I asked "Do I need to sign anything?"

"No she's signed everything, and she's fully covered. Go back to your room and don't worry…, she's going to be fine. Many younger people should wish they were in the shape she's in," she said.

"Thanks," I replied as I left. I had looked back at her and wished things were different. Even with that, she appeared to be resting without any trouble. I felt better and went out to the emergency waiting area.

They greeted me at the door, and I told them everything grandma had said. I also told them she had fallen asleep, and we might as well as leave. With nothing else to say or do we walked out to the parking lot and left for the hotel.

"I'll call your room and wait for Teri down here," Bill said.

He hadn't said much since leaving the hospital. I know he wanted to talk to grandma, but it wasn't in the cards. I personally felt it was better that way, so she could think her actions over.

"I'll stay here until she comes down," Martha told him. She smiled at me and added, "The least I can do is to tell her thanks for watching the kids."

When I saw her looking at me, I replied, "I'm not going anywhere."

"I just don't know what to say… I know I shouldn't be mad, but I can't help it" Bill said as he paced the floor.

"At least she got us together. She didn't have to do that you know," I reminded him.

"And that I'm to be happy, for" he said giving me a smile.

"Remember that goes both ways" I replied. I knew what he meant, but it was good to see him joking.

It wasn't long Teri was downstairs, and we said our goodbyes for now. Martha and I went upstairs not sure if I was looking forward to what was going to take place in the morning.

When we got back to our room, Martha said, "Bill has a point."

"I know I went through the same feelings he's probably going through. The difference is that I know her," I replied not knowing what else to add.

"A shame with all that had happened in the past year. Learning he had a grandmother, he didn't know as well as a brother. Then the two of you found your father and all of that…. It's really a shame it has to come down to this," she said as she sat on the edge of the bed.

"We'll be talking to him later. Once he cools off he'll see he has more to lose by cutting her off than it's worth," I added as I said a prayer.

"I hope so," she added as we went in, to say good night to the kids.

As I wrapped my arms around her, I told her, "Just think it only gets better tomorrow morning."

"Don't remind me" she replied."

CHAPTER THIRTEEN

The next morning-after breakfast, I got a call in our room. The message was to be downstairs in the Conference room at 9:00 A.M. Then Bill called to see if I had any idea what was going on. His problem was that he had called the hospital and found grandma wasn't registered.

Grandma had called me saying she was going to the airport. She had called so early all of it took me back a little. Then knowing her as I did it wasn't surprising. She had always been the one to go off and do her own thing. Before I could say anything she assured me, she was fine.

I assured him our grandmother was fine, and that she was on her way back home. Though shocked, he said it was just as well. We met downstairs, and we took our families to the conference room.

When we entered the conference room, we found Phil and a couple of attorneys waiting for us. Phil asked us, "Please, have a seat… Where is your grandmother?"

"She wasn't feeling good and went back home," I explained not going into detail.

"Just as well," he replied.

We took our seats and waited to see why he had called us together. I had an idea why, but I knew it wasn't worth the effort to second-guess him. As I kept my eye on him, I wondered if he might be why father didn't have anything to do with us boys. I knew if that was the case, I should hate him, but I knew it wasn't worth it. Father was old enough to make his own decisions so it really didn't matter what Phil thought of us or not.

Once he sat himself. He told us, "Eight nights ago Jake died of a massive stroke. As he had wished, I called all of you together. I guess I should add the day before he died, we talked about you two boys and the will. Somehow, he knew he was dying, and wanted me to pass a message to you.... He told me to tell you he was sorry he hadn't been a father to the two of you. I was also to tell you he understood that money could never make up for your loss. He knew his greatest love was money, and that he felt you two deserved something.... With that Mr. Armstrong will now read your father's will."

"I, Jake A. Allison, leave my fortune to my two sons, Jeffrey A. and William A. O'Connor...," the attorney said, reading the will. He added more mumble jumble then sat the will down. With a quick glance at it, he looked at the two of us and added, "I have a breakdown of your inheritance that I will give you. I don't see any reason to go into it right now.... You might want to contact your attorneys to have them give me a call. Of course all of this has to go through probate first, which gives us plenty of time. If at some later time you have any questions, please feel free to give me a call."

To me, having an attorney read the will was a waste of time. It was enough to know it said Bill and I would share in the inheritance, equally with one stipulation. All our father asked of us was that we would continue to contribute to the different organizations he had given to over the years. Without hesitation, Bill and I agreed to support the missions and the others as well. As to the rest of the money, we would talk it over.

I looked up from the table at Phil and asked him, "How long have you been with our father?"

"Thirty years," he answered. In answering me, he didn't look up but continued to put papers back into his briefcase. We knew he had nothing more to tell us when he shut the case.

I remembered I hadn't heard the attorney mention him in the will. I asked him, "I'm surprised, he didn't leave you anything... I would've thought he would have left you something. The two of you have been together for a lot of years."

"Don't worry he took good care of me…, and I do mean good care of me. We were more than employer and employee. Bill would know what I mean having lived in Frisco…. Your father and I were joint owners of everything, but we did have our own accounts. That's how he was able to will what he did to the two of you," he answered with a grin. Then, for some reason, he added, "You might say he gave me everything I needed long before he died."

"Oh," Bill got out as he gave me a funny look.

"Don't get me wrong I don't hold anything against him for giving what he did to the two of you," Phil added.

"It was his," Martha added with a disgusted expression.

I wanted to tell him I didn't care one way or the other. I had another idea come to mind, but I also let it drop. All of us left the conference room with their own thoughts. Then we went and had lunch to talk it over.

"Why didn't one of you ask where they buried him?" Teri asked.

"I don't think he wanted us to know…, and I don't think he thought we wanted to know. If he did Phil would have called us sooner," I answered.

Still in the Lobby, Bill asked, "What now?"

"We need to sit down and discuss what we'll do with our inheritance. I don't know if we need to do that right now, but we need to talk it over… I thought we might stay another night and have supper together," I suggested.

"Sounds good to me," Bill replied as he looked at his wife.

"I don't have anything planned," Teri told us.

"I also want to see Bertha before we leave," I told him.

"I'll go with you," Bill offered.

"Good… I thought I might send her and her family on a cruise," I suggested.

With a chuckle Bill said, "We have more than enough money…. You might want to visit someone else."

Not knowing who that might be, I asked, "Who's that?"

"John," he answered. Then, with a smile, he added, "He's become quite the cook."

"I might do that and see Carl while I'm there. We should tell him we'll continue to support the mission," I answered.

"Let's see Bertha first," Bill suggested.

"I would like to see her also" Martha said agreeing to the idea. She looked over at Teri and saw she agreed with her.

"I don't have any problem with that," I replied, agreeing with him.

"A thought just came to me," Martha announced.

I asked, "What's that?"

"The two of you might do one better than what your father did…. He didn't help financially, but he did help Mr. Kelly become what he is today. Why don't you set up a scholarship for down and outers? In doing so maybe they can become something."

"That's a good idea Martha" Bill's wife said.

"I like the idea" Bill replied.

I nodded my head and thought about it. I found myself thinking our father's life wasn't a total waste after all. If things were to work out right, many men might be happier than what they are now.

I'm sorry for blowing up like I did to our grandmother," he told me.

"I understand because I have wondered the same thing," I confessed.

"I guess we'll see you for supper. I might feel like eating," he said with a smile when we reached the elevator.

"Call the room when you're ready," I told him as I pushed the button.

"Yeah," he answered. Then turning from the elevator he turned and walked away with Teri.

Martha asked, "I wonder where they're going?"

"No Idea," I answered as the elevator doors closed.

All of us got together that night for supper. For some reason, I had the feeling there was a silent agreement not to talk about the events earlier in the day. We agreed after supper to meet for breakfast before Martha, the kids and I headed back for Los Angeles.

We went back to our rooms, and I knew it was over. I had walked in my father's footsteps and learned more about him than I expected. He might not have responded to me as I would have liked, but I did get to meet him. In my efforts to find him, I became a man, and I owed him that. While walking in his footsteps, I found him, and I found I had a brother. I realized I was left with learning what else my grandmother has kept from her grandsons.

As Martha and I got out of bed the next morning, I told her "I don't care."

She asked, "What are you talking about?"

"I fell asleep last night wondering what grandmother was still keeping from me...," I began to answer. I stopped in the middle of my thoughts remembering what our relationship had become since Bill, and I had found our father. Though she had walked out before the reading of his will, it was because she knew her dreams of seeing him again would never come true.

Still, when I returned from San Francisco, our relationship had changed for the better. She was pleased that we had found him, and I think it was from the fact that we seemed to become closer. There was some strain with her knowing I had learned how he had helped support me and pay for my college education. In doing what he did, meant she knew more about him than she had admitted to while I was growing up. Since I had done my best not to remind her of that fact, she was now telling me things about my father I had always wanted to know. So, I might have lost my father, I had a grandmother that was part of my life as well as my families.

Martha interrupted me by asking, "And?"

"It's just...most of my life, I have been asking question wondering about this and that. I don't think I care any more. I have a fantastic wife, some wonderful kids, a brother, and a good business. I have as much if not more than most. If she has anything else to tell me she can keep it," I told her.

With a teasing type of grin, she said, "You know what."

Seeing her expression, I hesitated to say anything. I finally asked her, "What?"

"I love you," she answered as she gave me a kiss.

"Not right now…we have to get the kids going, and then meet Bill and Teri for breakfast," I reminded her. Though the twinkle in her eye said she was offering more but it was not the time or place.

"I still love you," she said as she started to dress.

"And I love you," I assured her with a wink. Then silently to my father I said, "At one time I was as bad of a father and husband as you were…but through you, I'm the man I always wanted to be."

Note: Some time later, I erected a brass plaque in my front yard. The Plaque reads:

In honor of a Vietnam Soldier
My father and others like him
He may not have been what I needed
he still served our country with honor
but never got the respect
he rightly deserved.
Please remember him now

Author Ben Steinlage: Though born in California, he now lives in New Mexico with his wife. He is a father of six children, seven grandchildren. Professionally he was a consultant in the printing industry. Now that he is retired, he spends a good part of his time writing and helping other writers.

His writing began more than fifty some years ago as a hobby. This past time has led him to become a published writer. As a writer he likes challenges, which means he writes in a variety of genres. To date, he has written (though not all published) better than thirty stories of historical fiction, murder mysteries to fantasy. It wasn't until 2007 that his wife decided it was time to share his works with the world that he became a published author. To his surprise, he found that others enjoyed his stories as much as his family. In offering this story to the many readers out in the world, he hopes this story will be as enjoyable as his past stories.